# Indigenous Peoples

# Other Books of Related Interest:

## Current Controversies Series

Aid to Africa

The Global Food Crisis

Carbon Offsets

## Global Viewpoints Series

Famine

Poverty

## Introducing Issues with Opposing Viewpoints Series

Global Warming

Native Americans

Water Resource Management

## Opossing Viewpoints Series

The Environment

Latin America

**GLOBAL**VIEWPOINTS

# Indigenous Peoples

*Diane Andrews Henningfeld, Book Editor*

**GREENHAVEN PRESS**
*A part of Gale, Cengage Learning*

GALE
CENGAGE Learning

Detroit • New York • San Francisco • New Haven, Conn • Waterville, Maine • London

Christine Nasso, *Publisher*
Elizabeth Des Chenes, *Managing Editor*

© 2009 Greenhaven Press, a part of Gale, Cengage Learning

Gale and Greenhaven Press are registered trademarks used herein under license.

*For more information, contact:*
Greenhaven Press
27500 Drake Rd.
Farmington Hills, MI 48331-3535
Or you can visit our Internet site at gale.cengage.com

For product information and technology assistance, contact us at

Gale Customer Support, 1-800-877-4253
For permission to use material from this text or product, submit all requests online at
www.cengage.com/permissions

Further permissions questions can be emailed to permissionrequest@cengage.com

Articles in Greenhaven Press anthologies are often edited for length to meet page requirements. In addition, original titles of these works are changed to clearly present the main thesis and to explicitly indicate the author's opinion. Every effort is made to ensure that Greenhaven Press accurately reflects the original intent of the authors. Every effort has been made to trace the owners of copyrighted material.

Cover image by John Miles/The Image Bank/Getty Images.

**LIBRARY OF CONGRESS CATALOGING-IN-PUBLICATION DATA**

Indigenous peoples / Diane Andrews Henningfeld, book editor.
    p. cm. -- (Global viewpoints)
Includes bibliographical references and index.
ISBN 978-0-7377-4468-2 (hardcover)
ISBN 978-0-7377-4469-9 (pbk.)
  1. Indigenous peoples. I. Henningfeld, Diane Andrews.
GN380.I529 2009
305.8--dc22
                                  2009013594

# Contents

## Chapter 1: Confronting Past Treatment of Indigenous Peoples

# Chapter 2: Current Issues for Indigenous Peoples

# Chapter 3: Indigenous Peoples and Natural Resources

# Chapter 4: Preserving Indigenous Cultures

# Foreword

> *"The problems of all of humanity can*
> *only be solved by all of humanity."*
> *—Swiss author Friedrich Dürrenmatt*

Global interdependence has become an undeniable reality. Mass media and technology have increased worldwide access to information and created a society of global citizens. Understanding and navigating this global community is a challenge, requiring a high degree of information literacy and a new level of learning sophistication.

Building on the success of its flagship series, *Opposing Viewpoints*, Greenhaven Press has created the *Global Viewpoints* series to examine a broad range of current, often controversial topics of worldwide importance from a variety of international perspectives. Providing students and other readers with the information they need to explore global connections and think critically about worldwide implications, each *Global Viewpoints* volume offers a panoramic view of a topic of widespread significance.

Drugs, famine, immigration—a broad, international treatment is essential to do justice to social, environmental, health, and political issues such as these. Junior high, high school, and early college students, as well as general readers, can all use *Global Viewpoints* anthologies to discern the complexities relating to each issue. Readers will be able to examine unique national perspectives while, at the same time, appreciating the interconnectedness that global priorities bring to all nations and cultures.

Material in each volume is selected from a diverse range of sources, including journals, magazines, newspapers, nonfiction books, speeches, government documents, pamphlets, organization newsletters, and position papers. *Global Viewpoints* is truly global, with material drawn primarily from international sources available in English and secondarily from U.S. sources with extensive international coverage.

Features of each volume in the *Global Viewpoints* series include:

- An **annotated table of contents** that provides a brief summary of each essay in the volume, including the name of the country or area covered in the essay.

- An **introduction** specific to the volume topic.

- A **world map** to help readers locate the countries or areas covered in the essays.

- For each viewpoint, an **introduction** that contains notes about the author and source of the viewpoint explains why material from the specific country is being presented, summarizes the main points of the viewpoint, and offers three **guided reading questions** to aid in understanding and comprehension.

- **For further discussion** questions that promote critical thinking by asking the reader to compare and contrast aspects of the viewpoints or draw conclusions about perspectives and arguments.

- A worldwide list of **organizations to contact** for readers seeking additional information.

- A **periodical bibliography** for each chapter and a **bibliography of books** on the volume topic to aid in further research.

- A comprehensive **subject index** to offer access to people, places, events, and subjects cited in the text, with the countries covered in the viewpoints highlighted.

*Global Viewpoints* is designed for a broad spectrum of readers who want to learn more about current events, history, political science, government, international relations, economics, environmental science, world cultures, and sociology—students doing research for class assignments or debates, teachers and faculty seeking to supplement course materials, and others wanting to understand current issues better. By presenting how people in various countries perceive the root causes, current consequences, and proposed solutions to worldwide challenges, *Global Viewpoints* volumes offer readers opportunities to enhance their global awareness and their knowledge of cultures worldwide.

# Introduction

*"The growing migration of indigenous persons is another expression of globalization and of the inequalities and poverty generated by it. Indigenous migrants are particularly exposed to human rights abuses in agricultural and mining works, in the urban context and at the individual level. Forced migration of indigenous peoples is the result of the situation, often desperate, that they face in their places of origin."*

*Rodolfo Stavenhaven,*
*"Oral Statement on Human Rights,"*
*Sixth Session, United Nations Permanent*
*Forum on Indigenous Issues, May 2007.*

The term "indigenous peoples" encompasses widely diverse groups of people living on every continent in the world, except for Antarctica. According to the United Nations Permanent Forum on Indigenous Issues (UNPFII), there are approximately 370 million indigenous peoples worldwide, living in some 70 countries. Their numbers include, for example, the Inuit peoples of the far north, First Nation tribes and the Métis people in Canada, American Indian Tribal Nations in the United States, the Aboriginal populations of Australia and New Zealand, the Tupinikim and Guarani peoples of South America, the San people of the Kalahari Desert in Africa, and the Orang Asli people of Malaysia, among many, many other groups and tribes around the world. Indeed, most countries of the world have at least a remnant of an indigenous population living within their boundaries.

While indigenous groups are very different one from another in history, tradition, culture, and way of life, they hold one important thing in common: a special relationship with their traditional lands. This relationship is often spiritual, and it underpins the indigenous person's sense of self. Further, many groups depend on the land to sustain their cultures and their livelihoods. Presently, however, indigenous peoples often find themselves in settings quite different from those of their ancestors.

In some instances, indigenous peoples may find themselves living in an urban area simply because a city has grown up around their traditional homeland. Maggie Walter, for example, in her paper "Lives of Diversity: Indigenous Australia," presented to the Academy of Social Sciences in Australia in 2008, notes that in the city of Perth, a majority of the indigenous population "are Noongar people, the traditional owners of the land on which Perth and its surroundings sit." Rather than moving to a city in this case, Aboriginal peoples have found the city moving to them.

In many past cases, however, indigenous peoples were taken from their homelands and resettled in different areas by military or governmental institutions. For example, in the United States, American Indians were moved from their traditional lands and resettled on reservations, sometimes half a continent away. First Nations people in Canada and Aboriginal people in Australia endured similar experiences. Often, migrations of this sort forced a "settlement" lifestyle on indigenous groups, dramatically changing the employment, culture, and health of traditionally nomadic peoples.

In a more recent example of forced migration, the indigenous peoples of the Marshall Islands were relocated so that the United States could test nuclear weapons on their traditional homelands. The testing led, in many cases, to permanent destruction of the environment, so that the indigenous peoples could not return to their traditional lands.

Finally, very current examples of forced displacement of indigenous peoples occur when large, multinational companies are given development rights by governments. These companies may be mining for petroleum or other mineral resources, or they may be harvesting plants for cellulose production, among other possibilities. Regardless, as a result, governments may move indigenous populations out of their traditional lands in order to give the lands over to the development of natural resources.

In addition to forced relocation, much of the current indigenous migration takes place as a result of what scholars call "push-pull" factors. Push factors include circumstances people experience on their traditional lands. These might include famine, warfare, and environmental destruction, among others. These circumstances make it difficult or impossible for indigenous peoples to continue to live in their homelands. Pull factors include perceived benefits in the new location. That is, people may choose to move to another location because of better employment, educational potential, or health care. In the first example, then, people are "pushed" out of their homelands because of factors that make their continued survival risky. In the second, people are "pulled" away from their homelands by the lure of improved quality of life available in the new location.

A consideration of the Inuit peoples of the far northern polar regions offers an example of the push-pull theory in practice. As the polar ice caps continue to melt at a rapid rate, Arctic indigenous peoples fear that the environmental conditions necessary for them to continue their subsistence level hunting and fishing are changing. Melting sea ice might mean an end to traditional forms of living. Faced with these circumstances, the Inuit would be pushed to move to other places, most likely urban areas. On the other hand, as revealed in a survey taken by the Inuit Tapiriit Kanatami in 2007, the leading reason Inuit peoples give for considering migration away from their communities is to seek new job opportunities, an example of a pull factor.

For whatever reason indigenous peoples choose to leave their traditional lands, the tendency is increasingly for them to move toward urban areas. *Statistics Canada*, for example, notes that the 2006 census indicated, "Aboriginal people in Canada are increasingly urban. In 2006, 54 percent lived in urban areas . . . up from 50 percent in 1996." For many indigenous peoples, however, the move to urban centers is one fraught with difficulty and challenges. As Amy Muedin reported to the Seventh Session of the UNPFII on April 4, 2008, "The migration process, including urbanization, of indigenous peoples, is often associated with a number of negative experiences that may affect their indigenous identity, belief systems, health, language and culture."

One of the most notable problems encountered by urban indigenous peoples is a deterioration of their health and quality of life. According to *Progress Can Kill*, a 2007 publication of the Cultural Survival organization, "Tribal people, living according to their traditions, on their own land, are typically healthy, happy, strong and vibrant, with low levels of the chronic diseases that plague western societies." However, according to the same source, once indigenous peoples move, or are moved, they suffer from poverty and diseases of the developed world: "The imposition of 'Western' society on tribal communities has passed on to them the worst impacts of this lifestyle without necessarily bringing them any 'affluence.'"

Indeed, across all measures of quality of life, urban indigenous peoples lag far behind non-indigenous urban dwellers. According to "Urban Indigenous Peoples and Migration: Challenges and Opportunities," a fact sheet prepared by the UNPFII, "Indigenous peoples that migrate to urban areas face particular and often additional challenges, most prominently unemployment, limited access to services and inadequate housing." Likewise, in a report prepared by the World Bank in

February 2007, "Economic Opportunities for Indigenous Peoples in Latin America," the writers note that "in urban areas, [indigenous people] are more likely to have informal jobs that lack security, access to social benefits, health care, and unemployment."

In an era of rapid climate change and increasing globalization, the subject of indigenous peoples and their ability to remain on their traditional lands is a vexing one. The viewpoints in this book explore many factors impacting indigenous peoples around the world today, including land, natural resources, cultural preservation, and interaction between indigenous and non-indigenous societies.

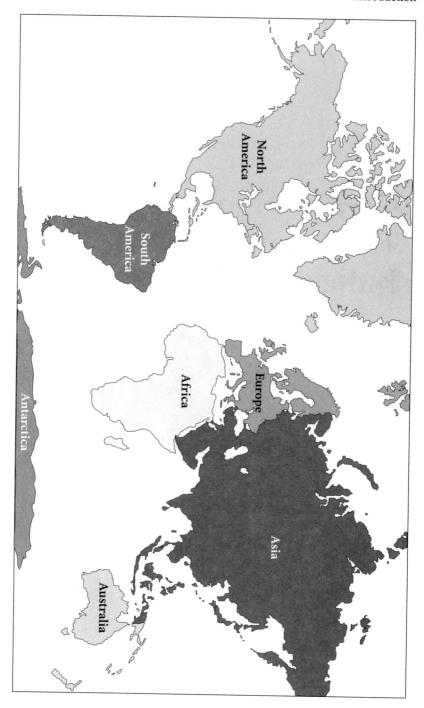

CHAPTER 1

# Confronting Past Treatment of Indigenous Peoples

# Identifying Indigenous Peoples: An Overview

## *The Secretariat of the United Nations Permanent Forum on Indigenous Issues/DSPD/DESA*

*According to the following viewpoint, although it is not possible to define what constitutes an indigenous person, it is possible to list specific characteristics that indigenous peoples have in common. These include self-identification as indigenous; historical association with a geographical location; strong links to land and natural resources; a distinct language and culture; and occupying a non-dominant position in society. The viewpoint contends that any development of natural resources on indigenous-held land must be done with their informed consent. The Secretariat of the United Nations Permanent Forum on Indigenous Issues serves as a clearinghouse for discussion and information concerning indigenous peoples.*

As you read, consider the following questions:

1. What is another name for the *Study on the Problem of Discrimination Against Indigenous Populations* cited by the authors of this viewpoint?

2. To what does Article 33 of the United Nations Declaration on the Rights of Indigenous Peoples refer?

3. What is one of the root causes of poverty and marginalization for indigenous peoples, according to this viewpoint?

The term "indigenous peoples" has become a general denominator for distinct peoples who, through historical processes, have been pursuing their own concept and way of human development in a given socio-economic, political and historical context. Throughout history, these distinct groups of peoples have tried to maintain their group identity languages, traditional beliefs, worldviews and way of life and, most importantly, the control and management of their lands, territories and natural resources, which allow and sustain them to live as peoples.

## Characteristics of Indigenous Peoples

The international community has not adopted a common definition of indigenous peoples and the prevailing view today is that no formal universal definition is necessary for the recognition and protection of their rights. However, there have been attempts to outline the characteristic of indigenous peoples.

The ILO's [International Labor Organization's] Indigenous and Tribal Peoples Convention, 1989 (No. 169) applies to:

- Tribal peoples whose social, cultural and economic conditions distinguish them from other sections of the national community, and whose status is regulated wholly or partially by their own customs or traditions or by special laws or regulations.

- Peoples who are regarded as indigenous on account of their descent from the populations which inhabited the country, or a geographical region to which the country belongs, at the time of conquest or colonization or the establishment of present state boundaries and who, irrespective of their legal status, retain some or all of their own social, economic, cultural and political institutions.

- The Convention also states that self-identification as indigenous or tribal shall be regarded as a fundamental criterion for determining the groups to which the provisions of this Convention apply.

## A Working Definition

The [United Nations] *Study on the Problem of Discrimination Against Indigenous Populations* (the "Martínez Cobo Study") offers the following "working definition":

"Indigenous communities, peoples and nations are those which, having a historical continuity with pre-invasion and pre-colonial societies that developed on their territories, consider themselves distinct from other sectors of the societies now prevailing in those territories, or parts of them. They form at present non-dominant sectors of society and are determined to preserve, develop and transmit to future generations their ancestral territories, and their ethnic identity, as the basis of their continued existence as peoples, in accordance with their own cultural patterns, social institutions and legal systems."

The *Working Paper on the Concept of "Indigenous People"* prepared by the [United Nations] Working Group on Indigenous Populations lists the following factors that have been considered relevant to the understanding of the concept of "indigenous" by international organizations and legal experts:

- Priority in time, with respect to the occupation and use of a specific territory;

- The voluntary perpetuation of cultural distinctiveness, which may include the aspects of language, social organization, religion and spiritual values, modes of production, laws and institutions;

- Self-identification, as well as recognition by other groups, or by State authorities, as a distinct collectivity; and

- An experience of subjugation, marginalization, dispossession, exclusion or discrimination, whether or not these conditions persist.

Self-identification as indigenous or tribal is considered a fundamental criterion and this is the practice followed in the United Nations and its specialized agencies, as well as in certain regional intergovernmental organizations. Article 33 of the UN Declaration on the Rights of Indigenous Peoples refers to the rights of indigenous peoples to decide their own identities and membership procedures.

In some countries, it is controversial to use the term "indigenous". There may be local terms (such as tribal, first people, ethnic minorities) or occupational and geographical labels (hunter-gatherers, pastoralists, nomadic or semi-nomadic, hill people, etc.) that, for all practical purposes, can be used to refer to "indigenous peoples". In some cases, however, the notion of being indigenous has pejorative connotations and people may choose to refuse or redefine their indigenous origin. Such choices must be respected, while at the same time, any discrimination based on indigenous peoples' cultures and identity must be rejected. This different language use is also reflected in international law. The UN Declaration on the Rights of Indigenous Peoples, adopted in 2007, uses the term "indigenous" in a widely inclusive manner, while the only international conventions on the subject—the ILO Convention on Indigenous and Tribal Peoples, 1989 (No. 169) and its 1957 predecessor (Convention No. 107) use the terminology "indigenous and tribal". While these are considered to have similar coverage at the international level, not all governments agree.

# Identifying Indigenous Peoples

The most fruitful approach is to identify, rather than attempt to define, indigenous peoples in a specific context. Indigenous peoples' representatives themselves have taken the position that no global definition is either possible or desirable. Identification is a more constructive and pragmatic process, based on the fundamental criterion of self-identification. The identification of indigenous peoples must thus be undertaken with the full participation of the peoples concerned. The purpose of the exercise is to gain a better understanding of the specific situations of exclusion, discrimination and poverty faced by particular groups of peoples so that public policies can address these issues by developing targeted programmes and inclusive processes. . . .

# Distinguishing Indigenous Peoples from Other Marginalized Groups

Indigenous peoples often have much in common with other marginalized segments of society, i.e., lack of or very poor political representation and participation, lack of access to social services, and exclusion from decision-making processes on matters affecting them directly or indirectly. However, the situation of indigenous peoples is different because of their history and their intimate relationship with their lands, territories and resources which, in many cases, not only provide them with the economic means for living but, more importantly, sustain them as peoples. As distinct peoples, indigenous peoples claim the right to self-determination, including the right to control their own political, social, economic and cultural development as enshrined in the United Nations Declaration on the Rights of Indigenous People, ILO Convention No. 169, and other human rights instruments. Furthermore, many indigenous peoples have a profound spiritual relationship with their land and natural resources. Indigenous peoples' rights to manage their traditional lands, territories and rel-

## The Diversity of Indigenous Peoples

Indigenous peoples worldwide number between 300–500 million, embody and nurture 80% of the world's cultural and biological diversity, and occupy 20% of the world's land surface. The Indigenous peoples of the world are very diverse. They live in nearly all the countries on all the continents of the world and form a spectrum of humanity, ranging from traditional hunter-gatherers and subsistence farmers to legal scholars. In some countries, indigenous peoples form the majority of the population; others comprise small minorities. Indigenous peoples are concerned with preserving land, protecting language and promoting culture. Some indigenous peoples strive to preserve traditional ways of life, while others seek greater participation in the current state structures. Like all cultures and civilizations, indigenous peoples are always adjusting and adapting to changes in the world. Indigenous peoples recognize their common plight and work for their self-determination; based on their respect for the earth.

*Sarah Hymowitz, et al.,*
*"The Rights of Indigenous Peoples,"*
*University of Minnesota Human Rights Center, 2003.*

evant resources are fundamental for their physical and spiritual survival. However, all too often, indigenous communities have been displaced and dislocated from their ancestral lands in the name of development, by oil and gas or other natural resource exploitation projects, the construction of dams, conservation parks, roads or other national development priorities, which have been designed without the free, prior and informed consent of indigenous peoples—and indeed, often without any form of consultation with them at all.

# Indigenous Peoples and Development

During the early history of the United Nations' development assistance work, there was a tendency to regard indigenous rights as a "marginal" issue in the broader development context. However, it is estimated that indigenous peoples constitute some 370 million individuals, representing more than 5,000 distinct peoples living in more than 70 countries. The vast majority of indigenous peoples live in the developing world. In both developing and developed countries, indigenous peoples are generally excluded from political participation; they are economically and socially marginalized and disproportionately represented among the victims of human rights abuses and conflicts. Very often, indigenous peoples have not been recognized as peoples in the Constitution or other national legislation, and they may not even have the right to identity papers in their own country.

*All too often, indigenous communities have been displaced and dislocated from their ancestral lands in the name of development . . . without the free, prior and informed consent of indigenous peoples—and indeed, often without any form of consultation with them at all.*

Among the many challenges faced by indigenous peoples is usually a denial of their right to control their own development, even though they hold their own diverse concepts of development, based on their own different values, visions, needs and priorities. Equally, their perception and interpretation of well-being may not be the same as that of the dominant society in which they live, as it often reflects their own worldview and values. In some countries, despite their contribution to the nation-building process, their loyalty to the country has been questioned because their view of development does not correspond to that of the dominant society.

Although representing 5 percent of the world's population, studies have indicated that indigenous peoples represent 15 percent of the world's poorest people. Inequality in income, education, access to basic public services (e.g., clean water, food, shelter and health) and political representation affect almost all indigenous peoples. The achievement of the Millennium Development Goals (MDGs)—as well as of the Poverty Reduction Strategy Papers (PRSPs)—is therefore particularly challenging for indigenous peoples in many aspects, in both developed and developing countries.

The UNPFII [United Nations Permanent Forum on Indigenous Issues] has consistently raised issues of crucial importance, such as the inclusion of indigenous peoples in development processes; the need for a human rights—based approach to development; and for indigenous peoples to be included in the monitoring mechanisms for the MDGs and PRSPs. Moreover, the UNPFII has reiterated that general indicators used to define and measure poverty do not necessarily reflect the reality of indigenous peoples' situations, nor do they correspond to the world views of indigenous peoples. It has been stated that one of the root causes of poverty and marginalization for indigenous peoples is the loss of control over their traditional lands, territories and natural resources. Denying them the right to live on their lands and territories and to manage natural resources in a sustainable manner has resulted in further marginalization and exclusion. At the same time, attempts to achieve the MDGs may drive governments and others to accelerate the expropriation of indigenous peoples' lands, territories and natural resources.

# Australia Apologizes to Indigenous Peoples for Past Wrongs

*Kevin Rudd*

*The following viewpoint is excerpted from a speech given to parliament in 2008 by Australian Prime Minister Kevin Rudd. Rudd argues that the members of parliament and the people of Australia must offer an apology to the indigenous peoples of Australia for government policies that harmed them. In particular, he urges parliament to apologize to the "Stolen Generations," indigenous children separated from their families and sent to white boarding schools or given to white foster families. He concludes that only through extending such an apology can Australia hope for reconciliation and a new beginning with its indigenous populations.*

As you read, consider the following questions:

1. Whose story does Prime Minister Rudd tell to answer the question, "Why apologize?"

2. What was the name of the report commissioned in 1995 by Prime Minister Keating?

3. What core value of the Australian nation does Rudd cite as a further reason for an apology?

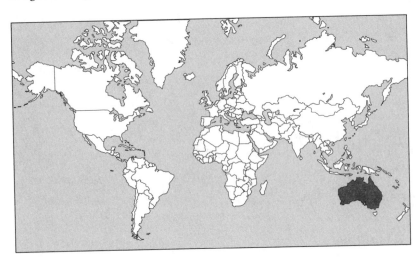

There comes a time in the history of nations when their peoples must become fully reconciled to their past if they are to go forward with confidence to embrace their future. Our nation, Australia, has reached such a time. And that is why the parliament is today here assembled: to deal with this unfinished business of the nation, to remove a great stain from the nation's soul and, in a true spirit of reconciliation, to open a new chapter in the history of this great land, Australia.

Last year [2007] I made a commitment to the Australian people that if we formed the next government of the Commonwealth we would in parliament say sorry to the Stolen Generations [generations of Aboriginal children forcibly taken from their homes]. Today I honour that commitment. I said we would do so early in the life of the new parliament. Again, today I honour that commitment by doing so at the commencement of this the 42nd parliament of the Commonwealth. Because the time has come, well and truly come, for all peoples of our great country, for all citizens of our great Commonwealth, for all Australians—those who are Indigenous and those who are not—to come together to reconcile and together build a new future for our nation.

# Why Apologize?

Some have asked, 'Why apologise?' Let me begin to answer by telling the parliament just a little of one person's story—an elegant, eloquent and wonderful woman in her 80s, full of life, full of funny stories, despite what has happened in her life's journey. A woman who has travelled a long way to be with us today, a member of the Stolen Generation who shared some of her story with me when I called around to see her just a few days ago. Nungala Fejo, as she prefers to be called, was born in the late 1920s. She remembers her earliest childhood days living with her family and her community in a bush camp just outside Tennant Creek. She remembers the love and the warmth and the kinship of those days long ago, including traditional dancing around the camp fire at night. She loved the dancing. She remembers once getting into strife when, as a four-year-old girl, she insisted on dancing with the male tribal elders rather than just sitting and watching the men, as the girls were supposed to do.

But then, sometime around 1932, when she was about four, she remembers the coming of the welfare men. Her family had feared that day and had dug holes in the creek bank where the children could run and hide. What they had not expected was that the white welfare men did not come alone. They brought a truck, they brought two white men and an Aboriginal stockman on horseback cracking his stockwhip. The kids were found; they ran for their mothers, screaming, but they could not get away. They were herded and piled onto the back of the truck. Tears flowing, her mum tried clinging to the sides of the truck as her children were taken away to the Bungalow in Alice, all in the name of protection.

A few years later, government policy changed. Now the children would be handed over to the missions to be cared for by the churches. But which church would care for them? The kids were simply told to line up in three lines. Nanna Fejo and her sister stood in the middle line, her older brother and cousin on her left. Those on the left were told that they had become Catholics, those in the middle Methodists and those on the right Church of England. That is how the complex questions of post-reformation theology were resolved in the Australian outback in the 1930s. It was as crude as that. She and her sister were sent to a Methodist mission on Goulburn Island and then Croker Island. Her Catholic brother was sent to work at a cattle station and her cousin to a Catholic mission.

Nanna Fejo's family had been broken up for a second time. She stayed at the mission until after the war, when she was allowed to leave for a prearranged job as a domestic in Darwin. She was 16. Nanna Fejo never saw her mum again. After she left the mission, her brother let her know that her mum had died years before, a broken woman fretting for the children that had literally been ripped away from her.

## All Mothers Are Important

I asked Nanna Fejo what she would have me say today about her story. She thought for a few moments then said that what I should say today was that all mothers are important. And she added: 'Families—keeping them together is very important. It's a good thing that you are surrounded by love and that love is passed down the generations. That's what gives you happiness.' As I left, later on, Nanna Fejo took one of my staff aside, wanting to make sure that I was not too hard on the Aboriginal stockman who had hunted those kids down all those years ago. The stockman had found her again decades later, this time himself to say, 'Sorry.' And remarkably, extraordinarily, she had forgiven him.

Nanna Fejo's is just one story. There are thousands, tens of thousands of them: stories of forced separation of Aboriginal and Torres Strait Islander children from their mums and dads over the better part of a century. Some of these stories are graphically told in *Bringing Them Home*, the report commissioned in 1995 by Prime Minister Keating and received in 1997 by Prime Minister Howard. There is something terribly primal about these firsthand accounts. The pain is searing; it screams from the pages. The hurt, the humiliation, the degradation and the sheer brutality of the act of physically separating a mother from her children is a deep assault on our senses and on our most elemental humanity.

> *Between 1910 and 1970, between 10 and 30 percent of [Australian] Indigenous children were forcibly taken from their mothers and fathers. . . . As a result, up to 50,000 children were forcibly taken from their families.*

These stories cry out to be heard; they cry out for an apology. Instead, from the nation's parliament there has been a stony and stubborn and deafening silence for more than a decade. A view that somehow we, the parliament, should suspend our most basic instincts of what is right and what is wrong. A view that, instead, we should look for any pretext to push this great wrong to one side, to leave it languishing with the historians, the academics and the cultural warriors, as if the Stolen Generations are little more than an interesting sociological phenomenon. But the Stolen Generations are not intellectual curiosities. They are human beings, human beings who have been damaged deeply by the decisions of parliaments and governments. But, as of today, the time for denial, the time for delay, has at last come to an end.

## Human Decency Demands That Wrongs Be Righted

The nation is demanding of its political leadership to take us forward. Decency, human decency, universal human decency, demands that the nation now steps forward to right a historical wrong. That is what we are doing in this place today. But should there still be doubts as to why we must now act. Let

## The Stolen Generation

The greatest assault on indigenous cultures and family life was the forced separation or 'taking away' of indigenous children from their families. This occurred in every Australian state from the late 1800s until the practice was officially ended in 1969. During this time as many as 100,000 children were separated from their families. These children became known as the Stolen Generation.

The separation took three forms: putting indigenous children into government-run institutions; adoption of children by white families; and the fostering of children into white families. The last two strategies were particularly applied to 'fair-skinned' children.

These forced separations were part of deliberate policies of assimilation. Their aim was to cut children off from their culture to have them raised to think and act as 'white'.

*"Indigenous Australia,"*
*Australian Museum Online, 2004.*
*www.dreamtime.net.au.*

the parliament reflect for a moment on the following facts: that, between 1910 and 1970, between 10 and 30 percent of Indigenous children were forcibly taken from their mothers and fathers. That, as a result, up to 50,000 children were forcibly taken from their families. That this was the product of the deliberate, calculated policies of the state as reflected in the explicit powers given to them under statute. That this policy was taken to such extremes by some in administrative authority that the forced extractions of children of so-called 'mixed lineage' were seen as part of a broader policy of dealing with 'the problem of the Aboriginal population'.

One of the most notorious examples of this approach was from the Northern Territory Protector of Natives [a government official], who stated, and I quote:

"Generally by the fifth and invariably by the sixth generation, all native characteristics of the Australian aborigine are eradicated. The problem of our half-castes—"

to quote the protector—

"will quickly be eliminated by the complete disappearance of the black race, and the swift submergence of their progeny in the white . . ."

---

*We apologise for the hurt, the pain and suffering, we, the parliament, have caused [Australian indigenous peoples] by the laws that previous parliaments have enacted. We apologise for the indignity, the degradation and the humiliation these laws embodied.*

---

The Western Australian Protector of Natives expressed not dissimilar views, expounding them at length in Canberra in 1937 at the first national conference on Indigenous affairs that brought together the Commonwealth and state protectors of natives. These are uncomfortable things to be brought out into the light. They are not pleasant. They are profoundly disturbing. But we must acknowledge these facts if we are to deal once and for all with the argument that the policy of generic forced separation was somehow well motivated, justified by its historical context and, as a result, unworthy of any apology today.

Then we come to the argument of intergenerational responsibility, also used by some to argue against giving an apology today. But let us remember the fact that the forced removal of Aboriginal children was happening as late as the early 1970s. The 1970s is not exactly a point in remote antiquity. There are still serving members of this parliament who were first elected to this place in the early 1970s. It is well within the adult memory span of many of us. The uncomfortable truth for us all is that the parliaments of the nation, individually and collectively, enacted statutes and delegated authority under those statutes that made the forced removal of children on racial grounds fully lawful.

## The Need for Reconciliation

There is a further reason for an apology as well: it is that reconciliation is in fact an expression of a core value of our nation—and that value is a fair go for all. There is a deep and abiding belief in the Australian community that, for the Stolen Generations, there was no fair go at all. And there is a pretty basic Aussie belief that says it is time to put right this most outrageous of wrongs. It is for these reasons, quite apart from concerns of fundamental human decency, that the governments and parliaments of this nation must make this apology. Because, put simply, the laws that our parliaments enacted made the Stolen Generations possible. We, the parliaments of the nation, are ultimately responsible, not those who gave effect to our laws, the problem lay with the laws themselves. As has been said of settler societies elsewhere, we are the bearers of many blessings from our ancestors and therefore we must also be the bearer of their burdens as well. Therefore, for our nation, the course of action is clear. Therefore, for our people, the course of action is clear. And that is, to deal now with what has become one of the darkest chapters in Australia's history. In doing so, we are doing more than contending with the facts, the evidence and the often rancorous public debate. In doing so, we are also wrestling with our own soul. This is not, as some would argue, a black-armband view of history; it is just the truth: the cold, confronting, uncomfortable truth. Facing with it, dealing with it, moving on from it. And until we fully confront that truth, there will always be a shadow hanging over us and our future as a fully united and fully reconciled people. It is time to reconcile. It is time to recognize the injustices of the past. It is time to say sorry. It is time to move forward together.

To the Stolen Generations, I say the following: as Prime Minister of Australia, I am sorry. On behalf of the Government of Australia, I am sorry. On behalf of the Parliament of Australia, I am sorry. And I offer you this apology without qualification. We apologise for the hurt, the pain and suffering we, the parliament, have caused you by the laws that previous parliaments have enacted. We apologise for the indignity, the degradation and the humiliation these laws embodied. We offer this apology to the mothers, the fathers, the brothers, the sisters, the families and the communities whose lives were ripped apart by the actions of successive governments under successive parliaments. In making this apology, I would also like to speak personally to the members of the Stolen Generation and their families: to those here today, so many of you; to those listening across the nation—from Yuendumu, in the central west of the Northern Territory, to Yabara, in North Queensland, and to Pitjantjatjara in South Australia.

I know that, in offering this apology on behalf of the government and the parliament, there is nothing I can say today that can take away the pain you have suffered personally. Whatever words I speak today, I cannot undo that. Words alone are not that powerful. Grief is a very personal thing. I say to non-Indigenous Australians listening today who may not fully understand why what we are doing is so important, I ask those non-Indigenous Australians to imagine for a moment if this had happened to you. I say to honourable members here present: imagine if this had happened to us. Imagine the crippling effect. Imagine how hard it would be to forgive. But my proposal is this: if the apology we extend today is accepted in the spirit of reconciliation, in which it is offered, we can today resolve together that there be a new beginning for Australia. And it is to such a new beginning that I believe the nation is now calling us.

# The United States Should Atone for Historic Wrongs Against American Indians

*A. Jay Adler*

*In the following viewpoint, A. Jay Adler argues that the greatest crime of human history is the genocide of indigenous peoples by European civilizations who invaded and colonized much of the world. He asserts that the injustices against indigenous peoples in the United States continue in the present through broken treaties and mismanaged American Indian trust funds. He concludes that in order for the United States to be a great nation, it must institute a national day of atonement and fully acknowledge the wrongs done to Native Americans. A. Jay Adler is a professor of English at Los Angeles Southwest College.*

As you read, consider the following questions:

1. What was the name of Dee Brown's 1970 book that told the story of the 1890 massacre of Sioux Indians?

2. What natural feature in South Dakota do the Sioux consider sacred?

3. With what current holiday does Adler suggest a national day of mourning and atonement might coincide?

A. Jay Adler, "Aboriginal Sin," *Tikkun*, vol. 23, no. 2, March/April 2008, pp. 15–20, 62. www.tikkun.org. Copyright © 2008 Institute for Labor and Mental Health. Reproduced by permission of the author.

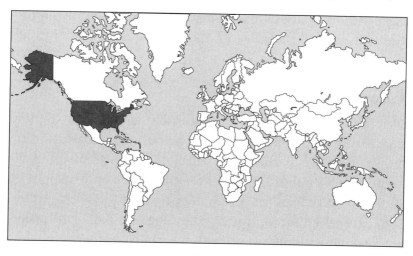

The original unredeemed social and political crime of human history is the displacement and genocidal destruction of aboriginal populations. Yet despite the powerful and irrefutable history of these events, overwhelming numbers of people in the Western world have yet to be moved by conscience. What is the reason for this demurral, and what is to be done about it? For those attuned to discordances in matters of social justice, this harsh reality is a historical given of the modern world. For others, whatever it is that may have occurred took place long ago—it is history, it is past, there is nothing to be done.

Recent events in the United States and elsewhere suggest otherwise, however.

During his visit to Brazil of May, 2007, Pope Benedict outraged many South American indigenous groups by suggesting that the deliverance of Christian faith to the native populations of South America had been a benefit of the colonial era—a benefit, indeed, for which the indigenous peoples had been "silently longing" and that had "shaped their culture for 500 years." Speaking defensively, and in denial of the historical record, he declared, "The proclamation of Jesus and of his

Gospel did not at any point involve an alienation of the pre-Columbus cultures, nor was it the imposition of a foreign culture."

## European Rationalization

Of course, the belief that European civilization and religious conceptions were superior to the native cultures, which were barely dignified as such, was what originally rationalized the subjugation of those cultures for those uncomfortable with purely materialistic motives. In Africa, the Western Hemisphere, and Oceania, notwithstanding the pain and loss—whole societies, millions of lives—the native peoples would be better off in the end. The cross or the sword had really been the cross and the sword. And now, in the twenty-first century, the leader of one of the world's predominant religions, that had in fact served as the handmaiden of conquest, that had offered spiritual balm to soothe cultural disembowelment, can still assert that no real crime was committed and the aboriginal peoples had been delivered a gift.

How does the conscience not reel?

Newspaper accounts reported the protests for a day or two and the world reacted with habitual indifference.

Around the same time HB0 premiered *Bury My Heart at Wounded Knee*, an Yves Simoneau film inspired by Dee Brown's seminal 1970 book of the same name. The book is a corrective account of the final act, in the second half of the nineteenth century, of the U.S. government's subjugation of the American Indian, its title drawn from the location on the Pine Ridge Indian Reservation in South Dakota wherein December 1890 the United States 7th Cavalry massacred over 300 Sioux Indians.

Despite the film's mediocre reviews, there is no reason to think that quality is the explanation for the film's failure to resonate in the American consciousness. Better films over the years, and a fairly complete revision in the scholarly histories of European-Indian contact, have served to undermine any serious, sustainable narrative of the expansion of the United States as, simply, a heroic and noble endeavor. Yet there has not been any fundamental alteration in the American sense of nationhood—no commonly accepted understanding of a sin concomitant with the nation's origin and development that demands some form of atonement.

Such crimes, however, are not mere history. In South America, for the past century up until the present day, miners, ranchers, and multinational corporations have overrun, despoiled, or committed murder among small indigenous societies in the Amazon rainforest. Throughout Latin America indigenous peoples have been bandied between the poles of oligarchic exploitation and demagogic tyranny.

---

*Though it is little noted by the American people, even today the U.S. government is actively deceiving and plainly stealing from Native Americans in lineal continuation of the deceptions and thefts of the nineteenth century.*

---

And what of the United States? Were the Native American tribes not so thoroughly conquered and diminished in the nineteenth century as to make any continuing assault on their dignity, culture, and lives effectively impossible? Unfortunately, no.

More than a century later all of the expected social afflictions and human maladies of a conquered and disintegrated culture are present: inadequate education, joblessness, drug dependence, despair, and poverty. The Pine Ridge Reservation itself is wholly within Shannon County, South Dakota, which is the second poorest county in the United States. The very poorest county is Buffalo County, South Dakota, which is mostly constituted by the Crow Creek Indian Reservation.

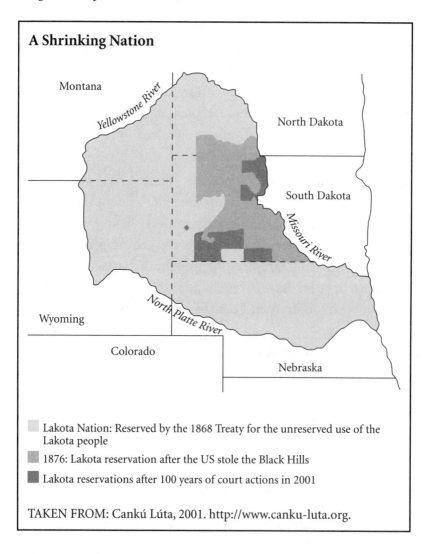

**A Shrinking Nation**

Lakota Nation: Reserved by the 1868 Treaty for the unreserved use of the Lakota people

1876: Lakota reservation after the US stole the Black Hills

Lakota reservations after 100 years of court actions in 2001

TAKEN FROM: Cankú Lúta, 2001. http://www.canku-luta.org.

## The Exploitation of American Indians Continues

It might be argued that these are the sad and unfortunate after effects of a regrettable past that we do not oppress and exploit the Indian today. We have, after all, the achievements of the Civil Rights and feminist movements behind us. Gay marriage is a subject of public and political debate. But what consideration is there of American Indians beyond occasional, unsympathetic arguments about naming athletic teams and mascots after them?

Indeed, though it is little noted by the American people, even today the U.S. government is actively deceiving and plainly stealing from Native Americans in lineal continuation of the deceptions and thefts of the nineteenth century. In fact, two current lawsuits brought by Native Americans against the U.S. Department of the Interior originate in obligations the government forced or coerced the tribes to accept during that long ago history of conquest. The conflict, we thought, had ended well over a century ago, but the end game is being played out today. A precursor lawsuit set the stage, though.

Among the most well-known deceits in an extensive history by the U.S government, the 1851 Treaty of Fort Laramie caused several Indian tribes, including the various Sioux tribes, to relinquish their customary freedom of movement and accept large tracts of the Great Plains as designated reservations for each tribe. In the successor 1868 Treaty of Fort Laramie, the Sioux were compelled to renegotiate the original treaty and accept as theirs a much-reduced expanse of territory, but which still included the Black Hills of South Dakota, land the Sioux consider sacred. After the discovery of gold in the Black Hills by prospectors who were already there illegally, the U.S. government broke the treaty and seized the Black Hills.

---

*While even the great sin of slavery is confessed, the genocide of Native Americans is not even discussed [by the United States government].*

---

In 1980, in *United States v. Sioux Nation of Indians*, the U.S. Supreme Court ruled in favor of the tribes of the Sioux Nation in their claim to the Black Hills. The monetary award was the $17.5 million market value of the land in 1877, which at 5 percent interest came to $105 million in 1980. The Sioux decided that they wanted not the money, but the land, and refused the award. Today, with continuing interest, the award money held in trust is in excess of $700 million dollars. However, the Black Hills trust money is very small compared to other Indian trust funds that the U.S. government has managed and institutionally embezzled for over a century. . . .

## A Painful Truth

How does this continue? How can the U.S. government—nearly 117 years after the Pine Ridge massacre, long after most Americans believe their nation began its struggle to repair the injustices that shadowed the ideals from which it was formed—continue its deceptions, its thefts, its oppression of Native Americans, and have its people still be silent? While even the great sin of slavery is confessed, the genocide of the American Indian is not even discussed. Can it be that the fundamental truth is too painful, too disillusioning to acknowledge? Slavery was an enormous and inconceivable crime. It cannot be undone any more than can any other crime. But we do not continue to perpetrate it. Yet every day, just by virtue of our presence in the lands we occupy—in the Western Hemisphere, in Australia—we affirm as real not just our political ideals and heroic myths, but the conquest and the genocide that enabled our cultural ascension. Still, we cannot undo them. We cannot give the land back. We cannot undie the dead.

The answer for too many is denial. The land was so vast, and they were so few. They could not use it all, did not need it all. And they simply did not understand. The conflict was inevitable. We were stronger, more unified, more ambitious. We *had* ambition. It is the sad way of the world. It was always so. But the world—we—are different now.

But we are not. The lawsuits are now. The money that could change the lives of so many Native Americans, still contending with their decline as the legacy of our ascension, the money is now, and it is theirs. We require the Germans to confess and pay for their genocidal crimes. We admonish the Japanese for refusing, still, to fully acknowledge theirs. Yet how well do we confront our own?

How can we be so great if the land is not ours?

Despite changes in scholarship, and the education of a segment of the population that might consider itself more historically enlightened, the public events of the past fifty years have achieved little for Native Americans. Events have not galvanized the American people or their government finally to concede the crime committed and to begin a policy of moral and social restoration. . . .

*If we are not familial, we are cultural descendents of those who committed this wrong [the genocide of Native Americans], and like any people of conscience, we must accept the full legacy that we inherit, all that is so great and kind and all that is not.*

## How to Address Wrongs

What can we do now to address the wrongs committed against aboriginal peoples?

In Australia, the course of conquest was strikingly similar to that of the United States. Again, all of the predictable social ills of a subjugated population struggling to overcome the loss of integral selfhood afflict aboriginal Australians today. Nonetheless, Australia has taken measures to acknowledge this history of subjugation, both substantively and symbolically, that cannot be observed in North and South America. On the symbolic level, in 1998, Australia instituted National Sorry Day as an annual acknowledgment of the wrongs that were committed against the indigenous population. So purely symbolic an act can easily be construed as pathetically inconsequential, but all acts of redemption must begin or end symbolically with acknowledgment of the wrong committed. When will the United States do as much?. . .

On the symbolic but very significant level, the United States should follow the lead of Australia and institute a national day of mourning and atonement in permanent recognition of the various crimes against the Native American population. At the appropriate levels, school curricula should more fully educate American students in the complex legacy that would call for such a day. The day might even be instituted to coincide with Columbus Day. As it is, an unacknowledged divide exists in the nation with respect to Columbus Day. Some casually look upon it as an honorific occasion for the origin of American history and culture, and others ironically, even bitterly, disdain the day. To join a day of atonement with Columbus Day would capture all of the contradictions and ambivalence with which a developed, mature, and confident nation and culture should regard human history. . . .

HBO's *Bury My Heart at Wounded Knee* has two unexpected virtues. The first is found in a dramatically absurd battlefield debate between the Sioux Chief Sitting Bull and Colonel Nelson Miles in which Miles argues forcefully that long before the white man arrived, the Sioux had warred with, conquered, and taken land from their Indian enemies. The second is in the portrayal of Henry Dawes, a U.S. Senator and white friend of the Indian, who, it is soon clear, was in the end only a patronizing pawn in the campaign of subjugation, offering the Indians help in giving up their land, culture, and language, as the only way for them to "survive." The lessons are that indigenous peoples need not be idealized to recognize the wrong that was done them, and there is no friendship in the unrefusable offer.

If we are ever to deserve the various appellations we take upon ourselves to claim we are unlike those who came before and would not do what they did, then we must freely acknowledge, without reservation, the sins of those who produced the world in which we live. We must do this not because we are personally guilty of the crime against native peoples. None of us lived when the genocide was committed, and in the United States most may not have ancestors who were even on the continent when these acts were committed. But if we are not familial, we are cultural descendents of those who committed this wrong, and like any people of conscience, we must accept the full legacy that we inherit, all that is so great and kind and all that is not. There need be no single set of ideas for how this may be done. In every nation the way may be different. Nothing lost can be reconstituted. Nothing can be restored except a form of balance. But we may be redeemed.

# Canada's Examination of Indigenous Residential Schools Is Controversial

*Nancy MacDonald*

*In the following viewpoint, Nancy MacDonald traces the formation of a truth and reconciliation committee (TRC) in Canada designed to address the abuse suffered by First Nations members who were forced to attend residential schools. At TRC hearings, Aboriginals will be encouraged to tell their stories. MacDonald argues, however, that such a process may not lead to reconciliation nor unify Canadian society. She notes that many of those assaulted while at the schools do not want to participate nor are they ready to reconcile with those who mistreated them. Nancy MacDonald is a reporter for the Canadian news magazine, Maclean's.*

As you read, consider the following questions:

1. Whose idea is the truth and reconciliation committee?
2. Why does writer Tomson Highway refuse to denounce the residential schools?
3. Who are two well-known Aboriginal leaders who have not decided if they will testify, according to MacDonald?

Will airing the truth heal old wounds or help create new ones?

Nancy MacDonald, "To Forgive or Forget," *Maclean's*, vol. 121, no. 24, June 23, 2008, pp. 24–25. Copyright © 2008 by *Maclean's Magazine*. Reproduced by permission.

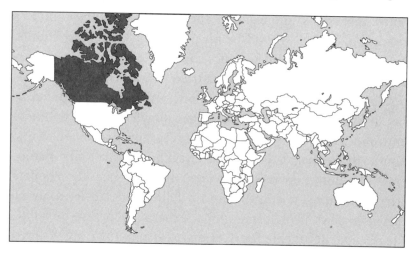

Twenty-five years ago, as Latin America was ditching its dictators and coming to grips with a legacy of death squads and "disappearances," Argentina tested a new way forward. It would let the guilty walk. Instead of mass prosecutions of crimes committed by the military junta, Argentina held hearings airing horrifying details of torture and the murder of as many as 30,000 leftist dissidents. Its final report, *Nunca Más* (Never Again), remains one of the country's best-selling books. It was the first ever "truth commission," and a hit well beyond Argentina's borders. Chile and El Salvador soon initiated their own. By the late '90s, truth commissions had almost become part of the cycle of war and peace, most famously in South Africa. Most often, they recommend reparation programs and legal reform. Today, four are under way, including one in Timor-Leste, the world's newest country. Now that the blood has dried, Kenya will get one too.

But Canada may beat Kenya to the gate: we're soon getting a truth commission of our own. Headed by Ontario Court of Appeal Judge Harry LaForme, and slated to launch cross-country hearings this year [2008] Canada's truth and reconciliation committee will come on the heels of the PM's [Canadian Prime Minister Stephen Harper's] official apology to native Canadians, and examine the sad history of the country's residential schools. It will be a world first—on several counts. No one has ever tried a truth commission in a fully democratic country. No one has ever tried one absent a war or political conflict. And no commission to date has attempted to revisit historical wrongs. Most begin shortly after the conflict's end and limit the scope to the preceding five to 10 years. South Africa's began 24 months after the country's first democratic election. Canada's has waited 40-odd years. Its mandate stretches almost a century and a half. That fact is drawing mixed reviews from some global experts, who fear our TRC [Truth and Reconciliation Committee] may turn out to be a monumental waste of time. Truth commissions aren't meant to heal wounds created a hundred years ago, they note. Will airing ugly truths so long after they've already been accepted as such accomplish anything? Will it create new issues?

## The Missing Chapter in Canadian History

The commission was the brainchild of Grand Chief Phil Fontaine of the Assembly of First Nations [AFN] and Calgary lawyer Kathleen Mahoney, chief negotiator for the AFN and Fontaine's long-time companion. Its point is to write the "missing chapter" in Canada's history, they say. That chapter might have stayed buried if not for Fontaine, who, in the fall of 1990, live from Winnipeg, blew the lid on the scandal on CBC Television's *The Journal*. Already among the country's most prominent native leaders, the elegant, 46-year-old head of the Assembly of Manitoba Chiefs told the late Barbara Frum that he, like his Fort Alexander Residential School classmates, had been physically and sexually abused, hinting that, "as the cliché goes," he himself had gone from abused to abuser. It was a chilling tale. At the time, no one inside or outside the Aboriginal community had any idea of the extent of abuse, says Fontaine, whose torment began at age eight, when his older brother was moved to an adjacent dormitory, leaving him without a protector.

Fontaine's explosive confession opened the "floodgates," says Saskatchewan historian J.R. Miller, author of *Shingwauk's Vision*, the definitive text on Canada's residential schools. "That someone as prominent as he was talking about some pretty painful experiences made it easier for victims to talk openly," says Miller. "He made it okay." For over a decade now, Fontaine and Canada's Aboriginal community have demanded redress. Two years ago, Ottawa and the AFN agreed to a $1.9-billion settlement; reparations averaging $30,000 began flowing this fall [2007]. "But money alone doesn't salve wounds," says Mahoney. She hopes Canada's unprecedented program in truth-telling and repentance just might.

---

*Slated to launch cross-country hearings this year [2008], Canada's truth and reconciliation committee will come on the heels of [Canadian Prime Minister Stephen Harper's] official apology to native Canadians, and examine the sad history of the country's residential schools.*

---

"It's not about making Canadians feel guilty," says Toronto MP Michael Ignatieff, who headed Harvard's Carr Centre for Human Rights before entering politics, and, in 1996, spent six weeks in South Africa filming a documentary on that country's TRC. "It's about making Canadians feel responsible—saying 'Yeah, this happened. And let's unite as a country and make sure it doesn't happen again.'" But that's nonsense, says Harvard's Robert I. Rotberg, director of the Program on Intrastate Conflict and Conflict Resolution at the Kennedy School of Government. "It cannot be repeated because the circumstances are so different; the preventive part of this simply doesn't exist. What's the point of going past reparations, to a review of all that happened? It's very unusual, very narrow—and very much after the fact. I can't imagine what its reconciliatory function is. What is the purpose of having a flagellation like this? Why is that good for Canada?"

# The Culture Climate of the Residential Schools

It's crucial to remember the cultural climate in which the schools existed, notes Clyde Ellis, a professor of Native American history at Elon University, highlighting the inherent challenge of pursuing historical justice. The schools are reprehensible by today's standards, but in their heyday were not unique. "Their assimilationist intellectual and cultural agendas reflected the same goals public schools had when it came to the education of immigrant children," he says.

Complicating the picture is the fact that many natives' experience of residential school is oddly ambiguous, says Miller. There is a number for whom the experience was "totally, unrelievedly horrific." But others will say, 'There were a lot of problems; I was hit, or I was abused. But there were some good things about it. I learned skills. I made friends.'

That's true of writer Tomson Highway, whose play *Dry Lips Oughta Move to Kapuskasing* features a scene involving a rape by crucifix. His novel, *Kiss of the Fur Queen*, has a six-year-old protagonist who speaks no English and meets violence couched as discipline by his residential school's overzealous missionaries. Yet, for the horror recounted in the semi-autobiographical novel, including the repeated sexual assault of the Okimasis brothers, Highway doesn't denounce the school system, which, he says, allowed him to become a concert pianist and his brother René—a company member of the Toronto Dance Theatre, who, at 36, died of AIDS—to become a dancer. "There were no grand pianos in northern Manitoba," says Highway.

# A Place to Tell Stories

Yet advocates argue a TRC will give victims a place to tell their stories, which may be important as last fall's [2007] payments [reparation payments made to victims of residential school abuse] have already dredged up bad memories. It may

# The Canadian Truth and Reconciliation Commission (TRC): What Is It and What Are Its Goals?

*There is an emerging and compelling desire to put the events of the past behind so that we can work towards a stronger and healthier future. The truth telling and reconciliation process as part of an overall . . . response to the Indian Residential School legacy is a sincere indication and acknowledgement of the injustices and harms experienced by Aboriginal people and the need for continued healing. . . . .*

- The TRC [Truth and Reconciliation Commission] was established in 2008 as a part of the Indian Residential Schools Settlement Agreement and will operate for five years.

- The TRC will provide . . . anyone affected by Indian Residential Schools with the opportunity of sharing their personal experiences.

- The TRC will witness, support, promote and facilitate truth and reconciliation events. . . .

- The TRC will [educate] . . . Canadians about the Indian Residential Schools system and its impacts.

- The TRC will identify sources and create as complete a historical record as possible of the Indian Residential Schools system and legacy. . . .

- The TRC will produce a report concerning the Indian Residential Schools system and experience, including the history, purpose, operation, and supervision of the system; the effects and consequences of the system . . . and the ongoing legacy of the residential schools.

*"The Truth and Reconciliation Commission Mandate,"*
*Indian Residential Schools Settlement Agreement,*
*Schedule N, May 8, 2006.*

also help Canadians to better understand the devastating impact of past practices. "Look, the risk of people just getting angry all over again exists," says Mahoney. "This is not fail-safe. But it's okay to be angry. Anger does subside; it's our hope that reconciliation will occur." For that to occur, experts agree the hearings need regular publicity. Generally, this requires hearing from perpetrators, a process that "completely shook" South Africa and Nigeria, where "virtually everyone was staying up till two in the morning watching reruns of the testimony," says Priscilla Hayner, the Geneva-based co-founder of the International Center for Transitional Justice and author of *Unspeakable Truths*, a guide to the world's TRCs.

Lacking the power of subpoena, however, Canadian officials have no compelling reason beyond grace or goodwill to come forward. And then, most are dead, as Fontaine admits. The commission will surely grab headlines when ex-students allege criminal deaths and hasty burials took place on school grounds. But the Privacy Act applies; perpetrators can only be publicly named if they've been convicted of a crime. In any case, the idea isn't to go up and start naming a bunch of names, says Mahoney. "This is supposed to be an exercise in reconciliation and forgiveness."

---

*Advocates argue a [truth and reconciliation committee] will give victims a place to tell their stories. ... It may also help Canadians to better understand the devastating impact of past practices.*

---

## Will Truth and Reconciliation Unite or Divide?

Still, airing accounts of atrocities doesn't always lead to reconciliation. A decade after South Africa's TRC, the enormous gulf between black and white persists, its amnesty pact remains deeply controversial, and several apartheid-victim groups are pushing for trials for murders committed under white rule. Five years ago, Argentina scrapped the amnesty laws that had spared commanders of its "dirty war" from prosecution; some victims now seek justice. Meanwhile, there are questions about the impact on survivors, who risk re-traumatization. And evidence contradicts the idea that addressing old wounds will erase divisions, says John Torpey, a New York-based expert on the politics of reparation. As a unique experience, suffering is more likely to differentiate or alienate victims, he explains.

But that's not the point. A truth commission cannot overcome a society's division, Ignatieff once wrote. "It can only winnow out the solid core of facts upon which society's arguments with itself should be conducted." That Argentina's military threw half-dead victims into the sea from helicopters is part of the public record—and of the country's conception of its history. To allow hatred and resentment to continue to simmer unexamined would be far worse.

In Canada, some of the best-known Aboriginal leaders, including Fontaine and Elijah Harper, the Manitoba MLA [Member of the Legislative Assembly] . . . haven't decided if they will testify. Highway, reached in Buenos Aires, where he and his partner are spending the winter, will not. "I can't think of a more effective way to waste time than to gripe about the past; all I have time for are the present and the future, both of which look pretty damn good." For others, the crimes of the past refuse to die. In 1959, Sylvester Green entered the Edmonton residential school where, over the next 10 years, he was repeatedly assaulted. His tormentor is dead. But Green, now in his 60s, lays waste to hollow clichés about turning the page and letting bygones be bygones. "I hope worms are crawling around in his frickin' head; I hope it's painful. That's where I'm at, now."

# Marshall Islands Indigenous Peoples Were Harmed by Nuclear Testing

*Tony de Brum*

*In the following viewpoint, Senator Tony de Brum, a member of the Republic of the Marshall Islands Parliament, describes the effects of nuclear testing on the Marshall Islands. According to de Brum, the U.S. government has detonated tons of nuclear weapons in the island nation, resulting in the forced relocation of indigenous peoples, serious deterioration of their culture, and devastating consequences for their health. He calls on the leaders of the world to stop further testing, and asserts that one nation does not have the right to destroy a society in the name of global security.*

As you read, consider the following questions:

1. What did a U.S. government study predict about the incidence of cancer in the Marshall Islands in 2005, according to de Brum?
2. The residents of what island were first repatriated when U.S. officials declared that it was safe to do so, and then removed when the U.S. government decided that the islanders were receiving too much radiation exposure, according to de Brum?

Tony de Brum, "Indigenous Presentation to the Delegates of the Seventh Review Conference of the Non-Proliferation Treaty," Nuclear Age Peace Foundation, May 11, 2005. www.wagingpeace.org. Reproduced by permission.

3. What happened to the people of Kwajalein when the United States began launching interceptor missiles from the Ronald Reagan Missile Defense Test Site on that island, according to de Brum?

I lived on the island of Likiep in the northern Marshalls for the entire 12 years [1946–1958] of the US [United States] atomic and thermonuclear testing program in my country. I witnessed most of the detonations, and was just 9 years old when I experienced the most horrific of these explosions, the infamous BRAVO shot that terrorized our community and traumatized our society to an extent that few people in the world can imagine.

## The Nuclear Legacy

While BRAVO was by far the most dramatic test, all 67 of the shots detonated in the Marshall Islands contributed one way or another to the nuclear legacy that haunts us to this day. As one of our legal advisors has described it, if one were to take the total yield of the nuclear weapons tested in the Marshall Islands and spread them out over time, we would have the equivalent of 1.6 Hiroshima shots, every day for twelve years.

But the Marshall Islands' encounter with the bomb did not end with the detonations themselves. In recent years, documents released by the United States government have uncovered even more horrific aspects of the Marshallese burden borne in the name of international peace and security. US government documents clearly demonstrate that its scientists conducted human radiation experiments with Marshallese citizens. Some of our people were injected with or coerced to drink fluids laced with radiation. Other experimentation involved the purposeful and premature resettlement of people on islands highly contaminated by the weapons tests to study how human beings absorb radiation from their foods and environment. Much of this human experimentation occurred in populations either exposed to near lethal amounts of radiation, or to "control" populations who were told they would receive medical "care" for participating in these studies to help their fellow citizens. At the conclusion of all these studies, the United States still maintained that no positive linkage can be established between the tests and the health status of the Marshallese. Just in the past few weeks [May 2005], a new US government study has predicted 50% higher than expected incidence of cancer in the Marshall Islands resulting from the atomic tests.

Although the testing of the atomic and thermonuclear weapons ended 48 years ago, we still have entire populations living in social disarray. The people of Rongelap Atoll, the inhabited island closest to the ground zero locations, remain in exile in their own country. I might also add that although the people of Rongelap were evacuated by the US government for earlier smaller weapons tests, the US government purposefully decided not to evacuate them prior to the detonation of the BRAVO event—a thermonuclear weapon designed to be the largest device ever detonated by the United States. The people of Rongelap were known to be in harms way but were not warned about BRAVO in advance and had no ability or knowledge of how to protect themselves or reduce their exposure.

---

*If one were to take the total yield of the nuclear weapons tested in the Marshall Islands and spread them out over time, we would have the equivalent of 1.6 Hiroshima shots, every day for twelve years.*

---

## Statistics, Lies, and the Destruction of Medical Records

Throughout the years, America's nuclear history in the Marshall Islands has been colored with official denial, self-serving control of information, and abrogation of commitment to redress the shameful wrongs done to the Marshallese people. The scientists and military officials involved in the testing

## The Marshall Islands

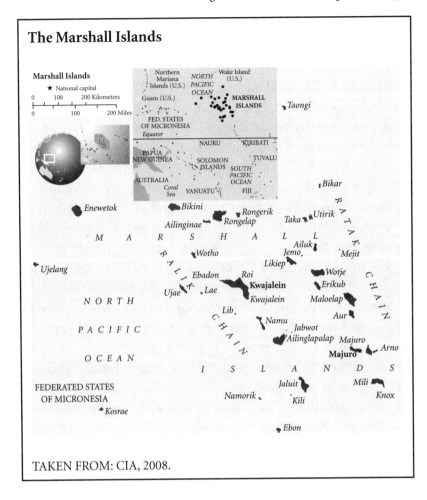

Marshall Islands

★ National capital

0   100   200 Kilometers

0   100   200 Miles

TAKEN FROM: CIA, 2008.

program picked and chose their study subjects, recognized certain communities as exposed when it served their interests, and denied monitoring and medical attention to subgroups within the Marshall Islands. I remember well their visits to my village in Likiep where they subjected every one of us to tests and invasive physical examinations which, as late as 1978, they denied even carrying out. In later years, when I was a public servant for the RMI [Republic of the Marshall Islands]. I raised the issue requesting that raw data gathered during these visits be made available to us. United States representatives responded by saying that our recollections were juvenile and did not consider the public health missions of the time.

For decades, the US government has utilized slick mathematical and statistical representations to dismiss the occurrence of exotic anomalies, including malformed fetuses, and abnormal appearances of diseases in so called "unexposed areas," as coincidental and not attributable to radiation exposure. We have been told repeatedly, for example, that our birthing anomalies are the result of incest or a gene pool that is too small—anything but the radiation. These explanations are offensive, and obviously wrong since these abnormalities certainly did not occur before we became the proving ground for US nuclear weapons. Selective referral of Marshallese patients to different military hospitals in the United States and its territories also made it easier for the US government to dismiss linkages between medical problems and radiation exposure. The several unexplained fires that led to the destruction of numerous records and medical charts for the patients with the most acute radiation illnesses further underscores this point. In spite of all these studies and findings, we were told that positive linkage was still impossible because of what they called "statistical insignificance."

## The Dog-and-Pony Show

I have been a student of the horrific impacts of the nuclear weapons testing program for most of my life. I served as interpreter for American officials who proclaimed Bikini safe for resettlement and commenced a program to repatriate the Bikini people who for decades barely survived on the secluded island of Kili. I accompanied the American High Commissioner of the Trust Territory just a few years later to once again remove the repatriated residents from Bikini because their exposure had become too high for the US government's comfort. I was also personally involved in the translation of the Enewetak Environmental Impact Statement that declared

Enewetak safe for resettlement. I voiced my doubts in a television interview at the time by describing the US public relations efforts associated with the Enewetak clean-up as a dog-and-pony show. Later, during negotiations to end the trust territory arrangement with the United States, we discovered that certain scientific information regarding Enewetak was being withheld from us because, as the official US government memorandum stated, "the Marshallese negotiators might make overreaching demands" on the United States if the facts about the extent of damage in the islands were known to us.

The outcome of our negotiations was the end of the United Nations Trusteeship and a treaty, which, among other things, provided for the ongoing responsibilities of our former trustee for the communities impacted by the nuclear weapons tests. This assistance provided by the US government for radiation damages and injuries is based on a US government study that purports to be the best and most accurate knowledge about the effects of radiation in the Marshall Islands. Our agreement to terminate our United Nations trusteeship that the US government administered was based largely on those assurances. We have since discovered that even that covenant by the United States was false. Today, not only is the US government backpedaling on this issue but its official position as enunciated by the current administration is to flee its responsibilities to the Marshall Islands for the severe nuclear damages and injuries perpetrated upon them.

## New Weapons Are Being Tested in the Marshall Islands

After spending decades of my life trying to persuade the US government to take responsibility for the full range of damages and injuries caused by the testing of 67 atmospheric atomic and thermonuclear weapons in the Marshall Islands, a new global arms system arrived at the door of the Marshall Islands. After years of ICBM [intercontinental ballistic missiles] testing, the Marshall Islands now has the dubious distinction of hosting the US government's missile shield testing program. The US government shoots Intercontinental Ballistic Missiles (ICBMs) at the Marshall Islands. From an area leased by the US Army on Kwajalein Atoll, the Ronald Reagan Missile Defense Test Site, the US launches interceptor missiles at the incoming ICBMs to test the ability of these interceptors to track and destroy incoming missiles. These tests impact every aspect of our lives . . . from the local people who are relocated from their homes, to the whales, sea turtles, and birds that have lived in harmony with human beings in our region of the world for centuries.

As history repeats itself in the Marshall Islands, the people of Kwajalein have been removed from their homelands, crowded into unbearable living squalor on a 56-acre island with 18,000 residents called Ebeye. This is the equivalent of taking everyone here in Manhattan and forcing them to live on the ground floor—can you imagine the density of Manhattan if there were no skyscrapers? The US Army base depends on Ebeye for housing its indigenous labor force, but the US Army has also erected impenetrable boundaries keeping the Marshallese at an arm's length; Marshallese on the island adjacent to the US base are unable to use the world-class hospital in emergencies, to fill water bottles during times of drought, or to purchase basic food supplies when cargo ships are delayed. One does not have to be a rocket scientist to suspect that the lands, lagoon, and surrounding seas of Kwajalein, are being damaged from depleted uranium and other substances. Unfortunately, our efforts to seek a clear understanding of the consequences of the missile testing program—data we need to make informed decisions regarding our future or the prerequisite rehabilitation of our lands before repatriation—have been spurned by the United States government. Perchlorate additives in the missiles fired from Kwajalein have been detected in the soil and the water lenses but to date no real data has become available for meaningful, independent study. The lands leased by the United States military are compensated far below market. Efforts by the Kwajalein leadership to deal with the realities which face them when the current agreement expires in 2016 have been largely ignored as the US openly and callously discusses the uses of our lands beyond 2016 and into 2086 ... all without our consent. Our Constitution specifically prohibits the taking of land without consent or proper compensation.

---

*A relatively few number of world leaders and decision-makers do not have the right to destroy the well-being and livelihood of any society, whether large or small, in the name of global security.*

---

We call upon the international community to extend its hands to assist the people of the Marshall Islands to extricate themselves from the legacy of the nuclear age and the burden of providing testing grounds for weapons of mass destruction. In the countries that produce these weapons we have come together to protest, if a person's land or resources become contaminated, persons so affected have the option to buy another house and move elsewhere. For indigenous people it is not that simple. Our land and waters are sacred to us. Our land and waters embody our culture, our traditions, our kinship ties, our social structures, and our ability to take care of ourselves. Our lands are irreplaceable.

When we talk about the importance of non-proliferation of weapons we also must include in our discourse the essential non-proliferation of illness, forced relocation, and social and cultural ills in the indigenous communities that pay disproportionately for the adverse consequences resulting from the process, deployment, and storage of weapons. A relatively few number of world leaders and decision-makers do not have the right to destroy the well-being and livelihood of any society, whether large or small, in the name of global security. Security for indigenous people means healthy land, resources and body—not the presence of weapons and the dangers they engender. Global leaders do not have, nor should they be allowed to assume the right, to take my security away so that they may feel more secure themselves.

# Periodical Bibliography

*The following articles have been selected to supplement the diverse views presented in this chapter.*

Philippa Fogarty — "Recognition at Last for Japan's Ainu," *BBC News*, June 6, 2008. news.bbc.co.uk.

Kathryn Fort — "The New Laches: Creating Title Where None Existed," *The George Mason Law Review*, vol. 16, no. 2, January 2009.

*Indigenous Peoples Indigenous Voices* — "Indigenous Peoples in the Pacific Region," United Nations Permanent Forum on Indigenous Issues, April 21, 2008.

Andrew Kindiger — "Native American Reparations Must Involve More than Money," *Truman Index*, November 29, 2007. www.trumanindex.com.

Veli-Pekka Lehtola — "The Multi-Faceted Land of the Sámi," Gládu Resources Center for the Rights of Indigenous Peoples, September 22, 2006.

Robert Murray — "A Dispossession Primer," *Quadrant*, vol. 51, no. 10, October 2007.

*Skwirk* — "Changing Rights and Freedoms: The Aboriginal People," 2009. www.skwirk.com.au.

Mary Stratton — "'Our Children Are Gone': Aboriginal Experiences of Family Court," *LawNow*, vol. 31, no. 3, January–February 2007.

José Tzay and Fanscisco Calí — "Discrimination Against Indigenous People: The Latin American Context," *UN Chronicle*, March 2007. www.un.org.

Maggie Walter — "Lives of Diversity: Indigenous Australia," Occasional Paper 4, The Academy of the Social Sciences in Australia, April, 2008.

## CHAPTER 2

# Current Issues for Indigenous Peoples

# The Rights of Indigenous Peoples: An Overview

## Kathrin Wessendorf and Lola García-Alix

*Kathrin Wessendorf and Lola García-Alix applaud the 2007 passage of the United Nations Declaration of the Rights of Indigenous Peoples. They argue, however, that putting the decree into practice worldwide will be a challenge. They further assert that indigenous peoples must be able to exercise free, prior, and informed consent for the uses of their lands and knowledge. Climate change, according to the authors, may also impact the rights of indigenous peoples by taking away their traditional lands and resources. García-Alix is the director of the International Work Group for Indigenous Affairs (IWGIA) and Wessendorf is the editor of the IWGIA yearbook,* The Indigenous World 2008.

As you read, consider the following questions:

1. What are some of the rights the United Nations Declaration on the Rights of Indigenous Peoples recognizes, according to Wessendorf and García-Alix?
2. Why were pastoralists evicted from their traditional lands in the Usangu plains in Tanzania?
3. What did the United Nations Human Rights Council decide to establish in December 2007?

With the adoption of the United Nations Declaration on the Rights of Indigenous Peoples on 13 September, 2007 has become a milestone in the history of indigenous peoples' struggles for their rights and recognition at international level. The Declaration had been discussed for more than 20 years in the former Commission on Human Rights and, later, in the General Assembly, and was passed with 144 votes in favor, 11 abstentions and 4 votes against. The text recognises a wide range of basic human rights and fundamental freedoms to indigenous peoples. Among these are the right to self-determination, an inalienable collective right to the ownership, use and control of lands, territories and other natural resources, rights in terms of maintaining and developing their own political, religious, cultural and educational institutions, and protection of their cultural and intellectual property. The Declaration highlights the requirement for prior and informed consultation, participation and consent in activities of any kind that impact on indigenous peoples, their property or territories. It also establishes the requirement for fair and adequate compensation for violation of the rights recognised in the Declaration and establishes measures to prevent ethnocide and genocide.

## Putting the Declaration into Practice

Indigenous peoples celebrated the adoption of the Declaration and used this historic moment to draw attention to their situation and raise awareness within their home countries. . . . It remains to be seen how governments and international institutions will follow-up on adoption of the Declaration and whether others will follow the example of Bolivia and transpose the declaration into national law. Unfortunately, some governments that voted in favor of the Declaration, such as Thailand for example, have already announced that the Declaration will only be implemented if subordinate to the laws and constitution of the country. The major challenge will be to put the Declaration into practice, to gain respect for and implement indigenous peoples' rights in all aspects of society and life.

In Latin America, and particularly in Ecuador and Bolivia, a tendency to include indigenous peoples' concerns in constitutional revisions can be observed. In Bolivia, the indigenous movement played an important role and contributed significantly to the constitutional process throughout 2007 and the ratification and transposition of the UN Declaration on the Rights of Indigenous Peoples into national law allowed the strengthening of indigenous issues in the Constitution. In Nepal, a country that ratified ILO Convention 169 in 2007, indigenous peoples tried to become involved in the constitutional developments throughout 2007. Unfortunately, an Interim Constitution signed in November did not adequately reflect indigenous peoples' rights and this led to protests by the indigenous movement. It is to be hoped, however, that the Declaration will play a role in future constitutional and legal developments and will thereby have a concrete impact on indigenous rights at national level.

*The major challenge will be to put the [United Nations] Declaration [on the Rights of Indigenous Peoples] into practice, to gain respect for and implement indigenous peoples' rights in all aspects of society and life.*

## Informed and Prior Consent Are Necessary to Protect Rights

One of the important principles of the UN Declaration on the Rights of Indigenous Peoples, . . . is free, prior and informed consent. Many country reports demonstrate that this principle is central to indigenous peoples' rights and well-being. It is therefore crucial that it should be actively implemented and included not only in the policies of states but also in those of industry and of financial institutions such as the World Bank.

Furthermore, and above all, any projects that have an impact on indigenous peoples' lands need to take indigenous peoples' collective rights to their lands and resources into consideration. And yet numerous examples show that states and industries do not prioritise this principle and, indeed, proceed with development projects on indigenous lands without consulting the people living on and from the land that they will affect. Natural resource use is expanding and indigenous peoples the world over live on lands rich in minerals, oil and gas and/or covered with forests. Many indigenous peoples are therefore affected by mining, hydroelectric dams, fossil fuel development, logging and agro-plantations, as well as tourism. . . .

At its 6<sup>th</sup> session in May 2007, the UN Permanent Forum on Indigenous Issues urged states to take measures to halt land alienation on indigenous territories through, for example, a moratorium on the sale and registration of land—including the granting of land and other concessions—in areas occupied by indigenous peoples. It also reaffirmed indigenous peoples' central role in decision-making with regard to their lands and resources.

---

*International and national climate change research and mitigation strategies . . . most often do not take indigenous interests into consideration and overlook their rights to their lands.*

---

## Indigenous Peoples and the Environment

At the same time, indigenous peoples are increasingly affected by a worldwide trend towards protecting the environment. The creation of national parks, conservation areas, wildlife protection and other measures can have a significant impact on indigenous peoples living on that land. The case of the violent eviction of pastoralists from their traditional lands in the Usangu plains in Tanzania due to the creation of a na-

# A Statement on the Rights of Indigenous People by United Nations Special Rapporteur Roldolfo Stavenhagen

In my last report to the Human Rights Council, I drew the attention to a number of trends in relation to the situation of the rights of indigenous peoples in various parts of the world, with a view to guiding the action by governments, international human rights bodies, and civil society in their efforts to provide a more effective protection of their rights vis-à-vis the new challenges they are facing.

One of the new trends that has been reinforced in recent years is directly related to the special theme of the Forum's current session. I am referring to the continuous loss of indigenous lands and territories, including their loss of control over their natural resources. This process has been intensified as a result of economic globalization, and especially with the intensified exploitation of energetic and hydric resources.

The environmental impact of extractive industries, such as in North America and Siberia; the extension of plantation economies, particularly in some areas of South East Asia and in the Amazon; the destruction of the last original forests of the planet due to indiscriminate logging, like in various countries in Equatorial Africa and Latin America, are all processes with a tremendous impact on indigenous peoples, leading to massive violations of their human rights.

*Rodolfo Stavenhagen, Oral Statement,*
*United Nations Permanent Forum on Indigenous Issues,*
*May 18, 2007.*

tional park to protect a water catchment area, which is providing water for a hydropower plant, illustrates just such a case. . . . This example also shows that environmental measures are often directly related to development or industrial projects. Other cases of displacement due to hydroelectric dams [occur in] . . . are Panama and Russia. Article 10 of the Declaration on the Rights of Indigenous Peoples states that "no relocation shall take place without the free, prior and informed consent of the indigenous peoples concerned. . . ." Unfortunately . . . relocation, resettlement and expulsion from their lands is a very common and widespread reality for indigenous peoples. Without their prior and informed consent, and without the real participation of indigenous peoples, who are the traditional owners of these lands, these people will also face further impoverishment, loss of culture and a decrease in their living standards in the future.

## The Importance of Traditional Knowledge

Indigenous peoples' traditional knowledge and their participation in policy development and their consent to any development taking place on their lands is of increasing importance in the current discussions on climate change. Indigenous peoples have shown remarkable capacity to adapt to a changing environment. Indigenous peoples interpret and respond to climate change in creative ways, drawing on their traditional knowledge of the natural resource base and other technologies to find solutions.

International and national climate change research and mitigation strategies, however, most often do not take indigenous interests into consideration and overlook their rights to their lands, thereby directly posing a threat to indigenous peoples' territories. Hydro-electric developments may form part of a government's mitigation strategy whilst at the same time leading to displacement, as the Tanzania case illustrates. Mono-crop plantations for bio-fuels affect the ecosystem, the water supply and the whole anatomy of the landscape on which indigenous peoples depend and this will be one of the biggest threats to indigenous peoples' livelihoods in the future. [In Indonesia], the various mitigation schemes appear to be a bigger threat to indigenous communities than climate change itself.

## Climate Change Threatens Indigenous Peoples Existence

To indigenous peoples, climate change is not simply a matter of physical changes to the environments in which they live. It also brings additional vulnerabilities and adds to existing challenges, including political and economic marginalization, land and resource encroachment, human rights violations and discrimination. The potential threat of climate change to their very existence, combined with various legal and institutional barriers that affect their ability to cope with and adapt to climate change, makes climate change an issue of human rights and inequality to indigenous peoples.

Unfortunately, having made considerable progress within the human rights bodies, the international arena lags behind in including indigenous voices in the discussions on climate change. This became clear during the 13th Conference of the Parties of the United Nations Framework Convention on Climate Change in Bali, where indigenous peoples' representatives were not allowed to present their statement at the opening ceremony. Hopefully, the thematic focus on climate change of the UN Permanent Forum on Indigenous Issues in 2008 will provide support to indigenous peoples' voices, at least at UN level.

The climate change issue, as a human rights issue, may also be a topic to be considered by a new human rights mechanism within the UN. The UN Human Rights Council decided in December 2007 to establish an "Expert Mechanism on the Rights of Indigenous Peoples". The new mechanism will consist of five independent experts on indigenous peoples' rights and will report directly to the Human Rights Council. This Council will be a forum in which indigenous peoples will have the possibility of reporting on their experiences of the severe marginalisation, discrimination and human rights abuses they still suffer.

# Indigenous Peoples of Latin America Suffer Economic Hardships

## Gillette Hall and Harry Anthony Patrinos

*Gillette Hall and Harry Anthony Patrinos (economists in the World Bank's Human Development Department, Latin America and the Caribbean Region) reveal in a 2005 study that Latin American indigenous peoples have not made substantial economic or social gains since an earlier study a decade prior. Poverty among indigenous peoples remained high while educational levels, access to health care, and earnings continued to lag behind those of non-indigenous peoples in Latin America. Gillette and Hall argue that addressing the problems of indigenous peoples in Latin America will require bilingual education programs, national health systems, and better social service delivery.*

As you read, consider the following questions:

1. What five countries in Latin America have the largest indigenous populations?

2. In Mexico, according to Gillette and Hall's study, what percentage of children are underweight? What percentage of indigenous children are underweight?

Gillette Hall and Harry Anthony Patrinos, "Latin America's Indigenous Peoples," *Finance and Development: A Quarterly Magazine of the IMF*, vol. 42, no. 4, December 2005, pp. 23–25. Copyright © 2005 by International Monetary Fund. Republished with permission of International Monetary Fund, conveyed through Copyright Clearance Center, Inc.

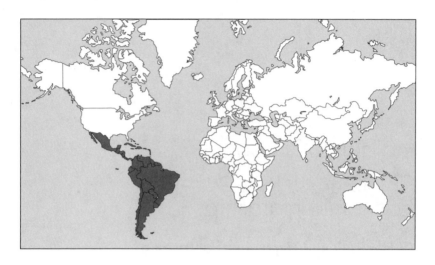

3. To ensure better health for indigenous peoples in Latin America, what should be the focus of efforts, according to Gillette and Hall?

In December 1994, the United Nations proclaimed 1995–2004 the International Decade of the World's Indigenous Peoples. In Latin America—where indigenous peoples comprise some 10 percent of the population—the ensuing decade coincided with an upsurge of indigenous movements exercising political influence in new and increasingly powerful ways. In 1994, the Zapatista Rebellion took place in Chiapas, Mexico. In Ecuador, indigenous groups took to the streets five times, leading to negotiations with the government and, ultimately, constitutional change; similar demonstrations in Bolivia led to the fall of the Sanchez-Lozada government in 2003. In Guatemala, home to Nobel Prize winner Rigoberta Menchu—an indigenous Mayan—the country's bitter civil war ended in 1996, with the Peace Accords that included an Agreement on the Identity and Rights of Indigenous Peoples. And Peru elected its first indigenous president, Alejandro Toledo, in 2000.

But palpable change on the economic front has been slower. In 1994, a World Bank report (Psacharopoulos and

Patrinos) provided the first regional assessment of living standards among indigenous peoples, finding systematic evidence of socioeconomic conditions far worse than those of the population on average. Ten years later, a major World Bank follow-up study (Hall and Patrinos, 2005) found that while programs have been launched to improve access to health care and education, indigenous peoples still consistently account for the highest and "stickiest" poverty rates in the region. This slow progress poses a major hurdle for many countries trying to reach the UN Millennium Development Goal (MDG) of halving the 1990 poverty rate by 2015.

Who are the indigenous peoples of Latin America? While there is great diversity among groups, they share certain characteristics, such as distinct language (even if many no longer speak it fluently), culture, and attachment to land—all stemming from the fact that their ancestry can be traced to the original, pre-Colombian inhabitants of the region. Estimates for the number of indigenous people vary from 28 million to 43 million. In the five countries that have the largest indigenous populations—Bolivia, Ecuador, Guatemala, Mexico, and Peru—indigenous peoples represent a significant share of the population (in Bolivia, they are the majority). There are literally hundreds of different indigenous groups. In Mexico alone, there are 56 recognized indigenous groups and 62 living languages.

*[A 2005 study] found that ... indigenous peoples still consistently account for the highest and "stickiest" poverty rates in [Latin America].*

# A Yawning Gap

The World Bank's 1994 report uncovered striking evidence of low human capital (education and health) as a driving force behind the high poverty rates, coupled with evidence of social exclusion via labor market discrimination and limited access to public education and health services. What does the picture look like now?

## Poverty

For the five countries with the largest indigenous populations, poverty rates for indigenous peoples remained virtually stagnant over the past decade—or where rates did fall, they fell less on average than for the rest of the population (see chart). In the three cases where national poverty rates declined (Bolivia, Guatemala, and Mexico), the rate for indigenous peoples registered a smaller decline, or none at all. In Ecuador and Peru, overall poverty rates increased, but for the indigenous, there was little change. This pattern suggests that indigenous peoples may be less affected by macroeconomic trends, whether positive or negative—although evidence from Ecuador suggests that even if the negative impact of a crisis is small for indigenous households, it takes them longer to recover. The poverty gap (average difference between the incomes of the poor and the poverty line) among indigenous peoples is also deeper, and shrank more slowly over the decade, compared to the same indicators among non-indigenous populations.

## Education

Education is one of the main factors that propel people out of poverty, yet indigenous peoples continue to have fewer years of education than non-indigenous ones. In Bolivia, non-indigenous children have 10 years of schooling versus 6 for indigenous; in Guatemala, the years are 6 versus 3. The good news is that in all countries the schooling gap shrank over the 1990s, following trends established in earlier decades. But the bad news is that the average increase in earnings as a result of each additional year of schooling (the private rate of return to each year of schooling) is slightly lower for the indigenous—in

# Latin American Indigenous Peoples' Poverty Rates Remain High

*Despite significant changes in poverty rates overall, the proportion of indigenous peoples living in poverty did not change much in most countries during the 1990s.*

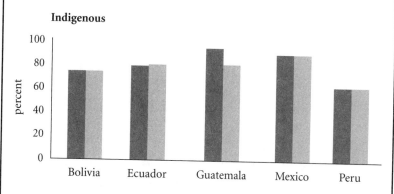

**Indigenous**

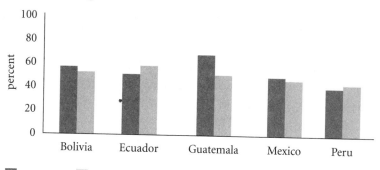

**Non-Indigenous**

■ Early year    ■ Last year

Note: Poverty headcounts are reported for the following years; Bolivia-1997 and 2002; Ecuador-1994 and 2003; Guatemala-1989 and 2000; Mexico-1992 and 2002; Peru-1994 and 2000.

TAKEN FROM: Gillette Hall and Harry Anthony Patrinos, "Latin America's Indigenous Peoples: A Decade of Disappointment," *Finance and Development: A Quarterly Magazine of the IMF*, vol. 42, no. 4, December 2005, p. 24. Copyright © 2005 International Monetary Fund. Republished with permission of International Monetary Fund, conveyed through Copyright Clearance Center, Inc.

Bolivia, it is 9 percent for the non-indigenous and 6 percent for the indigenous. Moreover, the gap is widening at higher schooling levels. What is behind this failure? The culprit may well be the quality of education that indigenous people receive. Recent standardized tests in the region reveal that indigenous students achieve significantly lower scores—from 7 to 27 percent lower—on reading and math tests.

## Health

Indigenous peoples, especially women and children, continue to have less access to basic health services. As a result, major differences in indigenous and non-indigenous health indicators persist, ranging from maternal mortality to in-hospital births and vaccination coverage. In all five countries, health insurance coverage remains relatively low, failing to surpass 50 percent of the population. In three of the five countries (Bolivia, Guatemala, and Mexico), coverage of indigenous families lags substantially behind the rest of the population. An important gap to emerge is that indigenous children continue to exhibit extremely high malnutrition rates, even in countries that have otherwise virtually eliminated this problem. In Mexico, just 6 percent of children nationwide are underweight compared with almost 20 percent of indigenous children.

## Labor

Evidence that indigenous peoples face significant disadvantages in the labor market is strong across the region. In late 2004, the portion of the difference in earnings between indigenous and non-indigenous peoples that is "unexplained"—perhaps due to discrimination or other unidentified factors—represented one-quarter to over one-half of the total differential, with the average at about 42 percent. This means that while about half of the earnings differential can be influenced by improvements in human capital (education, skills, and abilities that an indigenous person brings to the labor market), another half may result from discriminatory labor market practices or other factors over which the indigenous person has little control.

---

*In Bolivia, non-indigenous children have 10 years of school versus 6 for indigenous; in Guatemala, the years are 6 versus 3.*

---

## Starting to Make Headway

Over the past decade, significant political and policy changes have occurred with potential bearing on poverty and human development outcomes among indigenous peoples. These changes range from constitutional mandates and greater political representation to increased social spending and a proliferation of differentiated programs, such as bilingual education. Yet while some improvements have occurred in human development outcomes, particularly in education, these changes have yet to bring about the desperately needed reductions in indigenous poverty because of poor education quality, poor health outcomes for children, and limited opportunities once today's children reach the labor market. And although political representation of indigenous groups has increased in recent decades, they still cite lack of support from and a lack of voice in government as a substantive reason for their continued poverty.

Against that background, what shape should the future policy agenda take? Our results suggest that it must be broad enough to embrace issues such as land rights, labor legislation, and access to credit. On the human development front, we would suggest the following:

First, *more and better education*. Functional bilingual education programs are needed—including schools where teachers speak the same indigenous language as the students; teachers are prepared to teach in a bilingual classroom environment; and parents and the community participate in the design of curricular materials. Well-designed, well-implemented, and rigorously evaluated programs can produce significant returns. In Guatemala, indigenous students enrolled in bilingual schools tend to have higher attendance and promotion rates, and lower repetition and dropout rates. Bilingual education, despite the higher cost associated with teacher training and materials, may lead to cost savings through lower grade repetition and hence lower unit costs and more places generated for new students. In Guatemala in 1996, the cost savings were estimated at $5 million, equal to primary education for 100,000 students. Policymakers must also step up efforts to get all children in school, with incentives such as cash transfer programs. From 1997–99, Mexico's cash transfer program— *Oportunidades* (formerly *Progresa*)—resulted in higher school attainment among indigenous peoples and a significant reduction in the skills gap between indigenous and non-indigenous children.

---

*At present [2005], there is no systematic way of accurately identifying [Latin American] indigenous peoples in census or household surveys.*

---

Second, *better health*. Efforts need to be focused on the persistently high levels of malnutrition and associated high infant mortality rates, vulnerability to disease, and low schooling outcomes. Policies should promote equal opportunities for indigenous peoples—a sort of "head start"—including programs for maternal and child health and family planning. In some cases, it may be necessary to ensure that indigenous health practices that have proved effective be made available through national health systems. Ecuador, for example, is experimenting with combined services that offer a choice between modern and traditional medicine. It may also be necessary to train skilled providers in indigenous languages and cultural sensitivity.

Third, *better social service delivery*. The substantial progress in certain human capital inputs—such as quantity of school and health services—for indigenous peoples over the 1990s may not have led to a significant impact on earnings because of an insufficient voice in service delivery. Thus, there may be a need to explore strategies to strengthen the direct influence of beneficiaries on service providers. These could include enhancing client power or leverage of parents through choice or voice directly at the school level. Putting recipients at the center of service provision could also help by enabling them to monitor providers and amplify their voice in policymaking. Already, Mexico has been putting this idea into practice: the compensatory education program gives indigenous peoples a small but significant role in school management. Impact evaluations have shown this to be effective (Shapiro and Moreno, 2004).

In addition, better analysis of the conditions and needs of indigenous peoples, based on an improved data collection effort, would be essential. At present, there is no systematic way of accurately identifying indigenous peoples in census or household surveys. Thus, a list of standardized questions for surveys in different years and countries should be developed. It could include self-identification, language (mother tongue, commonly used language, language used at home, and secondary language), dominant group in the local community, and parents' mother tongues. Statistical agencies should also include a special survey module to delve deeper into the causes of poverty and constraints faced by indigenous peoples, as well as opportunities. That module could study traditional medicine practice, religious and community activities, land ownership, and bilingual schooling.

We hope that by building on the changes observed during the first indigenous peoples' decade, the next decade will bring them greater gains—in terms of human development, material well-being, and culturally appropriate economic and social development. The first step lies in setting realistic goals in terms of poverty reduction and human development, starting with disaggregated information on the MDG indicators. This would facilitate monitoring during the decade, coinciding with the culmination of the MDG period in 2015. Along with targets, monitoring, and evaluation, indigenous peoples—not just the leaders but community members and families as well—should participate in realizing these important goals.

In his 1934 book, *Fire on the Andes*, journalist Carleton Beals wrote "the uncut umbilical cord of South America's future is its duality, still the secret of political turmoil and national frustration. Until this duality is reconciled, [the region] can know no enduring peace, can achieve no real affirmation of its national life." The fact that 70 years later a report must still be written about this very duality signals the great depth of the inequalities, and the great magnitude of the task ahead.

## References

Hall, Gillette, and H.A. Patrinos (eds.), 2005, *Indigenous Peoples, Poverty and Human Development in Latin America* (Palgrave Macmillan, United Kingdom).

Psacharopoulos, George, and H.A. Patrinos (eds.), 1994, *Indigenous People and Poverty in Latin America: An Empirical Analysis* (Washington: World Bank).

Shapiro, J., and J. Jorge Moreno, 2004, "Compensatory Education for Disadvantaged Mexican Students: An Impact Evaluation Using Propensity Score Matching," World Bank Policy Research Working Paper 3334 (Washington).

# Nicaraguan Indigenous Children Have a Right To a Name and a Nationality

*José Adán Silva*

*In the following viewpoint, journalist José Adán Silva reports that Nicaraguan indigenous children who previously had no identity are being registered and given birth certificates through a United Nations Children's Fund (UNICEF) program, "Right to a Name and Nationality." Because children must have legal names and birth certificates to access educational and health services, the program is vitally important for these children, according to Silva. Silva is a writer for* La Prensa, *a Managua, Nicaragua newspaper.*

As you read, consider the following questions:

1. What is the goal for the UNICEF "Right to a Name and Nationality" program for the South Atlantic Autonomous Region, according to Silva?
2. What is one impact the program has had, according to the Supreme Electoral Council, as reported by Silva?
3. What percentage of Nicaragua's population are indigenous peoples, according to Silva?

Some 250,000 indigenous children and adolescents who had no legal identity in Nicaragua are now [2008] being registered, a step that may help them to achieve recognition of their basic human rights.

This was achieved by the "Right to a Name and Nationality" program run by Save the Children, Plan International, UNICEF [United Nations Children's Fund], Nicaragua's Supreme Electoral Council and regional and municipal authorities.

## Children Without Names

"A person who is not registered has no last name and not even a first name, because rural families and society call children whatever they want, which means children grow up without even having their own name," said UNICEF official Hugo Rodríguez, a consultant for the program.

Five years ago, human rights groups and universities in Nicaragua expressed concern about the fact that around 500,000 youngsters in indigenous communities in the eastern North Atlantic Autonomous Region and the South Atlantic Autonomous Region had no birth certificates.

*In indigenous areas on the Atlantic coast and in central and northern Nicaragua, researchers found native communities where 100 percent of the children and adolescents, as well as a portion of the adults, had never been inscribed in the civil register.*

An investigation indicated that nearly 40 percent of children in Nicaragua are not legally registered and thus do not figure in the country's demographic statistics, said Rodríguez, a statistician.

In indigenous areas on the Atlantic coast and in central and northern Nicaragua, researchers found native communities where 100 percent of the children and adolescents, as well as a portion of the adults, had never been inscribed in the civil register.

These findings led to the start of a mission that has registered 97,000 children and teenagers in the North Atlantic Autonomous Region, out of 100,000 minors without a legal identity, in the past four and a half years.

## Expanding the Effort to Register Children

The efforts expanded this year to the South Atlantic Autonomous Region, where the goal is to register 100,000 youngsters, and to the province of Nueva Guinea, south of that area, where about 50,000 minors have no birth certificates.

"There were communities where not even the parents were registered before, let alone their descendants, and the entire community had to get involved to help them remember dates, last names, addresses and other information about their relatives," said Susana Marley, a Miskito community leader in the village of Waspam, along the banks of the Coco River on the border with Honduras.

---

*Article 7 of the United Nations Convention on the Rights of the Child states, "The child shall be registered immediately after birth and shall have the right from birth to a name, [and] the right to acquire a nationality.*

---

Marley mentioned cases of people who traveled five days by river to register their children, and chose names and even last names for them on the spot, at the time of registration.

Last year [2007] in Waspam, the Health Ministry reported the births of 1,801 children, but only 144 figured in the records of the local civil register.

UNICEF staff and municipal authorities with whom IPS [Inter Press Service] spoke agreed that the main cause of the problem, besides the lack of education, is the extreme poverty plaguing the country's indigenous people, 80 percent of whom live on less than a dollar a day, according to United Nations figures.

"People can't afford to miss a single day of work in their fishing or farming activities, to leave the villages to register their children," Marley said.

## Making an Impact

The program has already had an impact. According to the Supreme Electoral Council, after the project was completed in the North Atlantic Autonomous Region, the voters list had expanded by between 33 and 45 percent in the different municipalities.

Supreme Electoral Council magistrate José Luis Villavicencio highlighted the progress made by the program and commented to IPS that the universal registration of births "is an important task for strengthening the country's institutional capacity."

"If a municipality does not have exact information on how many citizens live there, it is impossible to design accurate management plans for local development, and many people are left without the possibility of voting and exercising their citizen rights," he said.

Article 7 of the United Nations Convention on the Rights of the Child states, "The child shall be registered immediately after birth and shall have the right from birth to a name, [and] the right to acquire a nationality."

The program has been completed in the North Atlantic Autonomous Region, and the universal registration of births will continue in the future, thanks to training received by municipal authorities and community organizations, Rodríguez said.

## Children Are Receiving Birth Certificates

In the South Atlantic Autonomous Region, meanwhile, several municipalities have already been declared free of unregistered children. In late August, UNICEF reported that more than 8,000 minors in the municipalities of Corn Island and Bluefields had received birth certificates, as the first stage of the project came to an end.

The process of data collection, registration and the issuing of birth certificates was carried out by the Caribbean Coastal Center for Autonomous Human Rights, with the support of the other institutions involved in the program, said Olga Moraga, a UNICEF communications officer in Managua.

"My daughters learned to read and write, thanks to the solidarity of Christian monks, because the public schools wouldn't accept them since they had no birth certificates," said Marcia Cunninghan, who lives in Bilwi, the capital of the North Atlantic Autonomous Region. Like her three daughters, the 36-year-old mother had no documents either.

The program has given tens of thousands of children and adolescents an identity and has enabled them to gain access to health care and education, recreational facilities and civic participation, as well as to have their voices heard in their communities, said Argentina Martínez, acting director of Plan International Nicaragua.

## A Safeguard Against Human Trafficking

The registration of births is also a fundamental guard against human trafficking. Furthermore, once authorities have precise population statistics, they can draw up development plans and design accurate budgets, she said.

Miriam Hooker of the Caribbean Coastal Center for Autonomous Human Rights said that guaranteeing the right to a name and nationality "guarantees the autonomy of the indigenous peoples of the Caribbean coastal region," because autonomy is based on recognition of the identity of each ethnic group, which is also achieved through registering births.

## Nicaragua's Caribbean Coast: Homeland of Indigenous Peoples

- Economically the poorest region of Nicaragua
- Home to six ethnic groups speaking 4 different languages
- Indigenous peoples include the Mayangna (sumu), Rama, Garifunas, and Miskitu
- Other groups include English-speaking Creoles and Spanish speaking Mestizos
- Lowest level of literacy in Nicaragua
- 50% of national territory
- 10% of country's population
- Target of UNICEF "Right to a Name and Nationality" program

TAKEN FROM: United States Department of State, 2008. www.state .gov; and University of the Autonomous Regions of Nicaragua's Caribbean Coast, 2006. www.yorku.ca.

Indigenous people make up 8.6 percent of Nicaragua's 5.4 million people, according to the University of the Autonomous Regions of Nicaragua's Caribbean Coast.

The Miskito, Mayangna, Garifuna and Rama ethnic groups in the Atlantic coastal region, one of the poorest parts of the country, represent 5.3 percent of the population. The rest of the country's indigenous people are mixed-race descendants of the Nahua, Chorotega, Sutiaba and Matagalpa communities along the Pacific coast and in northern and central Nicaragua.

# American Indians Urge the United States to Adopt the United Nations Declaration on the Rights of Indigenous Peoples

*Editors of Indian Country Today*

*In the following viewpoint written before the 2008 U.S. presidential election, the editors of* Indian Country Today *assert that the next president of the United States should sign and support the United Nations Declaration on the Rights of Indigenous Peoples, adopted by the General Assembly on September 13, 2007. The authors argue that the United States must provide leadership in the international effort to secure human rights for all indigenous peoples. They believe such action will lead to greater peace and cooperation around the world.* Indian Country Today *is a newspaper that claims to be the world's largest news source for Native American concerns.*

As you read, consider the following questions:

1. Why did several African states want to defer the decision about the adoption of the United Nations Declaration on the Rights of Indigenous Peoples?

2. How many nations voted for the Declaration when it was presented to the General Assembly in 2007?

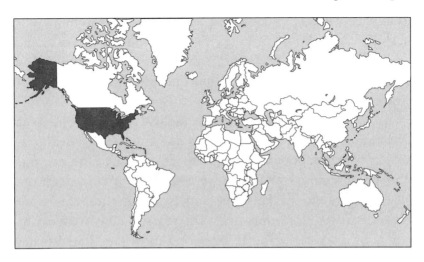

3. What government changed its negative vote on the Declaration and will now support its provisions?

Despite making strong statements supporting tribal sovereignty, none of the [2008] presidential candidates in their campaigns or senatorial statements have promised to lead the U.S. government to adopt the Declaration on the Rights of Indigenous Peoples, which was adopted by the U.N. General Assembly on Sept. 13, 2007.

The Democratic Party candidates, Sen. Hillary Clinton and Sen. Barack Obama, have named Native leaders as integral parts of their respective campaigns. GOP favorite Sen. John McCain has a long and respected history of supportive senatorial legislative, serving as the chairman of the Senate Committee on Indian Affairs. Nevertheless, none of the three front-running presidential candidates have stated they will work to ensure that the United States will change the nation's negative vote against the declaration and join the international community to support and implement its provisions.

## The United States Should Lead the Way

The United States should show international leadership by supporting and implementing the affirmation of human rights to indigenous peoples as agreed by the General Assembly. The next president should make a clear statement within party and presidential campaign platforms in full support and adoption of the philosophy and policy guidelines expressed in the Declaration on the Rights of Indigenous Peoples.

In June 2006, the U.N. Human Rights Council adopted the declaration over the objections of some nation-states with sizable indigenous populations. In the fall of 2006, the declaration was presented to the entire assembly for consideration. Negotiations on the language and issues of the declaration were discussed for more than 25 years. There were many points of discussion, and in many instances the United States opposed the language of the declaration, arguing that many aspects, especially treaty and land issues, would be difficult to implement. Several African states asked to defer the decision in the assembly to clarify language on self-determination and the definition of "indigenous" peoples.

Meanwhile, indigenous delegates from around the world, including many longtime international participants from the United States, lobbied the U.N. delegations from many countries. Some say a critical event was the winning over of the People's Republic of China, which also encouraged some African states to propose language changes and adopt the declaration.

---

*The United States should show international leadership by supporting and implementing the affirmation of human rights to indigenous peoples as agreed by the General Assembly [in 2007].*

---

## A Strong Show of Support for Indigenous Rights

Among diplomatic circles, there was talk that if the declaration did not pass in the 2007 session of the General Assembly, the declaration should be tabled. After more than 25 years of debate and discussion, the declaration would be set aside in the absence of international support and consensus about the rights of indigenous peoples. The declaration was in danger of indefinite tabling. But it was presented to the 2007 General Assembly (61st General Assembly Plenary, 107th and 108th meetings) by the delegation from Peru, a main sponsor, and passed with a vote of 143 nations in favor, four opposed and 11 abstaining. Even many indigenous representatives, working many years in the international arena, were surprised at the strong show of international support.

The dissenting nations included Australia, Canada, New Zealand and the United States. Their major objections to the declaration were over provisions providing for indigenous self-determination, supporting indigenous rights to land and resources, and encouraging veto power by indigenous peoples over land and resource decisions in their traditional territories. The United States, in particular, was discouraged because the approval of the HRC was carried without a consensus text with all nations in agreement. Without full consensus, implementation and further discussion of the declaration would be splintered and difficult. The United States said it could not lend support to the splintered agreement of both the HRC and the General Assembly. The Russian Federation and some allies abstained from the vote, also suggested that previous objections to the declaration in the HRC were not fully addressed.

The passage of the declaration gained international media attention. However, few if any major media outlets in the United States reported on the passage of the declaration or explained its implications for the indigenous peoples of the world, or its broadening of the human rights program of the United Nations and the international civil society. Since passage, the government of Australia changed its negative vote on the declaration and now will support its provisions. The recently elected labor party in Australia made a public apology for a history of mistreatment of Australian indigenous peoples and promised new policies and initiatives in support of indigenous peoples. The Russian Federation, although abstaining, has in its constitution a provision that it will uphold international standards in relations and treatment of indigenous peoples. By constitutional law, the Russian Federation will honor the provisions of the declaration.

---

*Creating greater consensus and agreement over human rights in the international arena is a pathway toward helping establish greater peace and mutual understanding.*

---

## A Major Step Forward

The General Assembly made a major step forward in recognizing indigenous collective and individual rights. The declaration is a non-binding text. The General Assembly has advisory powers only, but the provisions of the declaration create new moral ground and greater specificity of human rights and standards around the world. The declaration states that indigenous peoples have the right to observe treaty agreements made with nation-states and have basic human rights against discrimination, and encourages nation-states to enable indigenous peoples with full and effective participation in decisions that affect their self-determination, land, communities and cultures.

The U.S. government and its next president should be leaders in the universal human rights and indigenous rights movement. Creating greater consensus and agreement over human rights in the international arena is a pathway toward helping establish greater peace and mutual understanding. The United States and all presidential candidates should join in with the international community and agree to uphold indigenous and human rights and work to implement the policies and philosophies embodied in the declaration in the

# An Excerpt from the United Nations Declaration on the Rights of Indigenous Peoples

*Article 1*

Indigenous peoples have the right to the full enjoyment, as a collective or as individuals, of all human rights and fundamental freedoms as recognized in the Charter of the United Nations, the Universal Declaration of Human Rights and international human rights law.

*Article 2*

Indigenous peoples and individuals are free and equal to all other peoples and individuals and have the right to be free from any kind of discrimination, in the exercise of their rights. . . .

*Article 3*

Indigenous peoples have the right to self-determination. By virtue of that right they freely determine their political status and freely pursue their economic, social and cultural development.

*Article 4*

Indigenous peoples, in exercising their right to self-determination, have the right to autonomy or self-government in matters relating to their internal and local affairs. . . .

*Article 5*

Indigenous peoples have the right to maintain and strengthen their distinct political, legal, economic, social and cultural institutions, while retaining their right to participate fully, if they so choose, in the political, economic, social and cultural life of the State.

*Articles 1–5, United Nations Declaration on the Rights of Indigenous Peoples, September 13, 2007. www.un.org.*

nation's Indian policy. We invite the presidential candidates to revise their party and campaign platforms to include and provide implementation of the recent international affirmation of indigenous rights as stated in the declaration.

# Australians Are Divided over Government Control of Aboriginal Communities

## *Tim Johnston*

*Journalist Tim Johnston reports on the Northern Territory Emergency Response Bill, legislation passed by the Australian parliament to address problems in Aboriginal communities. Some indigenous peoples are unhappy with the measure, according to Johnston, and believe it is a return to the old paternalist treatment they have received in the past. They particularly dislike the provision that the government can take control of Aboriginal lands. Others believe that problems with education, child neglect, and drug and alcohol addiction among indigenous peoples are so severe that the government must intervene. Johnston is a writer for the* International Herald Tribune.

As you read, consider the following questions:

1. What are some of the requirements for Aboriginal people included in the Northern Territory Emergency Response Bill?

2. How does the life expectancy of an Aboriginal person compare with that of a non-Aboriginal Australian?

3. In what year was recognition of Aboriginal ownership of their own land recognized, according to Johnston?

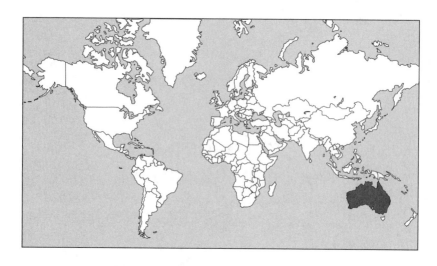

When Long Jack Phillipus, at the age of 12, walked out of Australia's vast Gibson Desert in 1934 and saw white people for the first time, he found that he had no rights.

Over the decades, he has seen his Aboriginal people win citizenship, then the return of some of their land. In time, as he watched, the authorities in Canberra promoted self-determination for his people.

## A Reversal of Government Policy

Then, last week [August 2007], at the age of 86, he saw the government abruptly throw the process into reverse. And he's angry.

"We should be the boss of our land, not that fellow from Parliament House," Phillipus said last week.

---

*Like many towns in the wide reaches of central Australia, Papunya was set up by the government in the 1950s as a distribution point for the rations it gave to Aboriginal people.*

---

Phillipus's land is the sun-baked heart of Australia. His home is in Papunya, 270 kilometers, or 170 miles, from the regional center, Alice Springs, and more than 100 kilometers from the nearest paved road.

For 40,000 years his people roamed free across the surrounding red sand scrub, and ties to the land still run deep. "I am the land, and the land is me," he said. Despite his age, he still occasionally sets off into the bush to shoot kangaroos and emus for the pot.

Like many towns in the wide reaches of central Australia, Papunya was set up by the government in the 1950s as a distribution point for the rations it gave to Aboriginal people. For residents, there is still a sense of being an unwilling subject in a cultural experiment.

There is a temporary feel to the town, with succeeding generations of government housing lying derelict. Plastic bottles and abandoned cars confirm that this ancient society has succumbed to the disposable culture.

Along with the trash, other ills—addiction, domestic violence, poor health and lack of education—have grown and festered, magnified by the isolation. Now the government has decided to act.

## The Northern Territory Emergency Response Bill

Last week Parliament passed the Northern Territory Emergency Response Bill. Among other measures, it requires welfare recipients to spend half their income on food, fines them if their children do not attend school, bans alcohol and pornography in Aboriginal areas and clears the way for the government to purchase five-year leases on Aboriginal town land.

The catalyst for the legislation was a report prepared for the Northern Territory government this year that uncovered widespread sexual abuse and neglect of children in indigenous Australian communities. But the legislation goes far beyond the direct protection of children.

Critics call it a return to the paternalistic policies that disenfranchised the country's Aboriginal population in the past. They note that the problems it is designed to address are not unique to indigenous communities and argue that the fact that it applies only to them makes it racist. The government, they say, would not dare curtail the rights of white Australians in the same way.

The bill lists 73 towns in which the legislation will apply, all of which have Aboriginal majorities. The towns are owned communally by their populations, with control in the hands of the town councils. But the new law will give the government control of the land within the town boundaries, as well as any local airstrips and water supplies.

Prime Minister John Howard has made sure that accusations of racism will not derail his initiative: the new law has a clause specifically stipulating that it may not be challenged under the country's Racial Discrimination Act.

In the past, Aboriginal leaders have accused the government of being neglectful at best and racist at worst. Relations were poisoned by a policy, formally abandoned in 1969, in which Aboriginal children—the "stolen generation"—were forcibly taken from their parents in an attempt to assimilate them into white Australian society.

---

*The indigenous population accounts for 2.7 percent of Australians, and by almost every measure they are worse off than the mainstream.*

---

## Lingering Guilt

In part because of lingering guilt over those practices, the government has been reluctant to take forceful action about the social problems in indigenous communities.

"It has always been too hard, there were no votes in it, and they were scared of creating another stolen generation," said

Alison Anderson, Long Jack Phillipus's granddaughter. She serves in the Northern Territory assembly as the representative of the 35,000 square kilometer constituency that includes Papunya.

The indigenous population accounts for 2.7 percent of Australians, and by almost every measure they are worse off than the mainstream. Life expectancy is 17 years lower than the average Australian's. They are 13 times as likely to be incarcerated, three times as likely to be unemployed and twice as likely to be a victim of violence or threatened violence. These indicators have gotten steadily worse since 1967, when indigenous Australians won citizenship and the right to determine their own futures.

"It's good to have rights, but you've got to have responsibility too, and I think we lost sight of that," Anderson said.

## Another Lost Generation?

In a society that places little value on accumulating material possessions, and in which the government provides all the basic necessities, there is little incentive to join the mainstream work force, especially if it means moving away from land and family, according to many who work with Aboriginal communities.

Though alcohol is banned in most indigenous communities in the Northern Territory, alcoholism is a severe problem, and marijuana addiction is widespread. "As a society we have been normalized to the behavior of people on alcohol and drugs, and we don't intervene anymore: this is one of the things that will have to change," Anderson said. "We've lost one generation to the government, and we're losing another to drink and drugs."

Anderson says Aboriginal leaders, including herself, have to shoulder some of the blame for not doing enough to help their people. She is torn about the bill: she says intervention is needed and applauds some of the measures, but thinks others may be counterproductive.

Even in the dusty streets of Papunya, a relatively stable community, there is a lassitude that many attribute to inadequate education and a scarcity of jobs for those who can read and write. The school has recently been upgraded, but on a recent Thursday only 25 of the 125 enrolled children turned up.

Many children are being brought up by their struggling grandparents, because their parents have moved to Alice Springs—many of them to feed their alcohol or drug addictions. Of Papunya's 360 residents, the overwhelming majority are entirely dependent on government money.

## Deep Misgivings About the Legislation

Despite these problems, in places like Papunya, the new legislation has stirred deep misgivings. "John Howard's trying to make us into white men," said Sammy Butcher, a founder of Aboriginal Australia's most successful rock group, the Warumpi Band.

---

*Almost everyone in the Northern Territory seems to agree that significant intervention is needed and most are resigned to the fact that it means ceding some powers and rights to the government.*

---

Many indigenous leaders say they weren't consulted about the bill, and the Northern Territory government was not told about the plan until after it was announced to the press. Community leaders believe many of its measures are fundamentally flawed, designed more to appeal to voters in the upcoming election than to solve their problems.

They are particularly critical of the stipulation that the government will purchase five-year leases on town lands. That issue, they say, has struck a particularly raw nerve among people whose ownership of the lands their people lived on for thousands of years was recognized only in 1967.

## A Comparison of the Indigenous and Non-Indigenous Population of Australia

| Indicator | Indigenous Peoples | Non-Indigenous Peoples |
|---|---|---|
| Age >15 years | 37.6% | 19.8% |
| Age <65 years | 3.3% | 13.3% |
| Median age | 20 | 37 |
| Home-owner | 43.1% | 64.8% |
| Renter | 60.2% | 27.2% |
| Households with 6 or more usual residents | 12% | 3.1% |
| Educated to 12th Grade | 19.4% | 44.9% |
| Post-high school qualifications such as college degree or technical certification | 20% | 44% |
| Unemployment rate | 15.6% | 5.2% |
| Median weekly individual income | $278 | $466 |

TAKEN FROM: 2006 Census, Australian Bureau of Statistics.

"I feel very sad that land is being taken away from Aboriginal society again and I don't know why: we don't have a fight with John Howard," said Long Jack Phillipus.

## New Schools, Health Clinics, and Police Stations

Sue Gordon, the head of the task force overseeing the government intervention, says the government needs the leases to build new schools, health clinics and police stations and upgrade existing facilities without interference.

"If they didn't have the lease of the land there would be too much red tape that would bog down redevelopment and reconstruction," said Gordon, herself an Aboriginal Australian and one of the "stolen generation."

Almost everyone in the Northern Territory seems to agree that significant intervention is needed, and most are resigned to the fact that it will mean ceding some powers and rights to the government.

But people like Jane Rosalski, who has worked with indigenous communities for seven years, say better legislation could have given the authorities as much latitude as they needed without inflaming sensitivities about land.

She says the risk is that local people will fixate on the land issue, making it harder to win community acceptance for the measures tackling child neglect, addiction and educational issues.

Some parts of the bill are less controversial. The proposal to put more police officers and health workers into Aboriginal towns answers longstanding demands from indigenous communities.

Even the more controversial measures have support among people frustrated with the lack of progress on Aboriginal problems. "Sitting down and talking has been tried so many times before, it just goes nowhere," Alison Anderson said. "Do you want them to go on living in the conditions they have now? I don't."

Even if some of the policies are misguided, she said, having the central government engaged with the problems of her people is better than the neglect of recent years.

"We're on a merry-go-round: every 30 years we seem to get off in the same place," she said.

# Mayan Survivors of Guatemalan Genocide Ask for Justice

*Kate Doyle*

*In the following viewpoint, Kate Doyle reports on a trial that took place in a Spanish court in 2008. Guatemalan officials had been charged under international law with "state terrorism, genocide, and torture" in a campaign against indigenous Mayan people. Survivors of the attacks by the Guatemalan army and civil patrols described their experiences and asked the international court for justice. Doyle is a senior analyst at the National Security Archive and a member of the North American Congress on Latin America's editorial committee.*

As you read, consider the following questions:

1. How many civilians died during Guatemala's 36-year civil war, according to Doyle?

2. When did the first massacre near the Chixoy Dam take place, according to Doyle?

3. For what purpose did the Guatemalan army form task forces in the military zone in Santa Cruz de la Quiché?

Kate Doyle, "Guatemala's Genocide: Survivors Speak," *NACLA Report of the Americas*, vol. 41, no. 3, May–June 2008, pp. 3–4. Copyright © 2008 by the North American Congress on Latin America, 38 Greene St. 4th FL., New York, NY 10013. Reproduced by permission.

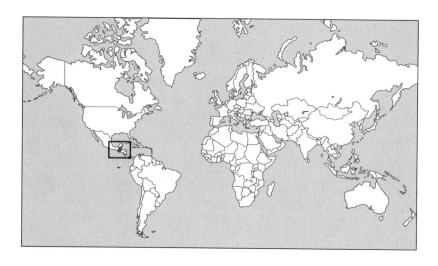

Guatemala took a small step toward justice on February 4, [2008] when an international genocide case charging eight former senior officials with crimes against humanity opened before Spain's federal court, the Audiencia Nacional, in Madrid. The suit was brought in 1999, when Mayan activist and Nobel Peace Prize winner Rigoberta Menchú Tum filed a criminal complaint charging the officials with state terrorism, genocide, and torture. Inspired by Spain's attempt in 1998 to try Chilean dictator Augusto Pinochet for human rights crimes, Menchú and other victims hoped to bypass the broken Guatemalan justice system and bring the defendants under the rules of "universal jurisdiction," which give any country the right to try cases involving crimes against humanity. Their targets included Efraín Ríos Montt, former head of state and architect of the scorched-earth policies of 1982–83, and former minister of the interior Donaldo Álvarez Ruiz. Over the course of the country's 36-year civil conflict—which began in 1960 and ended with the Peace Accords of 1996—more than 200,000 civilians died.

During five days of hearings, 17 Mayan survivors and one expert witness gave testimony and answered questions from Judge Santiago Pedraz. They described, in vivid and often wrenching detail, a state gone mad, as the Guatemalan army unleashed a sustained and savage attack against Mayan communities scattered across the rural highlands during the early 1980s. . . .

## The Testimony of Survivors

A witness to the massacres in the Quiché area testified about what life was for those who survived the attacks but fell under military control through the "strategic hamlets" the army established in the region. In 1982, the military's assaults on his village intensified. The army burned the houses, the fields, and the forests around them. When people tried to flee into the mountains, the troops would pursue and kill them. After his father disappeared, the witness, his mother, and two brothers decided to remain in the village, though it was occupied by the military. Daily life was strictly controlled; there were rules about how much food was permitted, what clothes one could wear, and when one was allowed to leave one's house. The rules were aimed not only at controlling the population but suppressing their Mayan culture. It was a hard life, in which, he said, "You had to be silent, completely silent. You were not free." The authorities used a local convent as an interrogation center. In mid-1982, the witness, then 10 years old, and his mother were tortured inside the convent, his mother raped. They survived and fled into the mountains, but life on the run was so harsh that they returned to their village in 1983.

---

*[Mayan survivors] described . . . a state gone mad, as the Guatemalan army unleashed a sustained and savage attack against Mayan communities scattered across the rural highlands during the early 1980s.*

---

## Massacres of Mayans

Another witness described the massacres carried out in and around the village of Río Negro in Baja Verapaz, where the government was constructing the hydroelectric Chixoy Dam. The first massacre took place on March 4, 1980, when soldiers and members of the military police force serving as security guards for the dam killed seven peasants who refused to leave their land, which was fertile but had been expropriated for the project. The violence mounted during 1981 and 1982. On February 13, 1982, a massacre near Xococ left 73 dead. On the morning of March 13, the witness was returning home from sleeping in the mountains for safety when his wife screamed to him from inside their house, "Go back! The soldiers are coming!" He dropped the wood he was carrying and ran, but stayed close enough to see soldiers corralling women and children. He could hear them crying as they were marched up a hill. The next morning he and other men went to the hill, where they saw clubs, machetes, bullet shells scattered on the ground. The bodies were piled there. Everyone in the witness's family was dead: his pregnant wife and two small children, his sister, his mother-in-law, and her other daughter. With other survivors from the zone, the witness fled to the mountains, where they organized themselves into small groups so they couldn't all be killed at once. People who did not remain in the mountains were captured and pressed into service on the Cobán military base or imprisoned there. The witness remained in hiding until 1986.

A survivor from Nebaj described his experience living as a refugee for years, hiding in the mountains above his home. The military began showing up in and around his community in 1981. The first time they came, they kidnapped four local leaders. In 1982, they moved through the area accompanied by members of the civil defense patrols (PACs), burning houses and destroying crops. The witness's house was burned to the ground in December 1982, and he and his family fled to the mountains. Neighbors who did not leave were killed. The witness was able to sow a small, hidden field with other families and planted corn, beans, vegetables, and fruit trees, but the army found it and destroyed it. "We had no more food," he remembered. "We ate the leaves of trees in the forest, wild sweet potato, and roots." The army would pass over the areas where the communities camped and bomb them; people also died of hunger and cold. On April 26, 1984, the army set fire to the woods where the people were hiding, and on the following day troops captured the witness's two sons, aged 9 and 12, and forced them to march with them carrying army backpacks. He never saw them again. They also caught his mother-in-law, who was 65 years old, tortured her, burned her hands and feet, and left her corpse. The witness and other surviving refugees escaped. They spent years on the run from the army, subject to constant attacks, bombing, and the destruction of the forest and fields.

---

*All of the survivors coincided in their descriptions of rape used by Guatemalan soldiers and members of the civil patrol to abuse and humiliate Mayan women.*

---

## The Treatment of Women

All of the survivors coincided in their descriptions of rape used by the Guatemalan soldiers and members of the civil patrol to abuse and humiliate Mayan women. The first woman to testify was from Rabinal, Baja Verapaz. She began her story by recounting the army's crimes against her and her people: She was raped by soldiers in Rabinal, her husband was forcibly disappeared, her mother was burned alive inside her house, her aunt and sister-in-law were raped, and the survivors fled the massacre in her village, where 32 people died. The witness then gave the judge the details of these crimes: She was taken to an army base and kept there, bound with rope and naked for 15 days, repeatedly raped by soldiers. Her uncle finally came to the base and rescued her. "I wanted to die," she told the judge.

## The Massacre of Indigenous Peoples in Guatemala

The Inter-American Court [of Human Rights, a branch of the Organization of American States] recently condemned the Guatemalan government for the July 18, 1982, massacre of 188 Achi-Maya in the village of Plan de Sanchez in the mountains above Rabinal, Baja Verapaz. In this judgment, and for the first time in its history, the Court ruled that a genocide had taken place. The Inter-American Court attributed the 1982 massacre and the genocide to Guatemalan army troops. This is the first ruling by the Inter-American Court against the Guatemalan state for any of the 626 massacres carried out by the army in its scorched earth campaign in the early 1980s—violence that took the lives of more than 200,000, mostly indigenous, Guatemalans. The Court has not yet announced the damages, expected to run in the millions, the Guatemalan state will be required to pay to the relatives of victims of the 1982 massacre. [In 2005, the Court awarded the survivors $7.9 million.]

*Victoria Sanford,*
*"The Inter-American Court Condemns Guatemalan*
*Government for 1982 Massacre," Network in Solidarity with the*
*People of Guatemala, July 23, 2004. www.nisgua.org.*

One of the witnesses served with the military as a member of the civil defense patrols and participated in the counterinsurgency campaigns in the Quiché. He testified as to how the army arrived in his community in May 1982, when he was 18 years old. Although some residents of his village decided to flee, his family and many others chose to stay in what became a military-controlled village. As a result, he and his brothers were forced to join the PAC. In 1983, the witness was taken as part of his group of patrollers to the military zone in Santa Cruz de la Quiché to form part of a "task force" with other units. The army created such task forces to destroy Mayan villages and kill or capture suspected subversives. The witness's company received four months of special training. "They would tell us, 'You have to be trained to kill your own family,'" he explained. "They said that everyone living in the Quiché was a guerrilla and so we had to kill all of them." The witness participated in numerous operations with the task forces. He said the soldiers always functioned through the chain of command: From military staff to senior officers, to junior officers, to troops, "the hierarchy was always followed."

The hearings in Madrid will resume at the end of May with testimony from six more survivors and several expert witnesses, including anthropologists Beatriz Manz, Ricardo Falla, and Charles Hale. Human rights advocates around the world are watching as one of the most important cases testing the principles and effectiveness of universal jurisdiction unfolds.

# Periodical Bibliography

*The following articles have been selected to supplement the diverse views presented in this chapter.*

Vanessa Baird

"Arise! Various Ways in Which Indigenous People Are Fighting Back," *New Internationalist*, no. 410, April 2008.

Hugh Blanco

"Indigenous Peoples and Our Environment," *Canadian Dimension*, vol. 42, no. 2, March–April 2008.

Rhett Butler

"Global Warming Solutions Are Hurting Indigenous People, Says UN," Mongabay.com, April 2, 2008. news.mongabay.com.

Christine Fiddler

"Government Refuse Support of UN Declaration on Indigenous Rights," *Windspeaker*, vol. 26, no. 2, May 2008.

*Indigenous Peoples, Indigenous Voices*

"Urban Indigenous Peoples and Migration: Challenges and Opportunities," United Nations Permanent Forum on Indigenous Issues, May 21, 2008.

Annie Kelly

"Global Warming: Hope Dries Up for Nicaragua's Miskito," *The Guardian*, May 29, 2007.

C. Richard King

"George Bush May Not Like Black People, But No One Gives a Dam About Indigenous Peoples: Visibility and Indianness After the Hurricanes," *American Indian Culture and Research Journal*, vol. 32, no. 2, 2008.

Haider Rizvi

"Climate Change: Indigenous Activists Decry Carbon Markets," Inter Press Service, May 7, 2008.

## CHAPTER 3

# Indigenous Peoples and Natural Resources

# Indigenous Peoples, Land, and Natural Resources: An Overview

## The Secretariat of the United Nations Permanent Forum on Indigenous Issues

*In the following viewpoint, the staff of the United Nations Permanent Forum on Indigenous Issues provides information on the connections among land, natural resources, and indigenous peoples. Indigenous peoples have deep spiritual and cultural connections to the environment. Many activities of developed nations threaten indigenous homelands. Successful land claims by indigenous peoples have been slow in coming. In addition, indigenous peoples are often not compensated for traditional knowledge about how to use natural resources. The United Nations Permanent Forum on Indigenous Issues is an advisory body to the Economic and Social Council of the United Nations.*

As you read, consider the following questions:

1. What are some Latin American countries that have led the way with constitutional reforms to the benefit of indigenous peoples?

2. Where is a vast reserve of petroleum, gas and coal, and heavy metals located? Why is this a problem for indigenous peoples?

"Backgrounder: Indigenous People—Lands, Territories and Natural Resources," *Sixth Session of the United Nations Permanent Forum on Indigenous Issues*, May 14–25, 2007. www.un.org. Reprinted with the permission of the United Nations.

3. What did two Indian scientists at the University of Mississippi try to patent for wound healing? Why was the patent overturned?

Around the world, indigenous peoples are fighting for recognition of their right to own, manage and develop their traditional lands, territories and resources. At the international level, their representatives are advocating for the adoption of the Declaration on the Rights of Indigenous Peoples by the UN [United Nations] General Assembly.

The Declaration—the result of more than two decades of negotiation—emphasizes that indigenous peoples' control over their lands, territories and resources will enable them to "maintain and strengthen their institutions, cultures and traditions" and to "promote their development in accordance with their aspirations and needs"....

## Indigenous Peoples Have a Deep Connection to Their Lands

Indigenous peoples' relationship with their traditional lands and territories is said to form a core part of their identity and spirituality and to be deeply rooted in their culture and history. Stella Tamang, an indigenous leader from Nepal, summarizes the relationship saying, "[I]ndigenous peoples ... have an intimate connection to the land; the rationale for talking about who they are is tied to the land. They have clear symbols in their language that connect them to places on their land ... in Nepal, we have groups that only can achieve their spiritual place on the planet by going to a certain location".

Indigenous peoples see a clear relationship between the loss of their lands and situations of marginalization, discrimination and underdevelopment of indigenous communities. According to Erica Irene Daes, a UN Special Rapporteur in 2002, "The gradual deterioration of indigenous societies can be traced to the non-recognition of the profound relation that indigenous peoples have to their lands, territories and resources."

Indigenous peoples are also acutely aware of the relationship between the environmental impacts of various types of development on their lands, and the environmental and subsequent health impacts on their peoples. Through their deep understanding of and connection with the land, indigenous communities have managed their environments sustainably for generations. In turn, the flora, fauna and other resources available on indigenous lands and territories have provided them with their livelihoods and have nurtured their communities.

---

*Indigenous peoples' relationship with their traditional lands and territories is said to form a core part of their identity and spirituality and to be deeply rooted in their culture and history.*

---

However, according to indigenous leaders this relationship is increasingly at risk.

Victoria Tauli-Corpuz, an indigenous Igorot leader from the Philippines and Chairperson of the UN Permanent Forum on Indigenous Issues, has stated that "With the increasing desire of states for more economic growth, senseless exploitation of indigenous peoples' territories and resources continues unabated."

Threats to indigenous peoples' ecosystems include such things as mineral extraction, environmental contamination, the use of genetically modified seeds and technology and monoculture cash crop production.

## Mixed Progression Land Rights

In recent decades, many countries have reformed their constitutional and legal systems in response to calls from indigenous movements for legal recognition of their right to the protection and control of their lands, territories and natural resources (as well as with respect to their languages, cultures and identities; their laws and institutions; their forms of government and more).

- Latin America has led the way with such constitutional reforms taking place in Argentina, Bolivia, Brazil, Colombia, Guatemala, México, Nicaragua, Panama, Paraguay, Peru, Ecuador and Venezuela, a number of which go so far as to acknowledge the collective nature of indigenous peoples (an essential element of land rights).

However, in his March 2007 report, the UN Special Rapporteur on the situation of the human rights and fundamental freedoms of indigenous people, stated that:

*Threats to indigenous peoples' ecosystems include such things as mineral extraction, environmental contamination, the use of genetically modified seeds and technology and monoculture cash crop production.*

"Although in recent years many countries have adopted laws recognizing the indigenous communities' collective and inalienable right to ownership of their lands, land-titling procedures have been slow and complex and, in many cases, the titles awarded to the communities are not respected in practice".

- For example, by 2005, the indigenous Aymara people in Bolivia—which make up 60 to 80 percent of the total population—had filed land claims covering 143,000 square miles, but due to the slow, under-funded titling process, only 19,300 miles had been granted by the end of 2006.

# Privatization of Indigenous Lands Is Increasing

Furthermore, the UN Special Rapporteur also noted that privatization of indigenous lands has been increasing.

- In Cambodia, a land law passed in 2001 recognizes the collective right of indigenous peoples to own their lands, yet over the last decade, some 6.5 million hectares of forest have been expropriated to large timber companies through concessions. A further 3.3 million hectares have been declared as protected land, leaving the indigenous communities with limited access to the forest resources necessary for them to survive.

- In Canada, the federal and provincial governments are negotiating agreements with First Nations peoples of British Columbia which recognize only a small portion of these communities' traditional lands as indigenous reserves, leaving the remainder to be privatized.

According to the Declaration on the Rights of Indigenous Peoples adopted by the Human Rights Council, Indigenous Peoples have the right to determine and establish priorities and strategies for their self-development and for the use of their lands, territories and other resources. Indigenous peoples demand that free, prior and informed consent must be the principle of approving or rejecting any project or activity affecting their lands, territories and other resources.

# The Fight for Natural Resources

According to Ms. Tauli-Corpuz, Chairperson of the UN Permanent Forum on Indigenous Issues the majority of the world's remaining natural resources—minerals, freshwater, potential energy sources and more—are found within indigenous peoples' territories. Access to and ownership and development of these resources remains a contentious issue.

- In the Russian Federation, laws adopted in 2001 permit private appropriation of lands yet procedures for access to ownership are so onerous that the majority of indigenous communities have remained excluded from the process. Central Siberia constitutes a vast reserve of petroleum, gas and coal and heavy metals and Russian and foreign companies are now competing for access to these sub-surface resources, presenting problems for the indigenous people in the districts of Turukhansk, Taimyr and Evenk in Krasnoyarsk Territory.

## The Forests of Indigenous Peoples

The situation of forest resources is particularly acute. According to a recent UN report, around 60 million indigenous people around the world depend almost entirely on forests for their survival. Indigenous communities continue to be expelled from their territories under the pretext of the establishment of protected areas or national parks. The report claims that forced displacement of indigenous peoples from their traditional forests as a result of laws that favour the interests of commercial companies is a major factor in the impoverishment of these communities.

- Indonesia is home to 10 percent of the world's forest resources, which provide a livelihood for approximately 30 million indigenous people. Of the 143 million hectares of indigenous territories that are classified as State forest lands, almost 58 million are in the hands of timber companies, with the remainder in the process of being converted into commercial plantations.

- In eastern Africa and the Congo Basin, the creation of protected forest areas has caused the displacement of tens of thousands of indigenous peoples and threatened their subsistence survival.

# Indigenous Lands Are at Risk from the Development of Natural Resources

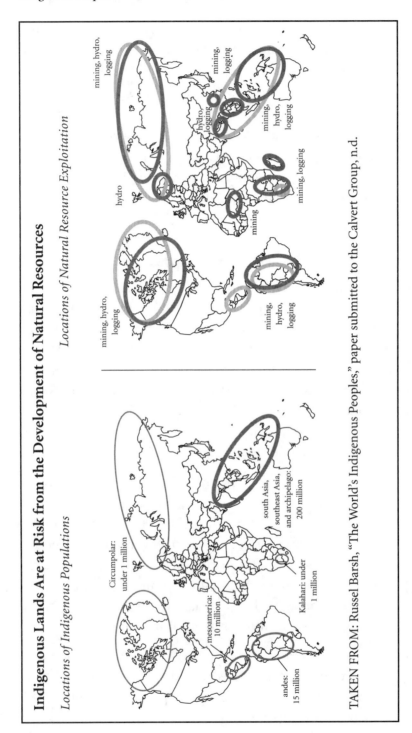

*Locations of Natural Resource Exploitation*

*Locations of Indigenous Populations*

TAKEN FROM: Russel Barsh, "The World's Indigenous Peoples," paper submitted to the Calvert Group, n.d.

# Profiting from the Knowledge of Generations Past

In recent years, the related issues of genetic resources and traditional knowledge have gained prominence on the international political agenda, with indigenous communities expressing fears over the expansion of biotechnology and bioprospecting.

Examples of indigenous traditional knowledge being used for commercial purposes include:

- An element of the Hoodia plant, used by the San people of southern Africa to stave off hunger and thirst during extended hunting expeditions, was patented in 1995 by the South African Council for Scientific and Industrial Research (CSIR). It was later licensed to a multinational pharmaceutical company for use in the development of a slimming pill. After the San people threatened legal action against CSIR, claiming their traditional knowledge had been stolen, the two groups reached an understanding whereby the San would receive a share of future profits from the sale of the drug.

---

*The related issues of genetic resources and traditional knowledge have gained prominence on the international political agenda, with indigenous communities expressing fears over the expansion of biotechnology and bioprospecting.*

---

- A frog poison which acts as a stronger painkiller than morphine and is used by indigenous communities in Brazil, has been the target of more than 20 patents in Europe and the United States.

- A patent awarded to two Indian scientists at the University of Mississippi for the "use of turmeric in wound healing" was overturned after the Indian Council of

Scientific Research argued that the use of turmeric for medicinal purposes had been around for thousands of years and was not "novel".

Two critical issues at the centre of this debate are:

- The requirement of outside actors to obtain the free, prior and informed consent of indigenous people for the use of their traditional knowledge and/or genetic material; and

- The establishment of arrangements for benefit sharing in the profits that flow from such developments.

The Convention on Biological Diversity—which highlights the need to promote and preserve traditional knowledge—sets out principles governing access to and benefit sharing from genetic resources and traditional knowledge, and efforts are being made to ensure such principles are incorporated into the international intellectual property regime.

# Indigenous Peoples Around the World Must Have Water Rights

*Ellen Lutz*

*In the following viewpoint, Ellen Lutz traces the loss of indigenous lands and water rights to major world powers who want to mine and exploit the natural resources present in these areas. Lutz illustrates how international law forbids such development; in addition, international law protects the water rights as well as the land of indigenous peoples. In areas where water rights have been violated, the result has been degradation of the environment, and at times, violence. Lutz is the executive director of Cultural Survival, a leading US-based organization defending the rights of indigenous peoples worldwide.*

As you read, consider the following questions:

1. From where does the oldest body of international law protecting indigenous rights come?

2. What group brought a complaint against Nicaragua for granting a company a permit to log within indigenous sacred grounds?

3. Where are indigenous peoples facing increasing competition for scarce water reserves?

Ellen Lutz, "The Right to Water: An Indigenous Struggle," *Canadian Dimension*, vol. 40, no. 5, September–October 2006, pp. 43–47. Reproduced by permission of the author.

Indigenous peoples worldwide face a long and sordid history of dispossession of their lands and resources, usually to benefit more dominant groups, or economic interests like mining, logging, oil drilling and pipeline construction. Sometimes they are evicted to make way for large-scale development projects like hydroelectric dams or even national parks. These activities universally have a destructive effect upon indigenous lives and cultures.

For many indigenous peoples, their connection to their territories and resources is spiritual. It is their "place" in the world—a place their ancestors lived before them or still reside in spiritual ways. It is home to their gods or spirits. It is where their food grows, and where the clay or thatch or other resources for constructing their material world can be found. Indigenous peoples' spiritual and cultural connections to their lands and resources are at the core of an emerging body of international law that recognizes indigenous peoples' rights and requires states to take steps to ensure that those rights are respected.

## Indigenous Rights and the International Labour Organization

The oldest body of international law protecting indigenous rights comes from the International Labour Organization (ILO), which as early as 1921 undertook studies on the working conditions of indigenous and tribal workers, especially forced labour in the colonies of major world powers. In 1957, the ILO adopted Convention 107 on Indigenous and Tribal Populations, which subsequently was ratified by 27 states. While that treaty incorporated numerous specific protections for indigenous peoples, like the requirement that both collective and individual ownership of traditionally occupied lands must be recognized, its overall focus on integrating indigenous peoples into the larger populace was problematic. In

1989, the ILO adopted a second treaty, Convention 169, to remedy the assimilationist orientation of the earlier treaty.

Seventeen nations, mostly in the Americas and northern Europe, have ratified ILO Convention 169. Today it is the leading standard on indigenous peoples' rights to land and resources. In the Americas, many of the states that have ratified it have also incorporated it into their constitutional or national law. In addition to recognizing the rights of indigenous peoples to own or possess the lands which they traditionally occupy, the treaty requires states to safeguard indigenous peoples' rights to natural resources on their territories, including the right to participate in the use, management and conservation of their resources. While it does not give indigenous peoples an absolute right to the mineral or subsurface resources beneath their territories, the convention does mandate that indigenous peoples shall have a say in any resource exploration or extraction on their lands, and shall benefit from those activities.

*Indigenous peoples' spiritual and cultural connections to their lands and resources are at the core of an emerging body of international law that recognizes indigenous peoples' rights.*

## The United Nations Draft Declaration on the Rights of Indigenous Peoples

Similar land and resource-rights protections are integral to the United Nations Draft Declaration on the Rights of Indigenous Peoples, which is likely to be adopted by the UN General Assembly, possibly this year [2006. The Draft was adopted in 2007.] While not a legally binding treaty, once adopted the Declaration will set the normative standard for states' duties to protect indigenous rights. Many international law scholars have already pronounced certain of the principles it contains to have crystallized into customary international law—law that is binding upon all states.

The UN Draft Declaration is important because it goes further than ILO Convention 169 by specifically recognizing the historical discrimination indigenous peoples faced from colonists and others who abused the rule of law to gain ownership over indigenous lands and resources. The Draft Declaration provides that indigenous peoples shall have "the right to redress, by means that can include restitution or, when this is not possible, of a just, fair and equitable compensation, for the lands, territories and resources which they have traditionally owned or otherwise occupied or used, and which have been confiscated, taken, occupied, used or damaged without their free, prior and informed consent." The Declaration also ensures that indigenous peoples shall have "the right to determine and develop priorities and strategies for the development or use of their lands or territories and other resources," and that "military activities shall not take place in the lands or territories of indigenous peoples.". . .

## The Work of the Inter-American Court on Human Rights

In addition to international legal documents specifically addressing indigenous rights, many international human rights and environmental law treaties have provisions relevant to the protection of indigenous peoples' lands and resources. For example, in a recent decision, the Inter-American Court on Human Rights, interpreting the American Convention on Human Rights provision on the right to property, found that states must actively adopt measures to protect indigenous claims to land and use of natural resources in accordance with their own use and relationship with the land. In this case, the Caribbean coast indigenous community of Awas Tingni brought a complaint against Nicaragua for granting a company a permit to log within the community's traditional sacred lands. In the first legally binding decision by an international tribunal to uphold the land and resource rights of indigenous peoples,

## Indigenous Peoples' Relationship to Water

We, the Indigenous Peoples from all parts of the world assembled here, reaffirm our relationship to Mother Earth and responsibility to future generations to raise our voices in solidarity to speak for the protection of water. We were placed in a sacred manner on this earth, each in our own sacred and traditional lands and territories to care for all of creation and to care for water.

We recognize, honor and respect water as sacred and sustains all life. Our traditional knowledge, laws and ways of life teach us to be responsible in caring for this sacred gift that connects all life.

Our relationship with our lands, territories and water is the fundamental physical cultural and spiritual basis for our existence. This relationship to our Mother Earth requires us to conserve our freshwaters and oceans for the survival of present and future generations. We assert our role as caretakers with rights and responsibilities to defend and ensure the protection, availability and purity of water. We stand united to follow and implement our knowledge and traditional laws and exercise our right of self-determination to preserve water, and to preserve life.

*"Indigenous Peoples Kyoto Water Declaration," Third World Water Forum, Kyoto, Japan, March 2003. www.indigenouswater.org.*

the Court held that Nicaragua must recognize the community's claim to their lands, and assist them to demarcate [distinguish] those lands so that they can be legally recognized. The Court also upheld indigenous peoples' right to enjoy the benefits of property without infringement by outside corporate interests.

# The Case of Mary and Carrie Dann

In another case, two Western Shoshone sisters, Mary and Carrie Dann, sought relief from the Inter-American Commission on Human Rights after the United States penalized them for failing to submit to a cattle-grazing permit system on their traditional lands. The Danns argued that the permit system, like the timber concessions in Awas Tingni, violated their land rights. In that case, the United States did not challenge that the lands had traditionally belonged to the Western Shoshone. Instead, it argued that Shoshone claims to the land had been extinguished through legal proceedings over the years. The Commission found that the Western Shoshone had been discriminated against because they did not have the same opportunity to be heard in those proceedings as non-indigenous property holders. It concluded that the Danns' right to their property had been violated.

In March, 2006, the United Nations Committee on the Elimination of Racial Discrimination (CERD) issued a ruling in another case filed by the Dann sisters. Of particular concern in that case was the U.S. government's stated intent to carry out nuclear-weapons tests on Western Shoshone lands. It called on the United States to freeze any plan to privatize ancestral Western Shoshone lands for transfer to multinational extractive industries and energy developers; to desist from all destructive activities on Western Shoshone lands that were planned to be carried out without their consent; and to stop imposing permit fees and other regulations on Western Shoshone for using their ancestral lands.

# Indigenous Peoples and Water Rights

International law also protects water on indigenous lands, as well as the water indigenous peoples have traditionally used. The Committee on Economic, Social and Cultural Rights, the body established by the United Nations to authoritatively interpret the meaning of the rights set forth in the International Covenant on Economic, Social and Cultural Rights (ICESCR), has declared that the "human right to water entitles everyone to sufficient, safe, acceptable physically and affordable water for personal and domestic uses." The Committee has declared that this right imposes on states the duty to ensure "that there is adequate access to water for subsistence farming and for securing the livelihoods of indigenous peoples." The Committee further declared that, "water should be treated as a social and cultural good, and not primarily as an economic good. The manner of the realization of the right to water must also be sustainable, ensuring that the right can be realized for present and future generations."

In addition, the Committee has called upon states to give special attention to individuals and groups who have traditionally faced difficulty in exercising their right to water. In particular, states should ensure that indigenous peoples' access to water resources on their ancestral lands is protected from encroachment and unlawful pollution. States should provide resources for indigenous peoples to design, deliver and control their access to water.

---

*International law also protects water on indigenous lands, as well as the water indigenous peoples have traditionally used.*

---

The burden falls upon states to ensure that the right to water is respected. Not only must states refrain from interfering with the enjoyment of the right to water, they also must prevent third parties, like large agricultural or corporate interests, from doing so. To ensure the right to water for future generations, states must adopt comprehensive and integrated water-management strategies, which may include:

- Reducing depletion of water resources through unsustainable extraction, diversion and damming;

- Reducing and eliminating contamination of watersheds and water-related eco systems by substances like radiation, harmful chemicals and human excreta;

- Monitoring water reserves;

- Ensuring that proposed developments do not interfere with access to adequate water;

- Assessing the impacts of actions that may impinge upon water availability and natural ecosystems' watersheds, like climate change, desertification and increased soil salinity, deforestation and loss of biodiversity; and

- Establishing competent institutions and appropriate institutional arrangements to carry out the strategies and programs.

These are the precise sorts of measures that indigenous peoples called for in the Indigenous Peoples Kyoto Water Declaration, which they delivered at the Third World Water Forum in Kyoto, Japan, in 2003.

## Indigenous Water Rights Are Often Violated

All too often indigenous peoples' rights to water are honoured in the breach. Throughout the Andes, in India and in the Philippines, indigenous peoples are facing increasing competition for their scarce water reserves from agricultural plantations, as well as from hydroelectric power, mining and drinking-water companies. In Chile the government's privatization of water, combined with its failure to provide its indigenous peoples with timely and adequate information about how to register their water rights, sold their right to water out from under them. On Black Mesa, the ancestral homeland of the Hopi and Dine (Navajo) peoples in the American Southwest, mining by the Peabody Coal Company has nearly depleted the aquifer upon which these Native Americans rely for their drinking water. In the Pacific Northwest, mercury from abandoned gold-rush-era mines and PCBS and other contaminates dumped into rivers by the U.S. military have polluted the water supply and made fish—a staple of the traditional diet—unsafe for human consumption.

Hydroelectric dams and other large-scale development projects also threaten indigenous peoples' right to water. A study carried out by the United Nations Special Rapporteur on the Situation of Human Rights and Fundamental Freedoms of Indigenous Peoples found that, where such developments occur in areas occupied by indigenous peoples, it is likely that their communities will experience profound and unforeseen social and economic changes that devastate their ways of life. The Embera-Katio in Colombia, a portion of whose ancestral territories was flooded without their consultation in 1992 to build a hydroelectric dam, were forced to move into an area that is heavily ravaged by the country's ongoing armed conflict. Many of their homes and property have been destroyed, several of their leaders have been assassinated or forcibly disappeared, and many have consequently been displaced a second time.

*On Black Mesa, the ancestral homeland of the Hopi and Dine (Navajo) peoples in the American Southwest, mining by the Peabody Coal Company has nearly depleted the aquifer upon which these Native Americans rely for their drinking water.*

## Violation of Water Rights Leads to Violence

Violation of the right to water can itself lead to violent conflict. In Bolivia the government, at the behest of the World Bank, turned over management of the Cochabamba city water and sewage system to a single-bidder concession of international water corporations in 1999–2000. Under the arrangement, which was to last for forty years, water prices increased immediately from negligible rates to approximately twenty percent of monthly family incomes. Citizen protests were eventually met with an armed military response that left at least six residents dead. The protests continued until the consortium was forced to flee the country.

Of more immediate concern is the situation in Darfur, Sudan, where decades of drought and desertification have intensified competition for scarce resources, particularly water. State interference with traditional dispute-resolution mechanisms and the superimposition of highly corrupt state administrative agencies have compounded underlying inter-group tensions. Over time, these flared into anti-state sentiment that turned violent as a result of the rebels' easy access to modern weapons. With its attention taken up by peace negotiations in the south of Sudan, the government turned to its supporters among Arab nomadic herders to act in its place. In short order, this government-backed contingent, which lacked land and were looking to settle, became a marauding force, the Janjaweed. The Janjaweed has targeted the civilian population with infamous abuses that include mass murder, the burning of villages and displacement of entire communities, and the rape of women and girls. Nearly a year after massive international attention, the situation refuses to abate.

# The Loss of Lands Leads to Damaged Health for Indigenous Peoples

*Jo Woodman and Sophie Grig*

*In the following viewpoint, Jo Woodman and Sophie Grig argue that although today many indigenous peoples suffer from chronic ill health, they were not unhealthy before contact with outsiders such as European explorers and invaders. In addition, according to the writers, those indigenous peoples who have been able to retain their ancestral lands remain in better health than those who have lost their lands. They offer examples of groups of indigenous peoples whose populations have dropped dramatically as the result of relocation. Woodman and Grig are researchers with Survival International, a London-based organization working on human rights for indigenous peoples.*

As you read, consider the following questions:

1. According to the viewpoint, to what is the life satisfaction rating of the Maasai compared?

2. Why are the life expectancies of hunter-gatherers now lower than they would have been at the turn of the 20th century, according to Woodman and Grig?

Jo Woodman and Sophie Grig, "Introduction: Land and Life," *Progress Can Kill: How Imposed Development Destroys the Health of Tribal Peoples*, edited by Jo Woodman and Sophie Grig, London, United Kingdom: Survival International, 2007, pp. 1–9. Copyright © Survival International 2007. Reproduced by permission. Full report and bibliography available at: www.survival-international.org.

3. By how much and for what reasons did the child mortality rate among the Andamanese increase between 1978 and 1985?

A cross the world, from the poorest to the richest countries, indigenous peoples today experience chronic ill health. They endure the worst of the diseases that accompany poverty and, simultaneously, many suffer from 'diseases of affluence'— such as cancers and obesity—despite often receiving few of the benefits of 'development'. Diabetes alone threatens the very survival of many indigenous communities in rich countries. Indigenous peoples also experience serious mental health problems and have high levels of substance abuse and suicide. The Pikangikum Indians of Ontario, for example, have a suicide rate nearly 40 times the national Canadian average.

## Land and Health

But indigenous peoples have not always been so unwell, and those who live independent lives on their own lands, eating traditional foods, continue to be healthy and strong. These groups may be poor in monetary terms, but are rich in many other ways. They typically have many of the characteristics that have been found to raise happiness, including strong social relationships, stable political systems, high levels of trust and support, and religious or spiritual beliefs, which give their lives meaning. A study exploring happiness and 'life satisfaction' found a high score among a traditional group of Maasai who had resisted colonial attempts to change their way of life and who had largely avoided the market economy. The Maasai had a similar life satisfaction rating to those on the Forbes list of the 400 richest Americans.

Tribal peoples who have suffered colonisation, forced settlement, assimilation policies and other forms of marginalisation and removal from ancestral lands almost always experience a dramatic decline in health and well-being. Dislocation from their land is almost always coupled with rising illness. . . .

There are many factors that can tip a group from an independent, healthy life to dependency and early death, but underlying them all is a loss of rights over their ancestral land and poverty created by the loss of an independent livelihood.

Improving indigenous peoples' health cannot be achieved through clinics and medications alone: the major factors causing their poor heath are social, economic, political and legal. International, national and local action is urgently needed to enable indigenous peoples to reconnect with their lands, rebuild their shattered lives and gain control over their futures. . . .

---

*Tribal peoples who have suffered colonisation, forced settlement, assimilation policies . . . and removal from ancestral lands almost always experience a dramatic decline in health and well-being.*

---

## Why Do Indigenous People Lose Their Land?

In many countries indigenous peoples have become a minority with little influence over policies that affect their lives. Their lands may be taken 'in the national interest' for dams, mines, conservation projects, and other schemes which promise 'development' but leave the land's true owners marginalised. Without a strong voice in political processes or recognition of their inalienable legal rights to their lands, it can be difficult—if not impossible—for tribal communities to influence these projects and protect their independence.

In other cases, indigenous peoples are removed from their land, often forcibly, in order to integrate them into national society and bring them 'development'. This often happens when there are valuable resources on or under the land. These policies are frequently born of a racism towards tribal communities that sees them as "backward" and in need of being 'brought into the modern world'. Changing these stereotypes and racist attitudes is essential for the long-term health and survival of tribal peoples. Whatever the factors that cause tribal peoples to be removed from their ancestral lands, the physical impacts are often similar: short-term shock and exposure to disease and long-term suffering from chronic mental and physical illnesses.

## Historic Health of Indigenous Peoples

There is, understandably, a lack of data on the health of uncontacted tribal groups, but clear patterns can be seen all over the world: independent, mobile peoples who live mostly by hunting and gathering are usually healthier than their settled neighbours who live in crowded, urban environments, eat a 'Western' diet and exercise less. No indigenous group is free of disease, but isolated tribal peoples are largely well adapted to the parasites and germs to which they have historically been exposed. . . .

Child survival rates and life expectancies vary greatly, but are often lower for tribal groups than for rich, Western populations. However, they are typically higher for tribal communities than for their non-tribal, poor neighbours. It is important to make realistic comparisons; when they are settled, tribal peoples do not suddenly have health statistics comparable to Western averages. . . .

---

*Whatever the factors that cause tribal peoples to be removed from their ancestral lands, the physical impacts are often similar: short-term shock and exposure to disease and long-term suffering from chronic mental and physical illnesses.*

---

Typically, life expectancies decrease when hunter-gatherers are settled, not increase. Their life expectancies are thought to be lower now than they would have been at the turn of the

20th century because of the negative impacts of outsiders, such as the stealing of land, the depleting of food stocks and the spreading of diseases.

## The Role of Infant Mortality

The major factor contributing to low life expectancies is commonly a high infant mortality rate. This means that those who survive infancy can expect to live longer than might seem apparent from a statistic of life expectancy at birth.

Looking specifically at infant mortality, there is great variation in rates among different tribal peoples. Where population densities are low, contact with external societies and their diseases is minimal and food is abundant, rates of child mortality are relatively low. Where there has been high exposure to external diseases, vaccination programmes are necessary to protect against epidemics. Among many tribal peoples, child mortality increases when they are settled, especially when highly mobile peoples are moved to crowded, unsanitary camps or shanty towns, as is common. For example, the Onge of Little Andaman Island, who were settled by the government in 1976, experienced a doubling of infant mortality rates in the seven years between 1978 and 1985. This was largely due to malnutrition following the change from a varied diet of meat, fish, fruits and honey to a diet of government rations, and due to exposure to diarrhoeal diseases.

## Reports by Early Explorers

Colonial explorers visiting isolated peoples regularly reported how strong and healthy the people were, recording 'fine teeth', 'excellent skin' and 'muscular physiques'. But contact with outsiders has brought exposure to new diseases and corrosive changes to the livelihoods and practices that had maintained the health of the community. Historical accounts by some of the first European settlers in Australia note that the Aboriginals they met were physically healthy, 'lively' 'active and nimble', with 'compleat setts' of 'even and good' teeth. *The Aborigine population then was around 750,000, although it was rapidly reduced to just over 70,000 by the 1930s.*

It is important to note that most of today's tribal peoples are living in very marginal environments, from the Arctic circle to the Kalahari desert, some having been pushed to these extremes by more numerous, powerful populations. The availability of resources has decreased for even the most isolated people due to loss of land and freedoms. Even the most isolated peoples have often been exposed to diseases and violent contact in the past. The health of many of today's hunter-gatherer peoples must be assessed in this light.

The Inuit certainly had some health problems before regular contact and sedentarisation, including unusual cancers, but early explorers remarked on the vigorousness and healthiness of Inuit peoples. They had some resistance to illnesses such as arthritis and diabetes because of their diet, levels of exercise and genetic adaptations. Similarly, there were some common diseases among the Amazonian Yanomami before waves of miners invaded their land. There was tetanus in the soil and viral infections like herpes and yellow fever, but those diseases were at a low level and were rarely fatal. Measles, malaria, whooping cough, influenza, polio, TB, rubella and chicken-pox were among the diseases to which they had no immunity and to which they were first exposed when gold-miners invaded.

## The Effects of Contact

Sudden contact with an alien society is devastating to remote tribal peoples, often involving shock, disease and violence, all of which can be deadly. The European invasion of the Americas wiped out 90% of the indigenous population. This devastation was caused partially by violence and slavery, but mostly by a lethal combination of epidemics and shock which led to a decline in total fertility and a loss of the will to live, often

## The Effects of Land Loss on an Indigenous People's Population

**Great Andamanese population**

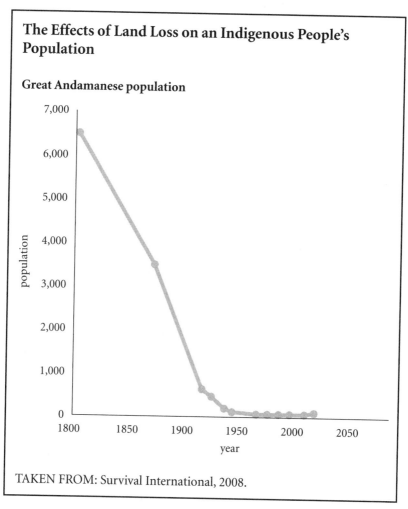

year

TAKEN FROM: Survival International, 2008.

resulting in suicides, even of children. The population of what is now Mexico, for example, fell from 20 million in 1518 to 1.6 million in 1618.

Between 1967 and 1975 one Yanomami community in Roraima, Brazil, was totally wiped out through measles. Other villages in the area suffered a dramatic population decline of up to 70% because of diseases spread by road builders. A fear of the supernatural forces that could cause such suffering immobilised people. Village life collapsed and suffering was increased by the lack of people able to bring water, hunt, care for the sick and prepare food. Such shock can have direct physical consequences, such as causing miscarriage in pregnant women.

In South America, South East Asia and Melanesia, there are some peoples who have deliberately chosen to remain isolated from outsiders, in an effort to save both their health and their ways of life from the impacts of contact. These peoples are incredibly vulnerable to complete extermination by invaders. The Peruvian indigenous federation, FENAMAD, has warned that, for the isolated Indians living upstream of the Timpia, Serjali and Paquiria rivers, 'contact by outsiders with these peoples would constitute a serious threat to their fundamental rights to health, cultural identity, well being and possession of land . . . and make possible their extinction as individuals and as indigenous peoples.' Importantly, however, first contact has a less devastating impact when people maintain control over their land. [According to researchers S. Foliaki and N. Pearce in a 2003 article,] 'Indigenous people experienced high mortality from imported infectious diseases mainly when their land was taken and their economic base, food supply and social networks were disrupted. When land was not taken in large amounts by European settlers the death rate was relatively low'. The Enawene Nawe of Mato Grosso, Brazil, have been able to hold onto most of their land, experienced contact relatively positively and have survived well as a distinct and healthy people.

## Disease and Devastation in the Andaman Islands

The Andaman and Nicobar Islands lie off the east coast of India and have been home to several distinct tribes for tens of thousands of years. Administration of the archipelago, first by Britain and later by India, has brought disaster for those tribes with whom they have had the most contact.

The Sentinelese [indigenous people living on nearby Sentinel Island] are self-sufficient hunter-gatherers whose isolated location and aggressive behaviour towards outsiders have saved them from the devastation that has been wrought on their neighbours, the Great Andamanese, whose population is now just 53.

---

*First contact [with outsiders] has a less devastating impact when [indigenous] people maintain control over their land.*

---

When the British first colonised the Andaman Islands, the Great Andamanese were a healthy people, but with little immunity to diseases such as measles and influenza. Since then, 99% of this tribe have been wiped out through battles with the British, transfer of diseases and the disastrous and cruel policy of taking children from their families to be raised in a children's home. *Of 150 babies born in the home, none survived beyond the age of two.* In 1970, the surviving Great Andamanese were moved to the tiny Strait Island by the Indian authorities, where they are now totally dependent on the government for food, shelter and clothing, with high rates of alcoholism and tuberculosis.

The Onge of Little Andaman Island have also suffered greatly. Before they were 'resettled' by the government, the Onge hunted, fished and gathered on Little Andaman island, and had diets rich in wild boar meat, fruits and honey. From the 1950s, settlers invaded their lands and the government logged their forests. Since being resettled in 1976, the Onge have become dependent on nutritionally poor government rations, with a drastic impact on child health. Between 1978 and 1985, the infant mortality rate doubled, with the most common cause of child deaths being from diarrhoea, dysentery and malnutrition. The Onge population fell from 670 in 1900, to 169 in 1961, to 76 in 1991. [As reported in a 2006 BBC article] 'This "resettlement" has set in motion the biological, social and cultural death of the Onge.'

The Onge's neighbours, the Jarawa, have maintained their independence and therefore suffered less through disease and removal from their lands. They are mostly still nomadic and self-sufficient, but they are at increasing risk from poachers and settlers who are continuing to use a road through their territory. The supreme court of India ordered that the road must be closed but, despite government assurances, the road remains open and poachers are not being stopped from accessing the area.

---

*When independent, mobile tribal people are suddenly shifted to a sedentary existence, surrounded by non-indigenous food and cultures and, especially, when they are removed to alien land, the health of individuals and communities suffers catastrophically.*

---

## The Loss of Indigenous Land to Development

All around the world indigenous people have their land taken from them for economic development projects such as mining, logging and plantations. Such projects are often imposed on the tribal landowners, ignoring their rights to their land. These activities can cause enormous environmental degradation leading directly to the loss of tribal land, hunting grounds, gardens and drinking water. For example, the Kamoro of West Papua have had one billion tons of tailings tipped into their river system from the American and British owned Grasberg copper and gold mine. Although the company claims that the quality of water passes international standards, even according to their own monitoring data supplied to the government, it breaches legal levels for dissolved copper. Total suspended solids in the Lower Ajkwa River are up to 100 times over the legal limit. The tailings also smother the vegetation causing trees and sago palms, the staple food of the Kamoro, to die. The Kamoro used to use the river for drinking water, fishing, navigating and washing and the forest, which is also being polluted by the tailings, for hunting.

## The Effects of Resettlement

When independent, mobile tribal people are suddenly shifted to a sedentary existence, surrounded by non-indigenous food and cultures and, especially, when they are removed to alien land, the health of individuals and of communities suffers catastrophically. This change rarely, if ever, affords tribal people a high standard of living but, rather, takes them to the edges of non-indigenous society—to slums and roadside squatter camps, underemployment, destitution or dependence. The shift towards higher-density living among mixed communities, often with domestic animals and usually in conditions of low sanitation, leads to diseases such as tuberculosis, intestinal parasites and cholera.

Sedentarisation causes a decrease in health in several direct ways: sanitation problems; contact with diseases from domestic animals; skin problems from clothing; 'crowd' diseases and epidemics such as measles, cholera and influenza; decreasing quality of diet; access to alcohol and other drugs; and a decline in social bonds and sharing. The shift away from tribal cultures and livelihoods can lead to chronic illnesses, including cancers, diabetes and heart disease, and social problems such as drug abuse, depression and violence. Divorced from their traditions and cultural coping mechanisms, individuals—especially the youth—can be led further away from their cultures and towards dependence on the non-indigenous society and the state. The power of Western medicine to conquer new diseases can often turn people away from their traditional cures and healers, thus undermining confidence in both leaders and their belief systems, leading to increased social decay. But the medical care available to indigenous communities tends to be of poor quality and low availability and is utterly insufficient compensation for the exposure to new illnesses.

# Canadian Indigenous Peoples Lose the Right to Log on Traditional Lands

## Thomas Isaac and Rob Miller

*In the following viewpoint, Thomas Isaac and Rob Miller summarize two Canadian Supreme Court cases, singly decided in* Marshall *and* Bernard. *The cases determined whether indigenous peoples in New Brunswick and Nova Scotia had title and treaty rights to log for commercial purposes on government lands. The Court ruled that they did not have such a right since they did not have title to the land and logging was not a traditional activity for the tribes involved. They further ruled that Aboriginal interests had to be weighed against the interests of Canadian society as a whole. Isaac and Miller are lawyers who specialize in Aboriginal law.*

As you read, consider the following questions:

1. What did the lower courts find in the case of Bernard, the Mi'kmaq Indian charged with the unlawful possession of spruce logs?

2. On what three grounds did the Mi'kmaq rely in the their assertion of Aboriginal title?

3. For what group does the decision of *Marshall and Bernard* pose inherent difficulty in proving title to land?

Thomas Isaac and Rob Miller, *Legal Update: Supreme Court of Canada: "Marshall and Bernard" Decision*," McCarthy Tétrault, August 2005. www.mccarthy.ca. Reproduced by permission.

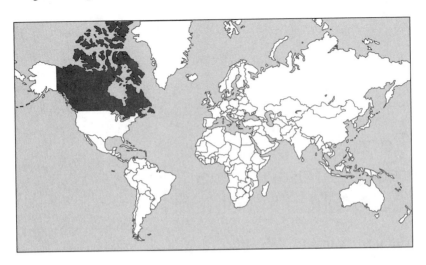

On July 20, 2005, the Supreme Court of Canada delivered its reasons in two cases: *R. v. Marshall*, and *R. v. Bernard* (*"Marshall and Bernard"*). The cases concerned claims of Aboriginal title and treaty rights to commercial logging in New Brunswick and Nova Scotia. In a single decision, the unanimous seven-member Court (a) allowed the appeals, (b) rejected the claims to Aboriginal title and the treaty right to harvest timber for commercial purposes, and (c) restored the convictions. While the decision deals with Aboriginal rights and title in New Brunswick and Nova Scotia, it has national implications for First Nations wishing to establish Aboriginal title, and for governments and businesses operating in areas where treaty rights or Aboriginal title claims are relevant.

## The Background of *Marshall and Bernard*

*Marshall and Bernard* deals with appeals in two cases. In *Marshall*, 35 Mi'kmaq Indians were charged with cutting timber on Crown [Canadian government] lands in Nova Scotia without authorization. In *Bernard*, a Mi'kmaq Indian was charged with unlawful possession of spruce logs he was transporting from the cutting site (on Crown land) to a local saw mill. In both cases, the accused argued that provincial authorizations were not necessary because the Mi'kmaq possess either a treaty right to harvest timber on Crown lands for commercial purposes or Aboriginal title over the cutting site.

The lower courts entered convictions in both cases, which were upheld by the summary conviction courts. The courts of appeal set aside both sets of convictions ordering a new trial in *Marshall* and entering an acquittal in *Bernard*.

---

*[Canadian Chief Justice Beverley McLachlin] stated that the conclusion that commercial logging was not a logical evolution of a traditional Mi'kmaq trace activity was supported by the expert and Aboriginal witnesses, as well as the documentation and the cultural and historical record.*

---

# The Decision: Part One

*No Treaty Right to Commercial Logging*

Writing for the majority, [Beverly] McLachlin C.J. [Chief Justice] began her analysis by examining the 1999 *Marshall* decisions from the Court dealing with the 1760–61 treaties, the terms of which were similar to those under consideration in *Marshall and Bernard*. All of these decisions involved an interpretation of the so-called "truckhouse" clauses which the British provided as a right to trade at truckhouses, [trading posts] but not the right to harvest the traded goods. Nothing in the clauses "comports a general right to harvest or gather all natural resources then used", as claimed by the Mi'kmaq. McLachlin C.J. found that the truckhouse clause in *Marshall and Bernard* does not protect the right to harvest, but the "right to practice a traditional 1760 trading activity in a modern way and a modern context."

The question then before the Court was whether commercial logging was a "logical evolution of a traditional Mi'kmaq trade activity." McLachlin C.J. concluded that it was not, and relied heavily upon the factual findings of the trial judge in each case. McLachlin C.J. went further and stated that the conclusion that commercial logging was not a logical evolution of a traditional Mi'kmaq trade activity was supported by the expert and Aboriginal witnesses, as well as the documentation and the cultural and historical record: "the evidence suggests that logging was inimical to the Mi'kmaq's traditional way of life, interfering with fishing which, as found in *Marshall 1*, [an earlier case] was a traditional activity."

## The Decision: Part Two

*No Proof of Aboriginal Title*

On the issue of Aboriginal title, McLachlin C.J. noted that the Mi'kmaq relied upon three different grounds for Aboriginal title: common law, the *Royal Proclamation of 1763* and *Governor Belcher's Proclamation*.

McLachlin C.J. began by stating that the Mi'kmaq in these cases were not asserting an Aboriginal right to harvest forest resources. Rather, they were asserting Aboriginal title simpliciter [a legal term meaning in a simple manner or degree], a right to the land itself.

As for the common law [law based on usage, custom, and/or earlier court decisions as opposed to statutory laws passed by government bodies], McLachlin C.J. noted that proven Aboriginal title can be infringed "for the good of larger society" which can be seen as a means of "reconciling Aboriginal interests with the interests of the broader community." The Court confirmed that both the Aboriginal and common law perspective of Aboriginal title must be considered in order to uphold the honour of the Crown. This required the Court to examine the pre-sovereignty Aboriginal practice and translate it into a modern right.

As for Aboriginal title, which is an Aboriginal right, it is established by Aboriginal practices that demonstrate "possession similar to that associated with title at common law." Accordingly, establishing Aboriginal title requires proof of exclusive physical occupation of the land (although exclusivity is not necessarily negated by occasional acts of trespass or the presence of other Aboriginal groups with consent). Where exclusive possession is not established, non-exclusive occupation may establish Aboriginal rights "short of title".

McLachlin C.J. expressly addresses the issue of whether nomadic or semi-nomadic peoples can establish Aboriginal title, particularly in light of the requirement of exclusivity. In short, it depends on the evidence. In each instance, it will depend on the "degree of occupation or use equivalent to common law title" that has been made.

In *Marshall and Bernard*, McLachlin C.J. concluded that both trial judges made no material errors in their analysis of whether the claim to Aboriginal title had been made out by the Mi'kmaq. As a result, she rejected the claim of Aboriginal title based on the common law.

# The Royal Proclamation of 1763

McLachlin C.J. rejected the notion that the *Royal Proclamation of 1763* (upon a review of the text, jurisprudence and historic policy) reserved the former colony of Nova Scotia to the Mi'kmaq. Likewise, McLachlin C.J. rejected the notion that *Governor Belcher's Proclamation* could serve as any basis to support the claim of Aboriginal title. She expressly endorsed the following tests as accurately reflecting the jurisprudence in respect of the burden of proof that must be satisfied to establish Aboriginal title:

- in *Marshall*, the provincial court found that "the line separating sufficient and insufficient occupancy for title is between irregular use of undefined lands on the one hand and the regular use of defined lands on the other"; and

# The Frustrating Message for First Nations Peoples

For First Nations, the message of *Marshall and Bernard* must be enormously frustrating. They were here before the Europeans arrived, living in an organized society that sustained itself from the land. They can prove their connection to, use of, and control over, specific territories, although not perhaps to every hectare within that territory. It is as if; to borrow an image from Tom Molloy, the Federal Chief Negotiator for the Nisga'a Agreement, [a 1998 land claim case involving the Nisga'a tribe of northern British Columbia] you came home one night to find strangers living in your house. "We'll share with you if you can prove the house is yours," they say, "but you have to prove it without using any title deeds, and, by the way, all the neighbours who have known you for more than twenty years have disappeared, and you can't have any legal aid to help you prepare your argument." Maybe you find pictures of family events that show you in front of the fireplace in the living room, or eating at the picnic table in the backyard, but when you point to the pictures as evidence that you occupied the house and the yard, the people in your house say, "Yes, but what about the kitchen? For all we know, you only passed through the kitchen on an irregular basis."

*Margaret E. McCallum,*
*"After Marshall and Bernard,"*
University of New Brunswick Law Journal,
*Sunday, Janurary 1, 2006.*

- in *Bernard*, the provincial court judge found that "occasional visits to an area did not establish title; [rather,] there must be evidence of capacity to retain exclusive control".

As a result, McLachlin C.J. rejected the claim of Aboriginal title at common law based on (i) the findings of fact of the provincial court judges, and (ii) the application of the appropriate tests by those judges:

> The trial judge in each case applied the correct legal tests and drew conclusions of fact that are fully supported by the evidence. Their conclusions that the respondents possessed neither a treaty right to trade in logs nor aboriginal title to the cutting sites must therefore stand. Nor is there any basis for finding title in the *Royal Proclamation or Belcher's Proclamation.*

## The Minority Opinion

LeBel J. [Justice] (with Fish J. concurring) agreed with the result set out by McLachlin C.J. but disagreed with the Chief Justice's statement that a right to harvest was not contemplated within the meaning of the truckhouse clause. He felt that such an interpretation rendered the trading right meaningless. However, on the facts before him, LeBel J. concluded that trade in forest products was not contemplated by the parties and that logging was not a logical evolution of Mi'kmaq traditional activities. He also thought that the approach to Aboriginal title adopted by the majority was "too narrowly focused on common law concepts relating to property interests."

## The Implications of *Marshall and Bernard*

*Marshall and Bernard* has broad implications for Mi'kmaq peoples in Nova Scotia and New Brunswick who have claimed the right to log on Crown lands for commercial purposes pursuant to treaty or Aboriginal title. This claim has been clearly rejected by the Court. The decision also places into better context the 1999 *Marshall* decisions by placing a very clear limit on the extent to which treaties will be interpreted generously. As the Court said in the *Marshall* decisions (reconsideration refused): "While treaty rights are capable of evolution within limits, . . . their subject matter . . . cannot be wholly transformed."

The decision confirmed the reasonably high bar set for proving Aboriginal title originally set out by the Court in *Delgamuukw v. B.C. ("Delgamuukw" [an earlier case concerning Aboriginal title])* The Court appears to be confirming that while Aboriginal rights to particular activities are one thing, the right to the land itself will be held to a reasonably high evidentiary standard. In this way, *Marshall and Bernard* represent an inherent difficulty for the Métis who may, as a general rule, have a difficult time meeting the indicia [circumstances] for proving title set out by the Court (e.g. exclusivity).

---

Marshall and Bernard *deals . . . with the Court's concept of the reconciliation of Aboriginal interests with the broader interests of society as a whole.*

---

*Marshall and Bernard* represents the first substantive post-*Delgamuukw* examination of Aboriginal title by the Court and as such, it is noteworthy that the claim of Aboriginal title, in this case, was rejected. The majority's discussion of the threshold for proving Aboriginal title and, that once proven, it can be infringed by the Crown "for the good of larger society" may prove to be beneficial to the process of negotiating treaties on Canada's east coast and in British Columbia in that the benefits of proving Aboriginal title as weighed against a negotiated settlement of claims are far from certain.

*Marshall and Bernard* demonstrates the Court's conviction to holding to its conceptual and legal framework for interpreting section 35 of the *Constitution Act, 1982* (which recognizes and affirms existing Aboriginal and treaty rights).

Finally, *Marshall and Bernard* deals, albeit briefly, with the Court's concept of the reconciliation of Aboriginal interests with the broader interests of society as a whole. In discussing the process of how the Crown can justifiably infringe proven Aboriginal title in "pursuance of a compelling and substantial legislative objective for the good of larger society", McLachlin C.J. noted that such a process can be seen as a "way of reconciling aboriginal interests with the interests of the broader community." In other words, when facilitating such reconciliation, the Crown must consider both Aboriginal and non-Aboriginal perspectives and interests, confirming that the recognition of Aboriginal rights and title is a process which requires the input of all potentially affected parties including First Nations, communities and industry.

# In the Torres Strait, the Indigenous Right to Hunt and Fish Is Endangering Wildlife

*Greg Roberts*

*Greg Roberts reports in the following viewpoint that bird, animal, and fish populations have declined dramatically in the Torres Strait region of Australia, largely due to over-hunting and fishing by indigenous peoples. Some indigenous peoples agree, but also assert that hunting and fishing are important to their culture, according to Roberts. The question of whether indigenous peoples should be limited in their hunting and fishing in national parks is a particularly difficult question. According to Roberts, both indigenous and non-indigenous peoples know that it is necessary to assess the sustainability of wildlife. Roberts writes for the Australian publication* The Australian.

As you read, consider the following questions:

1. What has ignited the debate over indigenous hunting, according to Roberts?
2. How many of the world's population of dugongs live in Australia?
3. About how many green turtles are killed annually for food in the Great Barrier Reef, according to the viewpoint?

Greg Roberts, "Hunting Towards Oblivion," *The Australian*, April 26, 2008. Copyright © 2008 News Limited. Reproduced by permission of the author.

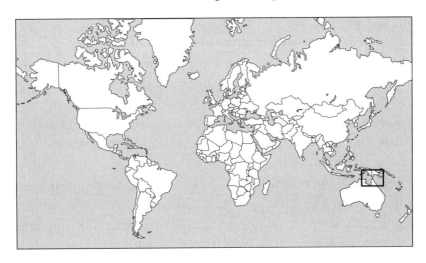

Peter Guivarra recalls how the sky would thicken at this time of the year with vast numbers of magpie geese that nested in swamps near his home settlement, Mapoon, on [Australia's] Cape York Peninsula's western side.

With thousands of geese being shot annually by indigenous hunters, Guivarra, chairman of the Mapoon Aboriginal Shire Council, says the bird population is a fraction of what it was 10 or 15 years ago.

Says Guivarra: "There were hundreds of thousands, but now it's thousands and the numbers get smaller every season. I want my sons and grandsons to be able to hunt, but at this rate they won't be able to."

Across the Gulf of Carpentaria, in the wetlands of Kakadu National Park in the Northern Territory, indigenous hunting of magpie geese with shotguns is so prolific that untargeted wildlife are suffering lead poisoning from spent lead shot ingested while foraging for food.

## Indigenous Hunting Is Excessive

Guivarra is among a growing band of indigenous leaders that believes hunting by their people is excessive and no longer sustainable. The leaders argue that a combination of increased human populations and the use of firearms, vehicles and motorboats has distorted traditional notions of hunting.

"It is easy these days for too many animals to be killed," Guivarra says. He adds that hunting is jeopardising plans by the Mapoon people to emulate Kakadu's success as an ecotourism destination. "We have the same wetlands and waterbirds, but soon there won't be anything for people to come and see," he says.

Debate over indigenous hunting has been ignited by Japan's move to attack as hypocritical [Australia's capital] Canberra's support for the indigenous harvesting of dugongs [large marine mammals similar to the manatee] in Australian waters. While Australia leads the charge against Japanese whaling, the number of minke whales killed annually by the Japanese—ostensibly for scientific research—is similar to the number of dugongs killed each year for food in the Torres Strait, about 1000. The Japanese point out that the world population of the minke whale is several times that of the dugong.

---

*[Indigenous elder De Nice] Gaia says hunting is culturally significant, but technology has reduced its relevance to the community's cultural fabric.*

---

Dugongs and sea turtles are traditional mainstays of the diet of Torres Strait Islanders and coastal Aboriginal communities in northern Australia, but on Palm Island, off Townsville, indigenous elder De Nice Gaia says her family refuses to hunt or eat them. Gaia says numbers of dugongs and turtles in local waters have fallen sharply. As elsewhere, they can be hunted only with harpoons, but there are no bag limits, set hunting seasons or other restrictions.

"It's not traditional hunting when you're chasing an animal in a dinghy with a 40-horsepower motor, and there's no way it can escape." Gaia says the killing is cruel; for instance, turtle carapaces are removed while animals are alive in the mistaken belief the meat will be more tender using this process. It is also wasteful. "I find turtles dead on the beach with holes in their shells that have been used as target practice."

Gaia says hunting is culturally significant, but technology has reduced its relevance to the community's cultural fabric.

"There is plenty of other meat available these days. Hunting has become a status symbol. Everyone wants the biggest turtle. If someone comes in with a big turtle, three or four boats go out the next day trying to get a bigger one."

## The Cultural Importance of Hunting

In the Torres Strait, Badu Island Council manager Manai Nona explains the cultural significance of hunting to islanders. Killing a dugong or turtle is part of the rite of passage to manhood for teenage boys. A feast of dugong and turtle is regarded as essential to the success of an important occasion, such as a wedding, funeral or tombstone unveiling. Hunting from boats is how islanders develop seamanship skills. Hunts and feasting ceremonies feature prominently in relationships between island communities. "Hunting is very important to our culture," Nona says. Dugong and turtle are a leading source of protein and fresh meat in often isolated communities where frozen meat imports are expensive and unreliable. "One dugong can feed an extended family of 10 or 12 people for a fortnight," Nona says. "Dugong and turtle is the best meat. I'll have it any day if the choice is rump steak or lamb chops."

However, Nona agrees that too many dugongs and turtles are killed. "We know there shouldn't be so many taken. The last thing we want is to wipe them all out."

## Is Indigenous Hunting Sustainable?

Central to the indigenous hunting debate is whether the harvesting of native animals is sustainable. Does it threaten the survival of species being targeted?

In the Iron Range area of eastern Cape York Peninsula, cassowaries—large, flightless birds found in the rainforests of north Queensland and New Guinea—have long been valued as food by the Lockhart River people. The wary cassowaries are difficult to stalk and kill by traditional means, but they are easily shot.

Large numbers of the once numerous birds were shot by indigenous hunters; today, cassowaries—an endangered species in Australia—are rarely seen and the future of the Iron Range population is uncertain.

Federal and state authorities are working to avoid a similar fate for dugongs and turtles. Federal Environment Minister Peter Garrett says the government is undertaking a strategic assessment of the Torres Strait turtle and dugong fisheries. Meanwhile, the available scientific evidence suggests that present levels of harvesting the sea animals are not sustainable.

---

*Central to the indigenous hunting debate is whether the harvesting of native animals is sustainable. Does it threaten the survival of species being targeted?*

---

Australia is home to 80 percent to 90 percent of the estimated world population of 100,000 dugongs. While the large sea mammals—listed by the International Union for Conservation of Nature as "vulnerable to extinction in the medium-term future"—range widely in the Indian and southwest Pacific oceans, their numbers have crashed due to hunting pressure and the loss of the seagrass meadows on which they feed. The species is especially vulnerable because it is slow-breeding; a female gives birth to a calf every five years on average.

A new study from James Cook University [JCU] researchers, commissioned by the federal Environment Department's Marine and Tropical Sciences Research Facility, reports that surveys in 2006 estimated a population of 23,500 dugongs in the Torres Strait and northern Great Barrier Reef, about 25 percent of the world total. This is close to the number estimated in surveys in 2000 and 2001, but substantially lower than numbers noted in 1996.

Modelling for the study suggests that killing more than 100 to 200 dugongs annually in the Torres Strait and 56 in northern reef waters—a fraction of the present harvest—is not sustainable. The study also says climate change may be affecting dugong numbers by increasing the incidence of seagrass dieback.

JCU dugong expert Helene Marsh says it is difficult to accurately measure dugong numbers because the animals roam over large areas in search of seagrass, but there are concerns about the harvest level in the Torres Strait. Says Marsh: "Scientific evidence suggests dugongs may be over-harvested by some Cape York communities and in the Torres Strait. The important thing is to work with indigenous people to ensure the harvest is sustainable."

Marsh adds that she disagrees with Japan's use of the dugong catch to defend its whaling practices. "Their whaling is a commercial harvest done under the guise of research. This is an indigenous harvest that goes back 4000 years."

## The Future of Green Turtles

Surveys indicate that about 5000 green turtles are killed annually for food in the northern Great Barrier Reef, the Torres Strait and adjoining Indonesian and Papua New Guinean waters. Queensland turtle research program manager Colin Limpus, one of the world's leading turtle authorities, says the regional breeding population, concentrated on Raine Island, was estimated at 50,000 10 to 20 years ago. Limpus says numbers have fallen significantly since then, with hunting accounting for more than half the loss.

# The Significance of Traditional Hunting to Indigenous Peoples

The economic, social, cultural and ecological significance of traditional hunting for many Indigenous people cannot be underestimated. Many Aboriginal and Torres Strait Islander people, particularly those living in urban areas, do not hunt at all and many others do so only as a recreational activity or as a chance to enjoy particular foods. Reliance on bush food has been lessened in most communities by the availability of processed food. Nevertheless, hunting is of continuing importance to the lives of people living in less-populated areas of Australia, such as northern and central Australia. The Australian Law Reform Commission reports that on the north coast of New South Wales where unemployment in Aboriginal communities is high, 'bush tucker' is heavily relied on for food. Bush meat and bush food in general can make up a significant part of the diet and in remote areas provide a fresher alternative to store-bought food. It also contributes to economic benefits through 'cash income equivalence'. It is also said to contribute to improved health through the physical exercise involved in the hunt, although the consumption of large amounts of fatty meats from hunts that are less physically demanding nowadays because of the use of modern technology (for instance the hunting of dugongs) is also believed to contribute to severe weight-related problems.

*Dominique Thiriet, "Tradition and Change—Avenues for Improving Animal Welfare in Indigenous Hunting,"* James Cook University Law Review, *vol. 8, 2004.* *www.austlii.edu.au.*

"When you can have a single village taking 100 to 200 turtles a year, it adds up to a lot of turtles," he says. "We have concerns for the population's viability."

Nonetheless, Marsh and Limpus are encouraged that indigenous leaders have begun to address the sustainability issue. Six Torres Strait communities are preparing management plans to limit dugong catches under a program funded by a $4.6 million commonwealth grant, although Marsh says more funds are needed to expand the program. Other communities are co-operating with authorities to control turtle harvesting. South of the Torres Strait, the Girringun people of the Cardwell area and the Woppaburra people of the Keppel islands have reached agreements with the Great Barrier Reef Marine Park Authority to ban the hunting of dugongs and restrict turtle catches. Hunting critics want to go further.

Legal researcher Rebecca Smith, who was commissioned to prepare a review last year on laws affecting dugongs for the Torres Strait Regional Authority, believes hunting is cruel: "Harpooning, a hideous death for whales, is no less hideous for dugongs and turtles. An adult male dugong takes up to two hours to die. People know these things, but they're afraid to tackle the issue."

*Indigenous hunting in national parks and other reserves is especially contentious, and management solutions are not easily recognizable when policies vary widely.*

## The Conservation Movement and Indigenous Hunting

The conservation movement, always sensitive about its relationship with the indigenous community, finds itself in a quandary over the hunting row. The Wilderness Society's northern Australia campaigner Lyndon Schneiders says the society does not oppose indigenous hunting in national parks when it complies with park management plans. However, as most plans allow hunting, Schneiders contradicts himself when he says the society opposes the use of guns and vehicles for hunting in all national parks.

Indigenous hunting in national parks and other reserves is especially contentious, and management solutions are not easily recognisable when policies vary widely.

In the Karijini National Park in Western Australia, Aborigines can shoot wildlife for food "for themselves and their families". In Katherine Gorge National Park in the NT, the Jawyn people can hunt freely with guns as long as visitor safety is not compromised. In Queensland's Barron Gorge National Park, no firearms can be used without permission and no endangered or vulnerable species can be hunted.

Says Queensland National Parks Association president John Bristow: "National parks are special areas that should be recognised by everyone. Nobody, including indigenous people, should be able to kill wildlife with firearms in national parks."

Mapoon's Guivarra says the crucial issue is not where hunting is restricted but whether it is sustainable. "Our people know that we have to get it right," he says. "We have been managing the country for a long time."

# Indigenous Peoples in Brazil Reclaim Land

*Isabella Kenfield*

*Brazilian-based writer Isabella Kenfield summarizes the story of indigenous peoples in Brazil who were successful in their attempts to reclaim their ancestral lands from agribusiness giant, Aracruz Celulose (AC). Kenfield asserts that AC is one of the largest paper pulp producers in the world, and that the company has had arrangements with the Brazilian government. In a surprising move, according to Kenfield, the Brazilian Minister of Justice set aside 27,000 acres of land for the Tupinikim and Guarani indigenous peoples in response to the growing unity of indigenous groups throughout the country.*

As you read, consider the following questions:

1. According to the viewpoint, how much paper does the United States, Europe and Brazil consume every year, on average?
2. How much water per day does Aracruz Celulose consume, according to figures in the viewpoint?
3. What happened on the morning of January 20, 2006?

Isabella Kenfield, "Taking on Big Celulose: Brazilian Indigenous Communities Reclaim Their Land," *NACLA Report on the Americas*, vol. 40, no. 6, November–December 2007, pp. 9–13. Copyright © 2007 by the North American Congress on Latin America, 38 Greene St. 4th FL., New York, NY 10013. Reproduced by permission.

In late August [2007] Brazilian Minister of Justice Tarso Genro shocked many with his decision to demarcate about 27,000 acres of land for Tupinikim and Guarani indigenous communities in the southeastern state of Espirito Santo. For almost 40 years, the land has been controlled by Aracruz Celulose S.A., or AC, the world's largest producer of Celulose made from bleached eucalyptus pulp. Genro's decision testifies to the growing capacity and organization of the country's rural civil society, which continues to put Brazil on the map as an epicenter of resistance to agribusiness.

"It is still difficult to believe," says Winnie Over-beek of the Federation for Social and Educational Assistance (FASE), an NGO [non-governmental organization] based in Vitoria, Espirito Santo, which has supported the Tupinikim and Guarani in their struggle since the 1980s.

## A Surprising Move

The surprise comes because AC has enjoyed massive state support since its founding in the Aracruz region of Espirito Santo in 1972 as part of the military dictatorship's national economic development plan, which centered on agro-industrial production for export. The dictatorship both subsidized AC and granted it massive tracts of land for its eucalyptus plantations.

But the Aracruz region was also "the last refuge" of the Tupinikim, according to a 2002 report by the Brazilian Platform for Economic, Social, Cultural and Environmental Human Rights (DhESCA). In 1970, there were 40 Tupinikim aldeias, or villages, in Aracruz, according to Overbeek. And in the early 1960s a Guarani community arrived there after a decades-long migration from southern Brazil, where it had been dispossessed of its lands, and joined a Tupinikim aldeia [village] called Caieiras Velhas.

---

*[Aracruz Celulose] illegally appropriated land from the Tupinikim and Guarani, building its first factory in a [village] called Macacos. This was easy, since there were no formal registers of indigenous populations or their lands.*

---

Antonio dos Santos, 71, a Tupinikim chief living in the aldeia of Pau Brasil, remembers how as a child and married man with young children, he and his community lived from hunting, fishing, gathering, and small-scale agriculture in the coastal Atlantic rain forest. "It was a good life," he says. "We had our day-to-day survival. We had liberty to go into the forest and pass the entire day hunting and fishing, without problems. Our agriculture was in clearings, planting corn, beans, manioc, banana, potato, and yams. We planted everything and lived from that."

## Illegal Industrial Land Appropriation

AC illegally appropriated land from the Tupinikim and Guarani, building its first factory in an aldeia called Macacos. This was easy, since there were no formal registers of indigenous populations or their lands. Moreover, the corporation had the full support of municipal, state, and federal governments, and was able to acquire land through a variety of ways, including grilagem, or falsifying deeds.

"When AC arrived, it paid a functionary to go from village to village, house to house, to inform us that AC was buying the land, and that the land had been sold to AC," dos Santos remembers. "That functionary arrived and said, 'You have to sell. So-and-so sold, so you must too. Because if you don't sell, you are going to be a prisoner here. You are going to be without a way to leave.' Whoever sold was deluded, was deceived, and so sold. We had to leave. Because soon after, AC came with a tractor, a machine, that destroyed everything. AC gave a short time, and if the person didn't leave, it would go and destroy the house. Destroyed the home and the person."

In all, AC appropriated about 100,000 acres, or 41% of land in Aracruz, leaving just 100 acres for the Tupinikim. Those who remained found their land increasingly unusable and their livelihoods destroyed, because eucalyptus monoculture creates "green deserts," growing rapidly and in the process secreting an acid into the soil, killing native plants and animals, and depleting freshwater sources.

---

*With 380,000 acres throughout the state [of Aracruz], [Aracruz Celulose] is today the largest landowner in Espírito Santo, and together with its holding in [other Brazilian states] it owns more than 1 million acres.*

---

In the 1970s, AC continued its expansion to the north of Espirito Santo, where it invaded the territory of about 12,000 quilombola families, rural Afro-Brazilians descended from escaped slaves who had lived in the Linharinhos region since their ancestors migrated there.

With 380,000 acres throughout the state, AC is today the largest landowner in Espirito Santo, and together with its holdings in Bahia, Minas Gerais, and Rio Grande do Sul, it owns more than 1 million acres, most of which are planted with eucalyptus, according to Overbeek.

## Producing Pulp for Paper

In 2006, the company's production reached 3.1 million tons, amounting to 27% of the global supply. Its pulp factory in Barra do Riacho, Espirito Santo, is the largest in the world, annually producing 2.1 million tons. According to FASE [Foundation for Advancements in Science and Education] almost all of AC's pulp is exported to Europe, the United States, and China (each year, the United States consumes an average 728 pounds of paper per person, Europe 431, and Brazil 132). More than half of AC's pulp is used to produce toilet paper, tissue, and paper towels, while 22% is used to produce writing and printing paper. In the United States, companies including Proctor & Gamble and Kimberly-Clark purchase its pulp to produce brand-name products like Kleenex, Scott, Charmin, and Bounty. The company's net income in 2006 was $455.3 million, an increase of 25% from the previous year.

With the support of civil society organizations and rural social movements like the Movement of the Landless Rural Workers (MST), President Luis Inacio Lula da Silva was elected in 2002 on a platform that included agrarian reform, a crucial issue in Brazil, the country with the world's most unequal land distribution—1.6% of landowners control almost half the country's arable land, and 3% of the population owns two thirds of it.

Lula decried this in a 2000 interview with the magazine *Caros Amigos*. "This is unjustifiable in any place in the world!" he said. "This only occurs in Brazil because we have a coward president."

## The Role of Agribusiness in Politics

But Lula, who accepted more than $200,000 from AC for his two electoral campaigns, has increasingly backed agribusiness interests. Since taking power in 2003, his administration has maintained state support for, and ownership of, AC through the National Bank for Economic and Social Development (BNDES), which owns 12.5% of the corporation. (The majority of AC's shares are held by foreigners, with the Safra Bank of New York and the Norwegian Lorentzen Group each owning 28%. The Votarantim Group of Brazil also owns 28%.) In 2003, BNDES helped finance the construction of the Veracel factory in Bahia (owned jointly by AC and Stora Enso) with a $546 million loan, the largest given to a private company by BNDES under Lula.

"These companies are buying lands with public money from BNDES, lands that should be used for agrarian reform," says Idiane Pinheiro, 34, a member of the MST for 17 years. Agrarian reform, she adds, has virtually disappeared from the national agenda under Lula. Indeed, AC's desire for more land, coupled with its capacity to pay high prices, has driven up land values and increased ownership concentration, so that today agrarian reform is slower than under the previous administration of Fernando Henrique Cardoso.

"Today if you talk about family agriculture, talk about [agrarian reform] settlements, you come up against the problem of agribusiness," Pinheiro says. "They are two totally contradictory proposals."

## The Problems of Monocultures

AC's territorial expansion is part and parcel of the explosion of other monocultures throughout Brazil, including soy and sugarcane, controlled by other giant multinationals. "Every form of monoculture used by agribusiness," Pinheiro says, "is a problem for agriculture, biodiversity, and water."

Eucalyptus monocultures obstruct the viability of small producers on agrarian reform settlements, further compromising land redistribution. According to Maria Morais, another member of the MST, eucalyptus impedes various types of production. "The type of eucalyptus being planted here does not flower, and so does not produce honey because the bees can't collect pollen from the trees," she says.

---

*The loss of rural livelihoods caused by the expansion of [Aracruz Celulose] and other agribusiness corporations in rural Brazil has expelled rural families, forcing them to move to urban areas that are often plagued by unemployment and violence.*

---

The large amount of water consumed by eucalyptus plantations and Celulose factories also affects production, for example milk, an important source of income for settled families. According to FASE, in 2003 AC consumed 322,000 cubic yards of water a day—the same amount consumed by a city of 2.5 million. The company has never paid taxes on its water use.

AC also impedes agrarian reform by shrinking rural labor markets. According to a report published by the World Rainforest Movement in 2005, the company generates one job per every 455 acres of land, while family farming generates 2.5 jobs per acre. The loss of rural livelihoods caused by the expansion of AC and other agribusiness corporations in rural Brazil has expelled rural families, forcing them to move to urban areas that are often plagued by unemployment and violence.

## The Fight Against Agribusiness

Over the years, the MST, the Tupinikim and Guarani, and, more recently, the quilombolas, [descendents of escaped slaves] have led the fight against agribusiness and land concentration, primarily relying on nonviolent occupations to pressure the state and society. In 1979, the Tupinikim and Guarani occupied 500 acres of AC's land in Espirito Santo, leading to a proposal from the National Foundation for the Indian (FUNAI), the federal agency that oversees indigenous affairs,

---

### Indigenous Peoples and Brazil

| | |
|---|---|
| Total population of Brazil: | 180,000,000 |
| Total indigenous population of Brazil: | 734,127 |
| Size of Brazil in square kilometers: | 8,514,215 |
| Percentage of Brazilian territory held by indigenous peoples: | 12.74% |
| Estimated number of indigenous tribes: | 200 |
| Estimated number of tribal languages: | 110 |
| Population of Guaraní people in Brazil: | 34,000 |
| Population of Tupinikim(also spelled Tupiniquim) people in Brazil: | 1,386 |

TAKEN FROM: Compiled by the editor.

---

to demarcate 16,000 acres for them. But AC refused to relinquish the land and pressured FUNAI to retract the decision.

So the Tupinikim and Guarani "autodemarcated" the land with a second occupation in 1980. As a result, FUNAI demarcated 11,000 acres for them in 1988. Five years later, they returned to demand more land, forcing FUNAI to initiate the first of several technical studies, officially published in 1997, which concluded that they had a right to 45,000 acres in Aracruz.

## Disputed Land Claims

"FUNAI decided wrong," says Jose Luiz Braga, AC's legal director and general attorney. He argues that the land the Tupinikim are claiming was originally occupied by the Guaytaches, who were enemies of theirs. "It is not a question of returning the land," he says, "because those lands didn't, at any moment, belong to the Tupinikim."

In 1998, then minister of justice Iris Rezende demarcated only 6,300 acres and brokered a series of accords, as they were called, between the Tupinikim and Guarani and AC, which were essentially payments from the company in exchange for their land (AC says it has paid the communities about $13 million). According to the 2002 DhESCA [Brazilian Platform on Economic, Social, and Cultural Rights] report, Rezende's action was illegal under the Federal Constitution, which states that "the Minister has no legal power to reduce indigenous land already identified as such." In total, the Tupinikim and Guarani regained only 17,500 acres, or about 40% of the land FUNAI had decided was theirs.

According to Andreia Almeida, a Tupinikim living in Pau Brasil, all the accords did was alienate her community from the land that had provided the basis of their identity, making them dependent on the corporation. But not everyone gave up. In May 2005, about 100 families occupied the remaining 27,000 acres to pressure Marcio Tomas Bastos, Lula's first federal public minister, to demarcate it. They cut down the eucalyptus trees and built two large community buildings where the aldeias of Corrego d'Ouro and Olho de Agua had once been, and people began living there.

## United Communities Take Back Land

"It was really beautiful," Almeida recalls. "You saw the communities uniting in the decision to construct that aldeia, to recover the old aldeias, and to bring back the Indians who are no longer on the aldeias." Later that month, a federal judge ordered the property to be returned to AC, but the ruling was overturned by Espirito Santo's federal public minister because the Tupinikim had occupied an area that FUNAI had declared theirs.

Yet on the morning of January 20, 2006, about 120 federal police raided the two aldeias, attacking the Tupinikim and Guarani with rubber bullets and tear gas from the ground and from helicopters. Twelve were wounded. Valdir dos Almeida Silva, 44, a Tupinikim chief, was shot three times with rubber bullets, including once in the head.

## The Relationship Between Police and AC

Federal Deputy Iriny Lopes told the newspaper *A Gazeta* that the relationship between the federal police and AC in the action was "illegal and immoral." The police had stayed in an AC guesthouse the night before the attack and later used it to detain and interrogate several wounded indigenous leaders. The police also used AC-owned tractors to raze the Tupinikim's dwellings and then burned the remains. Dos Almeida Silva says the police even burned his shirt.

While the police action allowed AC to retake control of the area, it was politically damaging for the corporation, giving the indigenous struggle increased international attention and support. It also sparked outrage and indignation among the rural social movements, as it symbolized the state's complete betrayal to rural civil society under Lula.

## The Brazilian Indigenous Movement Unites

Two months later, during the second UN International Conference on Agrarian Reform and Rural Development in Porto Alegre, about 2,000 members of the Via Campesina, an international movement comprising more than 150 organizations, entered and destroyed AC's laboratory in Barra do Ribeiro, Rio Grande do Sul, uprooting more than 1 million eucalyptus tree seedlings and costing AC $400,000. Participants included members of the six Brazilian organizations that compose the Via Campesina, including the MST, the Movement of Campesina Women (MMC), the Movement of Small Farmers, the Movement of Those Affected by Dams, the Pastoral Land Commission, and the Pastoral Rural Youth. Several foreigners also participated.

The action, for which 38 people are being prosecuted, demonstrated the emerging alliance between Brazilian indigenous movements and those united under the Via Campesina, an alliance that strengthened after the police raid in Espirito

Santo. "Of course there are differences of organization, of the peoples, of the indigenous struggles for the demarcation of indigenous areas," says Pinheiro, who participated in the action. "But due to this process of the advance of agribusiness, and because agribusiness is taking control of the indigenous lands, the struggles of the indigenous become more similar to the struggle of the landless."

## Global Resistance to Agribusiness

Taking place on International Women's Day, the action also symbolized the increasing articulation of feminism within the Via Campesina, especially by the Movement of Campesina Women. But most importantly, it represented the growing global resistance to agribusiness. Perhaps because of the MST, Brazil has become a key battleground in this struggle, as multinationals commit crimes with impunity and social movements become increasingly militant. Less than two weeks after the action against AC, the Via Campesina nonviolently occupied Syngenta's experimental site in Santa Tereza do Oeste, Parana, which the MST controlled for almost one and a half years. These occupations came in response to these corporations' illegal introduction of genetically modified crops into Brazil. The Syngenta occupation also drew international support and resulted in state governor Roberto Requiao's attempt to expropriate the site from the multinational in November 2006, though this effort appears to have been stopped by the federal government.

Buoyed by the growing solidarity and force of the campesino movements, the Tupinikim and Guarani further radicalized their struggle. In September 2006, they cut and burned several hundred acres of AC's eucalyptus plantations, and for two days the following December, they and about 500 MST members occupied the port through which AC and three other corporations export Celulose, costing them an estimated $21 million.

Finally, in November 2006, ex-minister Bastos promised the Tupinikim and Guarani that he would demarcate their land by the end of the year. Yet by the time he left office in January, he had not done so. "Our perception is that the federal government is not interested in deciding this question," Overbeek says, noting that while Lula repeatedly refused to meet with indigenous representatives, he did receive Carlos Aguiar, the president of AC, in December 2006.

## The Tupinikim and Guarani Return to Their Land

The Tupinikim and Guarani returned to occupy the remaining 27,000 acres of their land in July of this year [2007], reconstructing the aldeias of Olho d'Agua and Corrego d'Ouro. The occupation had the full support and participation of the MST, indicating the movement's increasingly confrontational stance toward Lula. Indeed, the previous June, at its fifth National Conference, the MST refused to let the president speak and publicly revoked its support for him with a march of 17,000 through Brasilia to the Square of the Three Powers (judiciary, executive, and legislative), where it raised a banner that read "We accuse the three powers of impeding agrarian reform."

Given the overall advance of agribusiness interests in Brazil, Genro's decision in August [2007] to demarcate the 27,000 acres for the Indians was surprising to all. There is no doubt it resulted from the unrelenting pressure on the government from rural civil society, whose growing voice of discontent, especially from the MST, and the threat of further mobilizations and more radical actions, ultimately forced Genro to fulfill his predecessor's promise. His decision was a blow both to AC and to the power of agribusiness, which until then had seemed unstoppable. According to Overbeek, the MST's solidarity with the indigenous movement was crucial. "In the decisive moments of struggle by the Indians," he says, "the campesino movements were there."

## Nonviolence as a Powerful Tactic

The victory against AC also highlights nonviolent occupations as a powerful tactic to voice dissent and demand radical social and economic change for society's most excluded populations. It's a trend that took off in 2004, when various social movements occupied Monsanto's experimental test site in Ponta Grossa, Parana, where the MST remained for more than a year. With this latest victory under its belt, Brazilian rural civil society will likely be inspired to further amplify its struggle against agribusiness.

Yet the process of demarcation is far from over, since Lula must still ratify Genro's decision. It remains to be seen how the president will negotiate these contradictions; so far he has remained silent on the issue. With the latest global craze for Brazil's ethanol, especially in the United States, his administration is advancing Brazil's agro-industrial sector full-throttle. With interest in second-generation agro-fuels from eucalyptus growing, AC is set to reap some of the spoils. In May, the government licensed the company to experiment with genetically modified eucalyptus trees, a move that will undoubtedly advance its quest to produce ethanol. Moreover, restoring the Tupinikim's land, now reduced to a green desert, will take years of work and cost millions of dollars.

# African Indigenous Peoples' Knowledge Can Help in Natural Disaster Management

## United Nations Environment Programme (UNEP)

*In the following viewpoint, the writer argues that traditional knowledge makes it possible for indigenous peoples in Africa to survive serious natural disasters such as drought, floods, and insect infestations. These people use their knowledge of their natural surroundings to monitor the weather and animal movements, giving them early warnings for impending disasters. In addition, they mitigate the effects of disaster by using their traditional knowledge of plants and herbs as well as employing behaviors that they know will help them survive the disaster. UNEP seeks to enable nations and peoples to care for the environment and improve their quality of life.*

As you read, consider the following questions:

1. What are two ways that indigenous people in general react to natural disasters?

2. How many cattle died in the 1992 drought in Swaziland?

3. What are some ways that indigenous peoples in Kenya and Tanzania spread information about impending disasters?

"Application and Use of Indigenous Knowledge in Natural Disaster Management," *Indigenous Knowledge in Disaster Management in Africa*, edited by Peter Mwaura, Nairobi, Kenya: United Nations Environment Programme, 2008, pp. 56–75. Copyright © 2008 United Nations Environment Programme. Reproduced by permission.

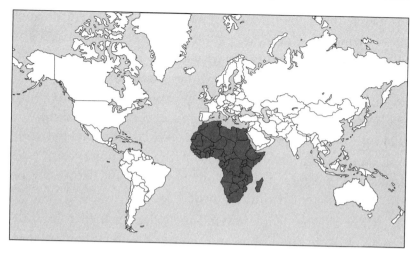

The repertoire of indigenous knowledge that communities in Kenya, South Africa, Swaziland and Tanzania draw on to deal with natural disasters is enormous. The stock of knowledge includes technologies, know-how, experiences, observations, beliefs and rituals. These range from the simple to the complex, such as relying on the water beetle to identify potable water in streams and ponds, using beanstalk ashes to preserve grain, reading signs on goat intestines to divine drought and famine, and immunizing cattle against rinderpest outbreak by smearing blood from infected animals in their nostrils.

## The Role of the Elders

This fund of knowledge served the communities well within the traditional power structures. The success was based on good prognosis, close observation and a thorough understanding of the environment. The people instinctively knew that they needed to understand their environment well to be able to foretell and cope with the occurrence of natural hazards. Elders undertook the responsibility of predicting disasters and guiding the people on the actions to take to prevent or mitigate the disasters.

179

Often the signs of coming natural disasters were obvious to everyone, in which case people instinctively responded and prepared for the coming events without the need for prompting from the elders. At other times, according to the study made in Kenya, the signs could be complicated and required the interpretation of the elders and experts. [According to a 2006 publication produced by the IGAD Climate Prediction and Application Center,] some of the interpretations "were known to engender major conflicts in opinion depending on the decisions that had to be made."

All in all, the people revered the elders in their role of divining climatic conditions and natural disasters. For instance, elders in Kenya's communities in Rusinga, Mfangano, Kano, Budalang'i, Lamu, Kwale and Makueni monitored the progression of hazards and gave advice, which governed the behavior of the communities. In the event of an ongoing disaster, the communities would do what was asked of them without question. If the elders told them to move to a designated place in the case of floods or droughts, they would do just that.

## Belief Systems Influence Responses to Disasters

The culture and belief system of a community influenced its responses to a disaster. The people of Mfangano Island in Lake Victoria, for example, strongly believed that disasters only came when one was not at peace with God and the spirits. They knew they could not stop the disasters once they were triggered by certain causes but they could mitigate their effects as every event, physical or spiritual, has a cause. The mitigation could take the form of measures that are preventive or remedial.

The attitudes to natural disasters by the people of Mfangano are typical among other communities. Among the people of South Africa, for example, there is also widespread belief that hydrological hazards are released by specific deities and

God in response to human misbehavior. Consequently, mitigation is sought in acts of repentance "to restore the divine balance".

## How African Indigenous Peoples React to Natural Disasters

In dealing with natural disasters, people would in general react in two ways. One way is to wait until the disaster strikes and then try to mitigate the consequences by utilizing indigenous knowledge. For instance, epidemics including cholera, dysentery, typhoid and other gastro-intestinal ailments are common during natural disasters such as floods. Early warning of the epidemic is only achieved, if at all, after some members of the community have contracted the disease. In that case the communities cope by resorting to traditional knowledge in medicine to cure afflicted individuals or by quarantining them. This is what might be called reactive or crisis management of disasters.

---

*Indigenous communities recognize that for them to be able to live with the natural disasters, they have to monitor the environmental conditions, including the weather, be able to make meaningful predictions and take appropriate actions to mitigate the disasters and associated hazards.*

---

The second way is to prepare for the disaster and take preventive action. If the disaster is perfectly predictable, then the community might take some preventive measures such as digging channels to divert floodwaters. This is what might be called risk management or anticipatory approach.

But the actual approach taken depends on the prediction of the disaster and its possible severity and consequences. If the disaster is impossible to foretell with certainty, or the consequences are manageable and not severe, the community might adopt a wait-and-see position. If the occurrence of the disaster can be foretold with certainty and the consequences are known to be severe, then appropriate preparations are made. The community might, for example, start preserving food in anticipation of a prolonged drought or famine.

## Disaster Prediction, Preparedness, and Prevention

Relying on indigenous knowledge, the communities are able to anticipate most of the disasters that afflict them. Disaster prediction and early warning leads to preparedness and other responses, and when the disaster impacts are brought under control recovery starts. The main aim of the recovery phase is to return the community back to normal. Recovery is usually made up of post-disaster activities. Recovery then gives way to the mitigation phase, which deals with developmental issues that ensure less vulnerability of the community to the disaster. For example, using indigenous knowledge to divine water, the community might dig wells to reduce its vulnerability to drought in future. However, "there is no distinct point at which these phases change from one to the other", as the Kenya study [a part of the 2008 United Nations Environment Program's (UNEP) research on indigenous knowledge] notes. There are "lots of overlaps" and differences in approach from community to community.

However, the important thing to remember is that the indigenous communities recognize that for them to be able to live with the natural disasters, they have to monitor the environmental conditions, including the weather, be able to make meaningful predictions and take appropriate actions to mitigate the disasters and associated hazards. The communities are well aware of the disasters that could affect them and in most cases had the knowledge and administrative structures to cope with them. At the same time, the communities know that a well-conserved environment helps prevent the occurrence of natural disasters and also enables people to mitigate and cope with natural disasters when they occur. . . .

Kenya, South Africa, Swaziland and Tanzania suffer from a range of natural disasters including drought, floods, landslides, windstorms, thunderstorms, lightning strikes and epidemics. Drought, and the associated famine and poverty, is however the most ravaging of the natural disasters that afflict those countries. Floods and epidemics can also cause serious devastation and destruction but these are not as common or persistent as drought.

## The Effects of Drought

Drought affects all the countries in the [2008 United Nations Environment Program] study. In Swaziland, the areas that are most frequently affected are those found in the east and west of the country where rainfall is often very low even under normal conditions. Drought has had a devastating impact on the economy of Swaziland. For instance, in the 1992 drought, about 90,000 cattle died and that greatly affected the economy as cattle are a major source of wealth in the country. Because of the persistent droughts that occur in the country from time to time, food insecurity is high. Food insecurity is compounded by the prevalence of HIV/AIDS and has become one of the biggest problems facing Swaziland and possibly some of the other countries. According to figures by the United Nations Food and Agricultural Organization and United Nations World Food Programme . . . production of the country's staple food, maize, has been on a long-term decline, dropping by 70 percent over the last five years in some areas. This is due to the fact that much of the arable land is uncultivated because of delayed rains, the high risk of making a loss from agriculture and shortages of seeds for alternative crops, among other reasons. In the 2004–05, cropping season the Lowveld farmers ploughed just 10 percent of their arable land. Lowveld is characterized by gently undulating terrain that is vulnerable to drought and high temperatures.

The situation in the other countries is not much better. Makueni in Kenya suffers from frequent drought that is equally devastating for the locals. Prolonged drought can be particularly disastrous in the district. In fact, the famines that are best remembered in Kenya are associated with drought. In western Kenya, the most severe famines have names that suggest the severity of the drought and famine, such as iamasero ("the famine of eating animal skins"), owukuyo ("the famine of eating fig tree fruits") and owugeke ("the famine of eating dry potatoes"). Some of the best remembered famines include those experienced in 1905, 1931, 1940 and 1949.

## Floods and Famine

Periodic floods affect most of the communities in all the areas studied. In Kenya and Tanzania the worst floods were recorded in 1961/62 and 1997/98. It is only Makueni District that rarely suffers from floods in Kenya. In contrast, communities in the Kano plains and Budalang'i in western Kenya, the Rufiji delta in Tanzania and many areas in Swaziland are affected by floods almost every year. In Swaziland, in particular, many parts of the country are prone to severe flooding during torrential rains.

---

*The indigenous knowledge on disaster prediction and early warning is based on keen observation of the behaviour of animals, birds, insects, vegetation, trees, winds, air and water temperatures, clouds, earth movements and celestial bodies.*

---

The Kano plains experience heavy flooding which causes loss of lives, livestock, household property and crops, and brings water-borne disease during the long rains in April–May. However, it is Swaziland which best illustrates the destructive nature of floods. A majority of the rural population in Swaziland is a high risk and extremely vulnerable to floods.

# Indigenous Knowledge Is a Great Treasure

It is widely assumed that poverty is an unavoidable consequence of climate change such as drought. For centuries, however, indigenous knowledge has provided Africa's tribal peoples with practical solutions to the problems of a fluctuating climate. As an example, the Maasai pastoralists of northern Tanzania and southern Kenya traditionally know where to find water, and green shrubs that can be fed to young calves, even during long periods of drought. Likewise, in Ethiopia, often regarded as inevitably dependent on Western aid, the threat of famine can be overcome by local expertise. . . .

In our opinion, the greatest threat to the economic stability of the African continent is not its changing climate. Rather, it is the gradual erosion of indigenous knowledge and the accompanying destruction of natural wealth—plants, animals, insects, soils, clean air and water—and human cultural wealth, such as songs, proverbs, folklore and social co-operation. This robs people of their ability to respond to social and environmental change, both by removing the resource base, and by attacking the foundations of human identity.

*Gemma Burford, et al.,*
*"Education, Indigenous Knowledge and Globalisation,"*
*Science in Africa, March 2003.*
*www.scienceinafrica.co.za.*

The floods unleashed by Cyclone Domonia in 1984 washed away and killed a number of people and destroyed farmlands, houses and infrastructure including roads, electricity and telephone lines. Swaziland was also severely ravaged by torrential rains in 2000, which led to flooding in many parts of the country and destruction of property and health risks due to pollution of water sources.

Famine and food insecurity, caused mainly by drought and floods is a major concern in all the countries. Famine, of course, can also be caused by other disasters such as invasion of locusts, armyworms and other pests and diseases. However, most incidences of famine are associated with drought.

## Disaster Prediction and Early Warning

Each community had an array of early warning indicators and well-developed structures through which the wisdom of the community was applied to deal quickly and efficiently with disasters. The structures included a council of elders which, had at its disposal "the speed and strength of numerous warriors that could be used to investigate a particular phenomenon or to pass on urgent messages upon need [according to the UNEP study]"

The indigenous knowledge on disaster prediction and early warning is based on keen observation of the behaviour of animals, birds, insects, vegetation, trees, winds, air and water temperatures, clouds, earth movements and celestial bodies. However, the sets of indicators used in each community are homegrown. A brief look at the early warning systems in the different communities shows how localized the systems can be. . . . [I]t is not always clear when disaster prevention and preparedness ends and mitigation and recovery begins. There is no distinct point at which these phases change from one to the other, as there is a lot of overlapping depending on the nature of the disaster. A brief look at some of the responses to natural disasters will demonstrate this.

## Drought-Tolerant Crops and Famine Preparedness

In all the communities, technologies and know-how in cultivating indigenous drought-resistant and early-maturing crops played a critical part in preparing for famines caused by prolonged drought or other natural calamities such as invasion of locusts or armyworms. Such crops included hardy species such as cassava (Manihot esculenta), pumpkins (Cacumis melo), cowpeas (Phaseolus multiflorus) and sorghum bicolor (Elesine corocana). So important was the cassava for famine preparedness, for example, that along the lakeshores of Lake Victoria and in river basins every family had a cassava plantation. . . .

In Tanzania, the cassava is viewed as equally important as a drought crop. . . . [C]assava not only has the attributes of being drought-resistant but can also be left in the field unharvested for a long time without spoilage, thus serving as a famine safety crop that can be harvested at any time as needed. The cassava leaves are also eaten as relish after being prepared appropriately using indigenous knowledge since certain species of cassava plants contain a quantity of hydrogen cyanide which can be fatal to humans. For the cassava roots, villagers in Tanzania use indigenous techniques of kuvundika (fermentation) and kuloweka (soaking in water) to detoxify them as they also contain hydrogen cyanide.

Cassava, jugo beans, bambara groundnuts, sweet potatoes, sorghum and pumpkin are grown particularly in drought-prone Lowveld and Lubombo regions of Swaziland. . . .

---

*Technologies and know-how in cultivating indigenous drought-resistant and early-maturing crops played a critical part in preparing for famines caused by prolonged drought or other natural calamities such as invasion of locusts or armyworms.*

---

## Spreading Information

The various communities had different ways of disseminating information on impeding disasters. The methods included specific beats of drums and sounding of horns by clan elders.

In western Kenya, the drums and horns were used to alert people to come together at known meeting points where the specific warning, instructions or advice was communicated and appropriate actions decided upon. In Tanzania, communities used a mortar known as kinu to warn distant villages about the occurrence of a calamity. This was achieved by beating the mortar with heavy sticks to make a cacophony that clearly signified danger. This was done in the evening or at night when the still, cool and quiet atmosphere enabled the sound to travel far and wide. In other areas, a drum known as lamgambo was beaten by a chief's drummer. This would produce a characteristic tune that signaled to villagers to assemble at the chief's home at the earliest opportunity for some important announcements. This gave rise to a Swahili saying: Lamgambo likilia ujue kuna jambo ("When the lamgambo makes a sound know that there is an important event around").

## Indigenous Responses to Natural Disaster

All in all, soon after a disaster, there was always the need to deal with the immediate calamity. The aim of such response was to provide relief and safety of the affected people, to meet their basic needs until more permanent and sustainable solutions could be found. However, in nearly all cases preparedness was critical, which made early warning extremely useful. A brief look at the approach taken by the Budalang'i community of western Kenya gives an insight into some of the strategies for preparedness. Though the details of the strategies are peculiar to this particular community, they nevertheless illustrate the nature of the application of indigenous knowledge in natural disaster management. The Budalang'i community had to observe or carry out, among others, the following in preparation for any impending disasters:

- Each homestead has to have a dugout canoe for transport in case of heavy flooding.

- Elders should dig trenches to control the water around the homestead and around farmlands.

- People in higher grounds should accommodate the people from flood prone areas.

- No ploughing is permitted along the shores when heavy flooding is predicted.

- Land preparation starts in November–January when it is dry. This plan was based on observing the nature of the winds and changes in fauna and flora.

- Plant maize, millet, peas, beans and cowpeas in February. The cues for this activity are associated with wind patterns, the kind of birds and the changes in vegetation and constellation.

- Harvest in July–August when the dry winds are experienced, the sky is covered with bright stars and days have long periods of sunshine under which grains harvested are dried.

- After harvesting, plant cassava and sweet potatoes which need little rain to survive. Sweet potatoes mature very fast and become a backup for food security.

- Stock enough fuel wood for food preservation and cooking during the rainy season in April–August

- Catch fish during April–August rainy period when they are plentiful and preserve them by drying and smoking.

The communities in the areas studied [by UNEP in 2008] face many natural hazards but the major ones are drought and floods. These invariably cause famine, food insecurity and poverty. Over the years, however, the communities have evolved indigenous knowledge technologies, know-how, experiences and beliefs that aid them not only in predicting the natural disasters but also in devising techniques and coping mechanisms to deal with the disasters. The communities focus on disaster prevention and preparedness. Thus, they take measures such as growing drought-resistant and early-maturing indigenous crop varieties, gathering wild fruits and vegetables, wetlands cultivation, transhumance, livestock diversifying and splitting, preserving and storing food for use in times of scarcity. All these measures enabled the indigenous communities to live with climatic hazards with little or no support from the outside world.

# Periodical Bibliography

*The following articles have been selected to supplement the diverse views presented in this chapter.*

Christopher Alcantara "To Treaty or Not To Treaty? Aboriginal Peoples and Comprehensive Land Claims Negotiations in Canada," *Publius*, Spring 2008.

Henry Gottlieb Alm "Indians Lose Claim for Lands Lost Two Centuries Ago," *The Legal Intelligencer*, May 29, 2008.

Zainab Amadahy "The Role of Settler in Indigenous Struggles: Questions Arising from the Six Nations Land Reclamation," *Canadian Dimension*, vol. 41, no. 3, May–June 2007.

Klaus Dodds "Canada: Indigenous Cree Peoples' Land Settlement with the Government," *Geographical*, vol. 79, no. 12, December 2007.

*The Economist* "This Land Is My Land: Canada," vol. 380, no. 8495, September 16, 2006.

Jens C. Hansen, et al. "Dietary Transition and Contaminants in the Arctic: Emphasis on Greenland," *Circumpolar Health Supplements*, no. 2, 2008.

Peter Jull "Reconcilation Constitution for Northern Territory?" *Arena Magazine*, June–July 2007.

Teresa Mitchell "A Lonely Limb: Today's Trial: Six Nations Aboriginal People Land Claims," *LawNow*, vol. 31, no. 4, March–April 2007.

*The New Zealand Herald* "The Right to Fish," August 2, 2008.

Terry O'Neill "The Bear Facts: Canada's Inuits Say the Polar Bear Isn't Threatened by Global Warming or Hunting," *Western Standard*, vol. 4, no. 3, April 23, 2007.

## CHAPTER 4

# Preserving
# Indigenous Cultures

# Indigenous Peoples Must Protect Their Cultures' Intellectual Property Rights

*Peter N. Jones*

*In the following viewpoint, Peter N. Jones argues that the traditional knowledge indigenous peoples have developed to help them subsist in their traditional homelands is their intellectual property. Further, indigenous rights to intellectual property must be protected. When companies from around the world take such knowledge and profit from it without permission or consent of indigenous people, Jones asserts, the companies are committing biopiracy. He urges consumers to make choices that support the retention of intellectual property by indigenous peoples. Jones holds a PhD in anthropology and is the director of the Bauu Institute.*

As you read, consider the following questions:

1. What is one example of intellectual property held by indigenous peoples?
2. How do people in the industrialized world protect their intellectual property?
3. What diet drug comes from a cactus found in the Kalahari Desert?

Peter N. Jones, "Intellectual Property Rights, Indigenous People, and the Future," *Indigenous People's Issues Today*, August 23, 2007. http://indigenousissuestoday .blogspot.com. Reproduced by permission.

One of the hotter issues that has emerged out of globalization concerns indigenous peoples and intellectual property rights. Intellectual property rights are those rights people or cultures have gained through their own experience or cultural knowledge. For example, the knowledge of how certain plants within an indigenous group's homeland are used to treat fever or diarrhea would fall under intellectual property rights. Likewise, particular understandings of the land, ecology, or environment of a certain area may also fall under intellectual property rights. The key point is that intellectual property rights refers to knowledge that otherwise would not be available. It is not knowledge gained through scientific experimentation, nor is it knowledge gained through empirical deductions. Rather, it is knowledge that is gained (some may say earned) through time, place, and experience.

## Indigenous Peoples Have a Right to Their Intellectual Property

Because indigenous peoples have lived in their homelands for hundreds or thousands of years, because they have subsisted in their traditional territory for just as long, and because they have experienced all of this they have developed certain intellectual property that they have a right to. That is, as a result of the long time spent in their homelands and the experiences they have accrued, the knowledge that they possess is unique and special. The same is true in the rest of the world, we just often don't think of the proper metaphors to make a logical connection.

In rock climbing there is something called "beta." To climb a route, it is often only possible when the climber knows the "beta" and does the correct sequence of moves. That is intellectual property, and climbers who have completed the route have a certain right to it. Hunters are the same. Many of them have certain tricks that they have learned over the years or a certain spot that they know will yield a good hunt. This is knowledge that has been learned or handed down for many years. This is intellectual property. In most of the industrialized world it is possible to apply for patents or some other form of guarantee that will protect these rights legally. Perhaps the most famous in terms of technology is Microsoft and its unwillingness to give up its intellectual property rights in terms of the Windows Operating System. Indigenous peoples, sadly, usually don't have the ability, nor the knowledge, that such a process actually exists.

---

*Biopiracy is a negative term for the appropriation, generally by means of patents, of legal rights over indigenous biomedical knowledge without compensation to the indigenous groups who originally developed such knowledge.*

---

## The Rich and Powerful Commit Biopiracy

Companies come from all over the world and visit indigenous peoples and their homelands in search of this intellectual property. When it focuses on some form of biological intellectual property, this phenomenon is known as biopiracy. Biopiracy is a negative term for the appropriation, generally by means of patents, of legal rights over indigenous biomedical knowledge without compensation to the indigenous groups who originally developed such knowledge. There are many debates about how bad such taking of intellectual property actually is. Some argue that it is not really knowledge that can be owned, and thus the knowledge is free for the taking and only the specific patents or chemical abstractions arrived at fall under any legal jurisdiction. Others argue the opposite, claiming that all knowledge was, and is, constructed by specific groups or individuals and thus is unique in the same way as chemical abstractions. The ethical and legal debates are very tricky and to some extent arbitrary. The ones with the power (and the money) will most likely carry the day.

# The Value of Traditional Knowledge

Globalization is jeopardizing the normal development of many indigenous peoples around the world in three main ways. First, it is creating sophisticated legal mechanisms to control the management of vast territories in the name of conservation. In spite of the fact that these so-called 'representative ecosystems' are, in as much as 60% of the cases, the 'homes' of indigenous peoples, their native inhabitants are generally disregarded from any conservation programs designed by governments. Second, globalization has exponentially increased the chances of acquiring first-hand information about (among other issues) the knowledge that indigenous peoples have of plants, animals, fungi and other living organisms, thus becoming medicinal prospects for pharmaceutical industries. Third, the intrusion of western styles in their traditional cultures and the exploitation of natural resources in their territories—a typical behavior of the western actor—have produced emigrations as well as the consequent subsuming of indigenous peoples as a whole.

This complex combination of factors has enhanced the erosion of TK [traditional knowledge], which in turn produces additional vulnerability of ecosystems. Pharmaceutical companies and other corporations are rather concerned about this: they would lose the opportunity to have direct information about medicinal plants, animals and even human genes. They have, therefore, embarked themselves in multi-million dollar projects to obtain as much traditional knowledge as possible about plants as possible before the TK disappears forever. . . .

*Mindahi Crescencio Bastida-Munoz and Geraldine A. Patrick,*
*"Traditional Knowledge and Intellectual Property Rights:*
*Beyond Trips Agreements and Intellectual Property Chapters*
*of FTAS," Michigan State Journal of International Law, 2006.*

## Consumer Choices Impact Indigenous Peoples

My point ... [is] more in line with simply getting the information out there and letting the consumer make the decision. People are beginning to realize that when they fill up their car, the gas came from somewhere real, and its extraction more than likely impacted a group of people. Drinking my coffee while writing this ... I'm reminded that the indigenous people of Guatemala farmed it for me. When young teenage girls pop Hoodia, they should (but don't) realize that their diet drug comes from a cactus found in the Kalahari Desert, and that the indigenous people of this area have not seen any benefits from the drugs mass explosion on the world market. The problem, however, is that people can grasp pollution, they can grasp environmental destruction, they can grasp deforestation—all of these are very visible and thus easier to understand. With intellectual property, to some extent the very heart and soul of a culture's history and experience, there is no visible entity to grasp and point to. Taking Hoodia pills gives one no indication that indigenous people in sub-Saharan Africa have been impacted. Well, I argue that they should.

The old saying goes, knowledge is all powerful. Well, here we are talking about knowledge, how it is appropriated and manipulated, and then spit out again as new knowledge. The only way to combat this is through more knowledge.

# Australian Aborigines Must Protect Their Ownership of Cultural Art

*Anthony O'Grady*

*In the following viewpoint, Anthony O'Grady describes the state of the Australian Aboriginal art scene, noting that the art has achieved high status among collectors. He argues that because there is no regulation of this market, artists and their communities are often unprotected and frequently are not adequately compensated. In addition, he notes, fakery is rampant with copies of Aboriginal art coming to market. However, O'Grady asserts, Aboriginal artists and their communities are finally seeing some of the wealth their culturally significant work is generating. O'Grady is a journalist who writes for the* Sydney Morning Herald.

As you read, consider the following questions:

1. What is the name of the art legal help initiative that is working with Aboriginal artists?
2. What happens to the money generated by reproductions of Aboriginal art in catalogues or prints if an artist dies without a will ("intestate"), according to the viewpoint?
3. How has the painting of Utopian women changed, according to O'Grady?

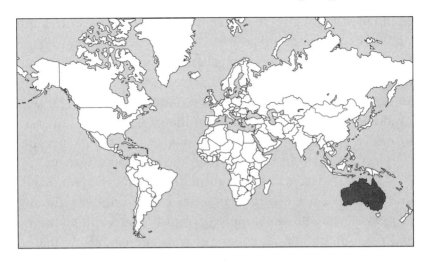

Originally, [Australian] Aboriginal art was practical, spiritual and ephemeral.

It was a mapping discipline: a row of goannas [an Australian monitor lizard], for instance, generally meant "bush tucker is plentiful here". It was ceremonial secret business espousing "the dreaming" that informs each tribe's cultural and spiritual identity.

It was ephemeral, drawn on sand or tree bark, to be returned to the earth.

First transposed to canvas by Papunya Tula artists in the early 1970s, Aboriginal art can be approached from a modernist perspective as daringly abstract. It can be appreciated as a traveller's guide to ancestral land. Many say they feel shock waves of spiritual energy from "the dreaming" within the art.

If none of the above applies, it can still be appreciated as a boldly stated, affordable embracement of indigenous values.

## The Complicated Process of Marketing Indigenous Art

Though its appeal is multi-levelled, Aboriginal art at source is a complex, often mysterious business. There are national organisations but no national standards. Most of the art is channelled through 116 art centres but no two centres are similar, or produce similar art.

More than 100 specialist galleries propagate and promote the art, but there is no national accreditation system, or guarantee of the art's authenticity. And, although the top 25 sales of indigenous artworks total more than $8.5 million, it is rare to find a successful artist who is not on Centrelink benefits [services provided by an Australian governmental agency].

"You just have to be here to understand," say overworked, under-funded art centre managers, explaining why the art process starts with the supply of canvas and paint to artists and relies on an honour system of consignment, rather than a written contract and copyright protection.

"We're sympathetic to that," says Robyn Ayres, executive director of the Arts Law Centre of Australia, which runs the indigenous art legal help initiative "Artists in the Black." "We're very aware that most art centres are dedicated to helping the communities. Our message is: we can help make the marketing of indigenous art more equitable for artists."

Artists in the Black started in 2003, after the Myer Report in 2002 sent shock waves through the indigenous art community. The report urged the introduction of copyright protection, resale royalties and major changes to legislation and the administration of art centres.

The report was timely, because the dollar value of the indigenous art market was doubling annually while the payback to artists remained somewhere near subsistence level.

---

*Channeling of cultural heritage [through art] has to be recognized in contracts presented to indigenous artists.*

---

## Aboriginal Art Expresses the Community's Culture

"But it's not as simple as introducing a new contract that doubles artists' fees," explains Ayres. "In many cases, Aboriginal art is an expression of community culture and is painted on behalf of the community."

This channelling of cultural heritage has to be recognised in contracts presented to indigenous artists.

"But contracts only bind the signatory parties," he says. "And though report after report has pointed out that here is an area where indigenous cultural rights should prevail, there has been no legislation to ratify this.

"Legislation was drawn up after the Myer Report to recognise indigenous community moral rights, but the bill was withdrawn to be redrafted. It has never been presented to Parliament."

## Aboriginal Artists Need Help with Wills

There is also an urgent need to formulate appropriate wills for Aboriginal artists.

Natalie Mason, a lawyer with DLA Phillips Fox [a large legal firm], drafted a sample will that has been circulated to art centres.

"It's important that copyright of the art—quite a lot of it now hanging in museums and earning sizeable income from reproduction in catalogues and prints—is recognised as belonging to the artist and handed down according to the artist's wishes," says Mason.

"If the artist dies intestate [without a legal will], that income is most likely retained by the current owner of the artwork."

Mason also included recognition of tribal marriage in the sample will, in lieu of legislation recognising such rites of indigenous culture.

But Mason, who worked as a midwife on Bathurst Island off the Top End [an outback region in the Northern Territories of Australia] before turning to law, agrees that emailing sample wills and contracts is no substitute to visiting art centres to explain their need to artists.

She points out most artists and art centre administrators are not even aware the artist retains a range of potential copyright income after the work has been sold and resold.

Artists in the Black has visited some 27 communities within the past two years (dealing with close to 1000 issues as a result), but that is just nibbling at the edges of a task that stretches through some 10,000 kilometres of northern Australia and encompasses at least 80 different tribal languages and individual cultures.

## Offering Free Legal Advice to Aboriginal Artists

"Artists in the Black was set up by the Arts Law Centre of Australia through a grant from the Australia Council," says Ayers. "We have funding for two full-time, indigenous legal staff and it is a great benefit to be able to draw pro bono [without charge] support from a range of law firms ranging from major to specialist.

"The sample will is step one of the process. The second step is to put together a team of lawyers, provide them with cultural awareness training if needed, and cover their travel to the centres and the cost of interpreters to implement the project.

"But to be able to utilise the pro bono expertise that is on offer, we first have to find the funds to visit the centres and evaluate the artists' needs."

Still, says Ayres, it is inevitable that properly constituted contracts will replace the honour system and verbal assurances that remain the standard deal for indigenous artists.

"A written contract makes terms clear. The problem with informal or oral agreements is, when results don't match expectations, it's most often the artist who feels ripped off."

Conversely, dealers and galleries have rejected or marked down the value of art produced by relatives of top-selling artists. "To the community, the art is legitimate," Ayres says. "An

## Indigenous Art Is a Critical Component to the Cultural Life of Australia

An important aspect of Creative Australia has to do with the role of the arts in the process of constructing our cultural identity. The changing face of Australia has always been portrayed and analysed by our creative artists—painters such as John Glover and Tom Roberts in the 19th century, poets such as Kenneth Slessor and Judith Wright in the 20th, together with novelists, playwrights, film-makers and so on. Many artists have come from diverse ethnic backgrounds and have helped to define an evolving picture of contemporary Australian culture through their creative work. Most importantly, the significance of Indigenous art as a unique expression of the world's oldest living culture, and as an inalienable component of a shared Australian cultural identity, cannot be overstated. In the 21st century ideas about Australian identity will continue to evolve, and the contribution of creative artists to this process will be absolutely critical.

*David Throsby, "Creative Australia: The Arts and Culture in Australian Work and Leisure," Academy of the Social Sciences in Australia, November 20, 2008. www.assa.edu.au.*

artist may feel it is time for someone else to continue painting the community's stories. The name on an artwork doesn't have the same significance to the tribe as it does to the fine art market. An appropriate contract would tell the community this is the way the market works."

## Legislation Must Establish Resale Royalties

Ayres says that legislation is needed to establish a resale royalty for indigenous art. "There is currently no mechanism for artists to share the windfall of rising prices for their work," she points out. "It's not uncommon for the market value of indigenous art to rise out of all proportion from its original sale price, sometimes within four or five years."

Johnny Warangkula Tjupurra's Water Dreaming at Kalipinyapa is an oft-quoted example. Sold by the artist in 1972 for just $150, it was most recently resold in 2000 for $486,500. A 5 percent resale royalty would have returned $24,000 to Tjupurra's community. In the past 15 years [since 1992] a 5 percent resale royalty would have benefited indigenous communities by $3.75 million, adding to or partially replacing the $13.5 million in government funding that now supports indigenous art.

The resale royalty cause does have political support, but not a lot from Coalition benches. Its most vocal supporter is Labor's Peter Garrett.

---

*In the past 15 years [since 1992], a 5 percent resale royalty [on Aboriginal art] would have benefited indigenous communities by $3.75 million, adding to or partially replacing the $13.5 million in [Australian] government funding that now supports indigenous art.*

---

Indigenous art has a fine art high end where entry level is above $10,000. This top end of mostly Top End art turns over some $100 million a year. The mass market, crafts end is also estimated at $100 million a year. This market is predominantly aimed at the tourist trade.

## The Cost of Fakery

Always a tough earn, it has been hit hard by the decline of tourism after September 11, 2001. It is also undercut by fakes, says Brad Parnes of Rainbow Serpent, which operates six Aboriginal Arts and Crafts stores, turning over $4.75 million last financial year.

Parnes bought an Indonesian-made didgeridoo on the Internet, paying $US17.34 (about $21.50 [in Australian currency]).

"Something like that," says Parnes, "would cost me $200 to buy and I would have to sell it for $500 or more."

Parnes says the fake plays just as well as the real thing. Yet, says Rainbow Serpent's Caroline Friend, the tourist trade demands ridgy-didge artefacts, at lowest possible cost. "We are constantly asked," she says, "whether we're selling genuine crafts and how much is going back to the artist."

This concern of integrity is particularly vital to the middle market for Aboriginal art, worth anywhere between $100 million and $300 million a year.

This market—for art between $500 and under $10,000—simply did not exist 20 years ago. A major reason for growth is that there are so many individual and community styles, it's hard to be a one-off buyer.

## The Evolution of Aboriginal Art

Also, artists constantly reinvigorate their style. Tim Jennings of the Mbantu Gallery near Alice Springs, which specialises in the art of the Utopia region, has observed the process.

"We had an exhibition of Utopia art last year," he says, "Three generations of painters were on display. It was amazing to see how each generation developed new art styles while still expressing traditional stories. The evolutionary process was very obvious."

Utopian artists (predominantly women) traditionally painted on fabric. Knowing that market was limited, Jennings gave the women canvas and acrylic paints.

"Originally they used traditional earth and wildflower colours," says Jennings. "Then they experimented with acrylic colours and the art changed dramatically."

A new, profitable era of Utopian art was launched, with work from the late Emily Kame Kngwarreye, Minnie Pwerle, Barbara Weir and Kathleen and Gloria Petyarre in ever-rising demand.

There is, to be sure, a degree of faddishness in the appreciation of indigenous art. Often, it seems, the more remote the tribe, the more prized the art. There is also a degree of reverse snobbery from tribal artists to indigenous urban artists who incorporate traditional techniques such as dot painting in their work.

## Indigenous Artists Should Share in the Wealth

"Basically though," says Tim Jennings, "the indigenous art market is potentially a thousand-million-dollar business per year."

America, Jennings says, is a virtually untapped market, showing all the signs of coming on board.

All that's needed is more effort from galleries and dealers and more support from the government in espousing the art's diversity and cultural significance.

Meanwhile, says Robyn Ayres, it is timely that indigenous artists begin sharing in the wealth already there.

## Australian Resale Royalties Long Time Coming

Labor was elected into Government in November, 2007 with resale proponent Peter Garrett given the ministerial portfolios of Environment, Heritage and Arts.

Garrett immediately pledged legislation would be introduced to establish the right of visual artists to receive a 5% royalty from the resale of their works.

The legislation, currently taking in submission stage by a standing committee, will take effect in July, 2009.

"We have put forward changes," says Robyn Ayres Executive Director of the Arts Law Centre of Australia, "because we believe there are significant problems with the bill in its present form."

Ayres points out that resale royalty operates in 50 countries and territories throughout the world starting with the first resale. Australian legislation stipulates royalties only from the second resale.

"Art works often are not resold a second time till forty or fifty years after original sale," says Ayres. "This represents a significant victory for art galleries and significant delay and loss of income for artists, their community and heirs."

"Also, Australian legislation as it stands only applies to works acquired after passing of legislation. In other territories resale royalties are payable on art acquired before and after commencement of legislation."

California is the only American state to have legislated an art resale royalty.

# The San of Southern Africa Are Preserving Their Traditional Knowledge

*Uwe Hoering*

*In the following viewpoint, Uwe Hoering follows the story of the San, an indigenous people who live in the Kalahari Desert of Southern Africa. After years of mistreatment and enslavement, the San are finally being compensated for their intellectual property. Through an agreement struck between the San and the South African Council for Scientific and Industrial Research (CSIR), the herb Hoodia will be developed and marketed. Hoering notes that while the San have the necessary knowledge, the CSIR has the means to turn that knowledge into profit. Hoering, a writer who specializes in development policy, is based in Bonn, Germany.*

As you read, consider the following questions:

1. What are some of the ways that plants from the Kalahari can be used in the home?

2. What does Petrus Vaalbooi say that the San need?

3. According to the World Health Organization (WHO), what percentage of the raw materials for modern medicine come from plants?

Uwe Hoering, *Biopirates in the Kalahari? How Indigenous People Are Standing Up for Their Rights*, Bonn, Germany: Church Development Service (EED) and Working Group of Indigenous Minorities in Southern Africa [WIMSA], 2004, pp. 5–24. Reproduced by permission.

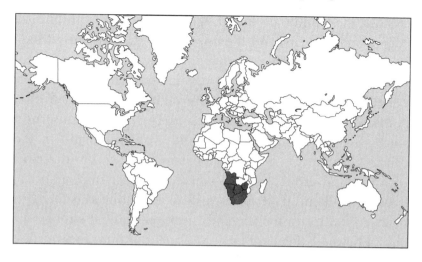

For once, the Kalahari Desert is green. In February and March [2004], heavy and prolonged rain fell, after three years of drought. The tall grasses, the creepers with pink, yellow and white blossoms, and the fresh foliage of camel-thorn trees and other kinds of acacia briefly belie the fact that, for most of the year, this is a hot and sandy wasteland, a hostile environment where little can survive. Scanning the surroundings intently, her eyes riveted to the ground, Magdaleen Steenkamp strides between the clumps of grass. Suddenly she stoops, and scoops out three or four handfuls of sand to uncover a small tuber, the colour and size of a new potato. To her well-trained gaze, just a few tiny cracks in the sandy soil advertise the presence of a buried Kalahari truffle. Despite its unassuming appearance, this edible fungus is a local delicacy, baked in hot ashes or boiled in salted water. Magdaleen, a member of the ‡Khomani San tribe, cheerfully admits that her gathering expeditions have also brought her face-to-face with a puff adder more than once.

## The Superstore Called Nature

The great outdoor superstore where Magdaleen 'shops' for supplies is on three levels: the basement, where buried delicacies like the truffles are found; the ground floor, with bushes, grasses and creepers; and the upper level, the treetops, including camel-thorns, other overhanging acacias, towering primeval baobabs and fruit-bearing marula and manketti trees. On every level, food is there for the taking—roots, cucurbits, beans, tubers, honey, seeds and leaves. The delicatessen section stocks tree fungi, morama nuts and mopane worms. In the drinks department—vitally important in a semi-arid region with low and erratic rainfall—there are water-storing succulents and tubers, fruit juices and melons, but also seeds to make coffee, leaves for tea, and sugary berries for stronger liquor. Elsewhere there are tobacco plants and horn for whistles, a range of cosmetics, and a full complement of hardware and construction materials like wood, clay and grass; there are tools, string made from plant fibres, and extra-hard wooden digging sticks. For the home, huge baobab fruits make water containers; grass and palm can be turned into baskets and wild cotton into pillows. There is even a small department for toys, jewellery, amulets and musical instruments, like rattles made of chrysalis cases, seed necklaces and bracelets, and ostrich-egg bowls.

## Knowing How to Find and Use Food and Medicine

The huge open-air pharmacy carries a wide array of medicinal plants and tonics, like the anti-inflammatory Harpago, or Hoodia to give sustenance, strength, motivation and stamina for the hunt. Close by, watch out for the poison cabinet, where deadly nerve poisons made from beetle larvae and roots are side by side with the materials for quivers, bows and arrows. And everything is free. You just have to find it—and know how to use it.

In the months after the rainy season, the store is fully stocked. The longer the drought, the more the risk that certain items will go 'out of stock'. Then the menu becomes increasingly poor. But even in September or October, fruits and nuts can still be found, along with roots and tubers which stay fresh under the ground for months. And there is always something from the live meat counter: kudu, eland antelope, springbok or warthog.

*The San (or 'Bushmen', the derogatory name given to them by settlers) were driven off their land, away from their ancestors' graves and their sacred sites, and enslaved.*

## The San: Expelled and Enslaved

Once the ‡Khomani, Khwe, !Kung, Hai[|o]m, Jul'hoansi and other San tribes were hunters and gatherers, with the freedom of the entire territory between the Atlantic, the Cape and the Indian Ocean. They are known to be the most ancient inhabitants of Southern Africa. Their language contains distinctive clicking sounds, which are written down with symbols such as !, [| ] or ‡. In thousands of rock paintings, some dating back over 20,000 years, they recorded scenes of daily life and hunting, hunters with bows and arrows and a multitude of wild animals, possibly as a tribute to the gods.

The first incursions into the region were made by nomadic pastoralists, African Bantu tribes from the north. From the mid-17th century, they were followed by European explorers, adventurers and colonialists. Portuguese voyagers landed in the west and the east, the Dutch and the English in the south. The Germans, as latecomers to colonialism, made their mark with a brief but bloody period of occupation in German South West Africa, present-day Namibia. From the coasts, these groups advanced towards the continent's interior, on their quest for land, water, and mineral resources—there were rich pickings of diamonds, semi-precious stones, gold, copper and uranium.

# Indigenous Knowledge and Modern Science

*Hoodia gordonii* is one species of the genus *Hoodia* an indigenous plant naturally occurring in South Africa in the semi-desert regions of the Northern Cape and Namibia. The San people call the plant *Xhoba*, and have traditionally used the plant as a substitute for food and water. *Hoodia* are spiny stem succulents resembling but unrelated to the cactus family.

South Africa, as a signatory to the Convention on Biological Diversity, is committed to protection and sustainable use of its biological diversity. Hoodia gordonii is threatened with extinction if international trade is not monitored and therefore it is listed under CITES (the Convention on the International Trade in Endangered Species of Wild Fauna and Flora). This means that *H.gordonii* cannot be exported from South Africa without a CITES certificate.

*Hoodia gordonii* is possibly the best known encounter of indigenous knowledge and scientific research that resulted in a benefit-sharing agreement between the CSIR [South African Council of Scientific and Industrial Research] and the San people in 2003. The CSIR isolated and patented the hunger-suppressing steroidal glycoside, known as P57 and the two parties agreed to share the benefits of the commercialisation of P57. With South Africa's rich indigenous knowledge from its biodiversity, this agreement sets a precedent of how owners of indigenous knowledge and practitioners of modern science can benefit in an equitable manner.

*"Technology for Sustainable Livelihoods," Department of Science and Technology, Republic of South Africa, 2008. www.dst.gov.za.*

# A Diminishing Population

The San (or 'Bushmen', the derogatory name given to them by settlers) were driven off their land, away from their ancestors' graves and their sacred sites, and enslaved. At times they were hunted like animals and murdered. They had their names, their languages and their culture taken away, and replaced with Christian names in Afrikaans or English. The apartheid laws in South Africa forced them to conceal their identity. Today there are only around 100,000 San left, probably less than one-tenth of the indigenous population in the pre-colonial era. Half of them live in Botswana, 36,000 in Namibia, and a few thousand in each of Angola, South Africa, Zambia and Zimbabwe—a dwindling minority everywhere. Nowadays very few are allowed to hunt like their forebears, with the exception of two thousand Jul'hoansi in the Nyae Nyae Conservancy in Tsumkwe District near the Botswanan border.

Although the San still live on their ancestral land, they have lost control over it and its natural resources, which were taken over both by the colonisers and by today's intruders. Some of the San became herdsmen on livestock farms, for meagre food and primitive lodgings. Others became servants. Often they ended up as bondsmen, similar to slavery. A few of them made use of their talent for tracking: their abilities were in demand by the army of the South African apartheid regime. They helped track down the fighters of the Namibian liberation movement SWAPO. In Namibia, this role is held against them to this day, and used as justification for the continuing discrimination they suffer, even though members of other ethnic groups such as the Ovambo or the Herero also collaborated with the white South Africans.

# Hoodia Holds Hope

"We need land and education," says Petrus Vaalbooi, Chairperson of the South African San Council, "in order to safeguard our rights and our traditions." A native succulent plant could help them to achieve this: Hoodia, a cactus-like plant which the ‡Khomani San call !Kkhoba. If everything works out, it could earn the San a lot of money. Then, instead of weaving baskets, working as day labourers or dancing to entertain tourists, they could buy land, give their children a good education, and revive their native language and their culture, once in perfect harmony with nature but now in danger of dying out. After years of oppression, discrimination and dispossession of their rights, Hoodia might hold out the hope of a better and happier future.

---

*After years of oppression, discrimination and dispossession of their rights, Hoodia might hold out the hope of a better and happier future.*

---

This promising turn of events is usually told as a 'good news' story, along the following lines: once there was a time when the 'Bushmen' of Southern Africa used Hoodia to stave off their hunger and thirst during hunting expeditions. One day, scientists came along from the South African statutory research council, the CSIR. They pinpointed and patented the active ingredient, without asking the San. The British company Phytopharm obtained the exploitation rights to P57, and the American pharmaceutical group Pfizer was awarded a production licence. The poor people's cure for hunger looks set to earn fat profits as an appetite suppressant for the wealthy but overweight: used fresh in salads, as a slimming drink, or a fat-busting pill. Luckily, the 'biopirates' were caught in the act. The South African San Institute, WIMSA [Working Group of Indigenous Minorities in Southern Africa] and the work of a committed lawyer, everything turned out for the best: the San were given a share in the income from the patent. "Doomed culture of the South African Bushmen saved by the pharmaceutical industry" the German television news reported gleefully. And they all lived happily ever after. . . .

# A More Complicated Story

But the real story is far more complicated, and raises any number of questions and problems.

For instance, whose property is the unique biodiversity of the Kalahari and Southern Africa, of which Kalahari truffles, Devil's Claw [a medicinal herb used to treat inflammation] and Hoodia are merely a few examples? The San may be the most ancient, but are not the only group today with knowledge of the effects of Hoodia and countless other plants. And South Africa is not the only country in which they grow. The answer has a commercial value, because natural resources, including genetic resources, contain vast potential for exploitation. According to estimates from the World Health Organization (WHO) for example, medicinal plants supply 70 percent of the raw materials for modern medicines. And with modern biotechnology and genetic engineering, the pharmaceutical and food industries have new tools for isolating and synthesising active ingredients, and for genetically modifying plants.

Most indigenous peoples and traditional communities have no concept of individual ownership of nature. Likewise, for the most part, their traditional knowledge about it is shared and made available to all. In industrialized countries, natural diversity was long considered to be the 'heritage of mankind', meaning that it belonged to everyone—or no-one. Collectors, researchers and breeders have repeatedly set out to scour nature's bounty, which is most abundant in certain countries of the South. However, when they turned a profit from their 'discoveries', as they did with Devil's Claw, the countries of origin and the people living there were left with little to show for it.

# Nations Have Sovereignty over Their Own Biodiversity

A clampdown on such practices came in the form of the Convention on Biological Diversity (CBD), passed in 1992 at the

United Nations 'Earth Summit' in Rio de Janeiro. For a start, it clarifies the matter of ownership rights. Under the Convention, each country of origin is assigned national sovereignty over its own biodiversity. This gives governments the right to rule on the use of flora and fauna occurring within their own territory. It covers not only whole plants and animals, but also all parts of them, including their genetic material.

By the same token, the Convention makes governments responsible for taking action to prevent the rapid loss of biodiversity, and for regulating the use of natural resources so that all exploitation—whether by national or foreign research institutions or companies—is on a sustainable basis. Profits from the use of biodiversity must be divided equitably among stakeholders. For instance, they could be shared between a pharmaceutical company and the country of origin.

## Benefit Sharing

Known as 'benefit sharing', this also has to be extended to indigenous peoples and traditional communities, because their ways of life and traditional patterns of use, including the cultivation of plants and breeding of animals, have contributed to the conservation and development of diversity. Added to that, their knowledge, experience, and traditions can be helpful to bioprospectors. Just as the San have an infallible eye for the plants they gather and the game or people they track in the bush, so they often give researchers vital clues about useful—and highly profitable—properties of nature. Just as they did with Devil's Claw a century ago. So, once again, the San's abilities as trackers are in demand. . . .

Hoodia's hunger-suppressing properties had first come to the attention of the South African army. Soldiers out on patrols with San trackers saw how they could keep going for days without eating any food, other than Hoodia. On learning of this, the CSIR set about conducting a systematic search for the active ingredient. If they help to separate the wheat from the chaff or to find the proverbial needle in a haystack, such leads are invaluable. They save time that would otherwise be wasted exploring blind alleys during systematic laboratory research—and that reduces costs.

Which brings us to the next question: what is an appropriate, equitable or fair share in the profits, whether for the San or any other provider of indigenous knowledge? How much credit should be given to the scientific achievement, and how much to the contribution of traditional knowledge?

---

*Just as the San have an infallible eye for the plants they gather and the game or people they track in the bush, so they often give researchers vital clues about useful—and highly profitable—properties of nature.*

---

## An Important Model

Sixty million rand [South African currency] were invested in Hoodia research, the CSIR contends; a sizeable stake to place on such a risky outcome. According to Roger Chennells, the lawyer facilitating the negotiations between the San and CSIR, this issue gave rise to some hard-nosed negotiating. But finally, in March 2003, the agreement on benefit-sharing was signed. As a result, the CSIR recognises the San as owners of the traditional knowledge, as well as the significance of that knowledge to the research. By the same token, it insists that isolation of the active ingredient was its own 'discovery', which it was legitimately entitled to patent. Under the agreement, the San become business partners and receive six percent of the royalties paid by Phytopharm to the research council for products containing the active ingredient P57. "So as a negotiator, I feel it ended fair for both sides—equally happy and equally unhappy," says Roger Chennells. The negotiations were made more difficult by the fact that, internationally, there are few comparable agreements to refer to. In any case, says the lawyer, depending on the success of the enterprise, six percent could be "a hell of a lot".

For Rachel Wynberg from the South African environment and development organisation BioWatch, however, the amounts seem like chicken-feed—"a miniscule sliver of a large, well-iced cake." She means that the San only receive a share of the CSIR's fee, not a share in the profits, let alone the revenues, from the product itself. What is more, they have to undertake not to make their knowledge about Hoodia available to any other commercial users. Nevertheless, even Rachel Wynberg sees the agreement between the CSIR and the San as a "historic breakthrough".

Indeed, many other indigenous groups and holders of traditional knowledge have been left empty-handed. With a cancer drug called Vincristine made from the Madagascar periwinkle, the American corporation Eli Lilly made annual revenues of 100 million US dollars. So far, the countries of origin have seen not a cent of it. . . .

## Both Parties Should Benefit

In collaboration with the San, the research council wants to gather all the known information on local medicinal herbs and other plants. That would also provide a body of evidence which the San could use as proof of their traditional knowledge, for instance in disputes with possible biopirates.

Despite the assurance that this data and its use "are subject to CSIR regulations, and legislation and conventions on bioprospecting," lawyer Roger Chennells thinks that considerable clarification is still needed. Bioprospecting is extremely complex and difficult to regulate. More to the point, it remains a legal 'grey area', with little relevant legislation yet in force. Namibia and South Africa are taking their time over national implementation of the Convention on Biological Diversity. Meanwhile, business in biodiversity is so lucrative that certain ruthless players will try every trick in the book. In such a climate, nobody wins concessions easily, least of all the San. Though the Convention requires states to recognise traditional knowledge and to promote its conservation, such obligations are of little help to the indigenous community in practice.

Organisations like WIMSA approach such agreements with great caution, unless there are adequate safeguards to prevent bioprospecting from crossing the line into biopiracy. So in future, all patents which derive from joint information gathering should be registered in both names, advises Roger Chennells, and be jointly owned by the CSIR and the San. Otherwise the San should withhold their consent.

In the light of the vast economic potential of biodiversity, one thing is clear: the CSIR and the state of South Africa had much more at stake than the imperative to clear their names of the biopiracy accusation by offering a 'fair' share of the proceeds. Throughout the negotiations on benefit-sharing with the San, big business deals were on the cards. Appetite suppressants and slimming aids containing Hoodia are no more than a tiny fraction of the great Kalahari superstore's true commercial potential. Far more lucrative ideas will follow: seed production, propagation, cultivation, processing and export of products by no means confined to Hoodia and Harpago. Numerous other plants and ingredients are likely to be covered under bioprospecting agreements with the San, and under a similar agreement between the CSIR and traditional African healers.

With their knowledge and experience, the San hold the key to these treasures—but the CSIR has the scientists, laboratories, and contacts, and since sovereignty over natural resources is assigned to states and their governments under international treaties like the Convention on Biological Diversity, it controls the instruments for profiting from them. It holds the power to turn the key into gold.

## Money Isn't Everything

In the film, *The Gods Must Be Crazy*, a cola bottle falls from the sky and lands in the midst of a San family in the Kalahari bush, remote from western civilisation. They admire and caress the magical, transparent, glittering object. Everyone wants to hold it—and an argument breaks out. At this, one of the men is charged with taking the ill-fated gift to the end of the world, and getting rid of it. It is the beginning of a daring quest through the bush and the modern world. Ultimately he tosses the bottle over a sheer precipice into the boundless waters of the ocean. And they all go back to their happy and contented lives. . . .

In the same way, the promising partnership with the CSIR more or less landed in the laps of the San. It resulted from research work in distant laboratories, negotiated by lawyers, governed by international agreements and reglations, all stemming from a worldview completely at odds with that of the San. Unlike the family in the film, the San decided to keep the alien, unexpected and fascinating gift, make use of it, and work together to make the best of it.

---

*As a consequence of the negotiations and developments of the past few years, the San in Southern Africa have become more experienced and confident.*

---

How much the San will receive in material terms remains to be seen. It is also unclear when there will be any actual money on the table. Whether it will be enough to fulfil all their wishes is doubtful. They are the last link in the chain, the group with the least influence. One thing is clear: the money will not offer a total solution to the San's wide-ranging economic, social and political problems.

In other respects though, they have gained a lot already: their organisation has grown stronger, even across national frontiers. Furthermore, "indigenous knowledge has received a huge boost of understanding," as Roger Chennells says. On the one hand, it has wrenched the San themselves out of their former oblivion and oppression. On the other hand, it does their self-confidence good to realise that their traditional knowledge is very valuable, even in far-off Europe, even for the invincible modern world. As a consequence of the negotiations and developments of the past few years, the San in Southern Africa have become more experienced and more confident. They want to learn more about their endangered traditions, languages and cultures, protect them and keep them in use. And they have grown warier and more reticent towards friendly visitors who show an interest in their traditions, medicinal plants, music and rock paintings, now that they know their potential value outside the Kalahari. Which means that biopirates will have it neither cheap nor easy in future.

# The Sámi of Northern Europe Are Rebuilding Their Culture

*Lander Arbelaitz*

*Lander Arbelaitz, a Basque journalist studying journalism in Denmark, describes in the following viewpoint the ways that the Sámi of Sweden, Norway, Finland, and Russia are preserving and rebuilding their culture. They have achieved some degree of political independence, according to Arbelaitz, through the establishment of Sámi Parliaments. In addition, Sámi schools are now teaching students in the Sámi language. Finally, media outlets including newspapers and radio and television stations are now using Sámi language for their articles and broadcasts.*

As you read, consider the following questions:

1. Who is Ole Henrik and why is he important to the Sámi?

2. What are the three languages young Sámi people learn in school?

3. How many hours per week is the Sámi language available on the radio in Norway?

Outside the temperature is below 0°C and it has been dark since 13:00. Since the first day of December the sun did not rise and now there are less than two hours of light per day. In one of the two supermarkets of Kautokeino—a village

Lander Arbelaitz, "The Silent Revolution," Gáldu Resource Center for the Rights of Indigenous Peoples, January 11, 2007. Reproduced by permission.

with 3,000 inhabitants, in the northeastern part of Norway—some people are doing their shopping. The supermarket is not very big and in total there are ten people inside. The atmosphere is calm and quiet. Suddenly the fridge is opened and a wrinkled hand takes some yogurts. It is an elderly woman and she is wearing warm colorful clothes. Those costumes are the Sámi clothes and she is not the only one wearing them. For some people the traditional clothes are still part of their modern life and that is a sign that the Sámi culture is still alive, at least in places like Kautokeino.

In the same town, a twelve-year-old child called Henrik goes everyday to the Sámi school. At 8:45 a.m. it is dark, and often, very cold. He wears a black thick coat and he hides his sleepy face under a black hat. He says that he does not like to go to school, but he does not realize how *lucky* he is that he can learn everything in his native language. That was not the case for Sámi before him.

Two generations—the woman in the supermarket and Henrik—are part of the same culture. Two generations sharing time and space. One is the experience, the other the future. Two generations where one suffered from the oppression of foreign cultures, and the other is too young to understand what happened. This comparison of generations is a clear example of the transition Sámi culture is going through. Despite not having accurate statistics, it is estimated nowadays there are between 70,000 and 100,000 Sámis in Sápmi—the name of the Sámi area that stretches into Norway, Sweden, Finland and Russia. In the recent years the Sámi are taking big steps forward, like creating more institutions to keep their culture going, for example, the Sámi Parliaments, schools and media in Sámi language.

## The Sámi Parliaments Support Sámi Culture

There is a picture of Ole Henrik Magga, the first president of the Sámi Parliament (*Sámediggi* in Sámi language), wearing

Sámi traditional clothes next to the King of Norway Olav V, taken in 1989. Most of the Sámi people know about this photo. It was photographed on the day the King of Norway went to Karasjok to inaugurate the Sámediggi. Today, Ole Henrik is a professor for the Sámi language at Sámi University College in Kautokeino and he also lives in the town. He remembers that day as "the happiest day" in his life, "the day the Norwegian king prayed for the Sámi people". He thinks that day is the symbol of the Sámi people's progress.

The Sámediggi is the highest representative body of the Sámis in Norway. There also are Sámi Parliaments in Sweden and in Finland, and even though they have an international cooperation to deal with some issues, they are different institutions. According to Aili Keskitalo, the current, and first female president of the parliament in the Norwegian part, it has different roles on promoting the Sámi culture. The first is to prioritize and distribute the funds; and the second to network and cooperate with cultural organizations and institutions like museums, the Sámi theatre, etc. Aili has set some goals for the future of Sámi culture. "Hopefully, we will enforce the work on our language. We will put more resources, because the eldest generation that are carrying the language, is getting older and we have to make sure the children will learn it."

---

*It is estimated nowadays there are between 70,000 and 100,000 Sámis in Sápmi—the name of the Sámi area that stretches into Norway, Sweden, Finland and Russia.*

---

Since its establishment, the indigenous Parliament in Norway has increasingly assumed the administrative responsibilities for Sámi matters. Since 1992, they gained further responsibilities. Today, the Sámediggi has the formal responsibility for the development and protection of the language, culture and heritage sites. They also took over the Sámi Educational Council's functions from the Ministry of Education. Besides,

The Sámediggi has the responsibility for the development of Sámi teaching aids with the allocation of an annual permanent grant for this purpose. The total budget from the Norwegian Government for 2006 was around 260 million Norwegian Kroner (around 32 million euros).

## Sámi Schools Ensure the Future of Sámi Culture

Henrik has many friends at the school. Even though they learn everything in Sámi, they can speak Norwegian perfectly. The young Sámi people are completely trilingual, since they also learn English at school. On the walls of the class they have a map of Sápmi drawn by the students in class. They have color coded each separate area of Sápmi and also shown a representation of the different gákti—traditional Sámi clothes. They learn what the Sámis in the Russian Kola peninsula wear or their neighbors on the Finnish side of the border.

Perhaps, in fifty years, Henrik and his friends will remember their school in a positive way. That does not count for the Sámi who had to go to Norwegian—or Swedish, Finnish and Russian—schools and be discriminated because they did not speak any other language but the one they learned at home. The researcher Tove Johansen made a collection of interviews with the Sámis who went to Norwegian schools, and as stated in his collection, to talk about school with elder Sámi people, is mainly, to talk about cultural repression and humiliation. In those times, some Sámis decided they should not teach their mother tongue to their children, to avoid problems. Still it is common to find some people who changed their original family name and invented a new one more similar to Norwegian. This way, they could hide their *Sáminess* in order to be accepted and at one stage, buy land. The children did not learn anything about their historic past, soon lost their identity and became completely Norwegian, especially those living in the coastal areas.

The school situation today is different [from] fifty years ago. The status of Sámi education has been determined in different ways in the legislation on compulsory schooling in Norway, Sweden and Finland. Now Sámi schools are one of the important engines for the revitalization of the culture and its survival. "It's really important that our children learn in Sámi, because we have to make sure our language will survive", says Kirsten A.G. Buljo, one of the teachers at the school in Kautokeino. There are many schools in the four states where the whole teaching is done in Sámi language and statistics show every year the number of children matriculated in those schools is rising. Nevertheless, to provide a good education, teacher Kirsten thinks they would need more school material in Sámi language.

## Media Are Re-establishing the Sámi Language

Near the cashier's desk, in the same supermarket where women are wearing traditional clothes, there are three different newspapers for sale. They inform about the news in Sápmi. On the one hand, *Ságat*—the biggest with 2,300 copies per edition—is in Norwegian and it is published twice a week. On the other hand, *Min Áigi* and *Áššu* are entirely in Sámi language and they are published twice a week 1,150 and 1,050 copies per edition, respectively. They are weekly newspapers due to the relatively small number of Sámis who are able to read in their own language. Actually, the readership is not large enough to maintain Sámi language newspaper solely through subscription and single-copy sales.

Nevertheless, those who were not allowed to be educated in their language have other alternatives to be informed about their issues. Since the Norwegian, Swedish and Finnish national broadcasting companies signed a treaty, for 15 daily minutes, the latest news in Sámi politics or other issues are broadcasted on TV. The news starts at 17:05 and focuses on

## The Sámi: One People in Four Countries

- 40,000 Sámi live in Norway
- 20,000 Sámi live in Sweden
- 7,500 Sámi live in Finland
- 2,000 Sámi live in Russia
- Sápmi is the traditional name for the Sámi homeland and is also the name of their language
- Formerly called "Lapps" or "Laplanders," Sámi now find these terms derogatory
- Although the Sámi are citizens of four countries, they also have semi-autonomous parliaments in Norway, Sweden, and Finland

TAKEN FROM: http://www.lepeupledusoleil.com/images/M/Sapmi.jpg; and "The Sámi People—A Handbook," 2006. www.galdu.org.

the whole Sápmi area. Since it is entirely in Sámi, subtitles are available in Norwegian, Swedish or Finnish, depending on which side of the border the viewer is located. "Our surveys say that we have about 70,000 viewers every day all over the year", confirms Nils Johan Heatta, the director and editor-in-chief of Sámi Radio. They are planning to present children's programs every day during five years from 2007 on and they are preparing to start with programs for youth.

---

*Two newspapers, a national Sámi radio and Sámi news on TV are notable signs that the Sámi language—and culture, at the same time—is in the process of normalizing.*

---

The Sámi language is also a radiophonic language. It was heard on radio for the first time in 1946, 15 minutes every week. It was the Norwegian Broadcasting Corporation's (NRK) decision. Nowadays, after 60 years, 30 hours weekly are available in the indigenous language and a NRK Sámi Radio Section is situated in Karasjok. Moreover, eight local offices are around the country.

Two newspapers, a national Sámi radio and Sámi news on TV are notable signs that the Sámi language—and culture, at the same time—is in the process of normalizing. In addition, Heatta thinks the role as independent media "is very important in building up and developing the rather young Sámi democracy".

The young Henrik and the women in the supermarket are part of an indigenous culture that was traditionally connected to exotic reindeer herding, *gákti-s*—Sámi traditional clothes—, *yoik-s*—Sámi chanting style—handicraft and midnight sun. Nevertheless, . . . having spent almost a century under oppression makes them look at the world from another point of view. The smallness and the satisfaction they have by knowing that they are doing well in their way, makes them strong. That could be one of the reasons why both Ole Henrik Magga and Aili Keskitalo—the former president and the actual president—see [the] future positively. Without making much noise, they are building up their culture and gaining the rights, which belonged to them long time ago. Some Sámi say this is a "silent revolution".

# The Orang Asli of Malaysia Assert Their Identity Through Music

*Tan Sooi Beng*

*Tan Sooi Beng writes in the following viewpoint about a young musical group, Akar Umbi, which is helping revive indigenous identity among the orang asli, of Malaysia. These Temuan-speaking indigenous peoples, according to Beng, have been the target of assimilationist tactics by the government as well as being pushed out of their traditional lands because of a large dam project and ongoing logging operations. The music of the group reminds the orang asli of their role as protectors of the rain forest. Beng is a professor of ethnomusicology at the School of Arts, Universiti Sains, Malaysia.*

As you read, consider the following questions:

1. What is the meaning of the Temuan phrase, "Akar Umbi"?
2. What does the song "Hutan Manao" describe, according to Beng?
3. On what is the Temuan culture dependent, according to Beng?

Tan Sooi Beng, "*Songs of the Dragon*, Indigenous Identity and Temuan Rights to the Forest," *Aliran Monthly*, vol. 25, no. 5, 2005. Reproduced by permission.

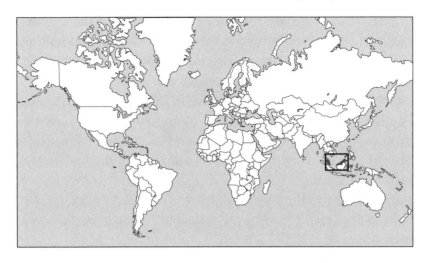

The *orang asli* (meaning "original people") are the indigenous minority people of Peninsular Malaysia whose ancestors inhabited the peninsula before the Malay kingdoms were established. They comprise 18 different groups, which make up 0.5 percent of the total population of 26 million. While a few have become professionals and businessmen and some work in factories in urban areas, the majority still live in the forest and forest-fringed areas. They depend on swiddening, hunting, gathering, fishing, and trading in forest products for survival.

## Cut Off from Ancestral Lands

To bring development, the government has adopted a policy of integrating and assimilating the *orang asli* into mainstream society, more specifically into Malay society. The Jabatan Hal Ehwal Orang Asli (JHEOA) or the Department of Orang Asli Affairs was set up for this purpose. Assimilation—together with increased deforestation and dislocation (as a result of logging and development projects)—has threatened to cut the *orang asli* off from their ancestral lands, the source of their livelihood and cultures.

The *orang asli* have responded to the state's assimilationist goal and the appropriation of their ancestral lands by uniting, lobbying politicians, and bringing their cases to the court. They formed organisations such as the Peninsular Malaysia Orang Asli Association (set up in 1976) and the Indigenous Peoples' Network of Malaysia, a network of indigenous peoples' organisations in Sabah, Sarawak, and the Peninsula. The *orang asli* began to claim an "indigenous identity" to "regain their cultural symbols" and to counter control by the state. In his book, *The Orang Asli and the Contest for Resources, Indigenous Politics, Development and Identity in Peninsular Malaysia*, Colin Nicholas, the co-ordinator of the Centre for Orang Asli Concerns, writes that the *orang asli* have come to realise that "an assertion of their indigenous identity is a prerequisite for their survival". There is a need to "assert both their personal and collective identity to counter the power of 'outsiders', particularly the state".

---

*Assimilation—together with increased deforestation and dislocation (as a result of logging and development projects)—has threatened to cut the* orang asli *off from their ancestral lands, the source of their livelihoods and cultures.*

---

## Asserting Cultural Identity Through Music

One of the ways to assert this identity is to set up cultural troupes (involving old and young people of the *orang asli* communities) to perform indigenous music and dance and their own versions of popular music. The various *orang asli* groups come together to perform and exhibit their handicraft at the annual International Indigenous People's Day events.

Akar Umbi (meaning "Tap Root") is an example of a cultural group of the Temuan, one of the indigenous *orang asli* groups living in Pertak, a forest reserve just outside of Kuala Kubu Baru (KKB). Akar Umbi is a musical collaboration which was initiated by Antares and Rafique Rashid, two musicians who moved to KKB in 1992. These two musicians encountered the rich culture of the Temuan and have been documenting the oral traditions, stories, and music of the Temuan which are in danger of disappearing.

Since its formation, Akar Umbi has presented live renditions of the songs of Mak Minah Anggong, a Temuan ceremonial singer who lived in Kampung Orang Asli Pertak. Mak Minah sang her songs at various concerts including the Second Rainforest World Music Festival in Kuching before she passed away unexpectedly on 21 September, 1999. To pay a special tribute to Mak Minah and to share her passionate love for the rainforest with others, Antares and Rafique assembled a CD of 10 tracks using whatever material that had been recorded at rehearsals and performances. The CD is entitled *Songs of the Dragon* (2002) as the dragon refers to Mak Minah's clan lineage whose totem is the Naga (the spirit guardian of rivers). The tracks include traditional Temuan songs with contemporary musical arrangements as well as healing ritual songs (*sawai* or *sewang*) with *buluh limbong* accompaniment. The *buluh limbong* are pairs of bamboo instruments struck on a long block of wood which are used in healing rituals and also to accompany other songs for entertainment by many *orang asli* groups.

## Singing Traditional Sacred Songs

In the CD, Mak Minah Anggong is the lead singer while Mak Awa, Mak Nai, and Mak Indah perform their traditional sacred songs on the *buluh limbong*. The Temuan women, who sing in the Temuan language, are accompanied by other Malay, Chinese, Indian, and Eurasian musicians performing on guitars, keyboards, and percussion. According to Antares, the music "breaks through traditional cultural barriers". Not only are the musicians multi-ethnic, the music is "a musical fusion."

In *Hutan Manao*, for instance, Mak Minah sings in the Temuan language using the traditional style of singing with a narrow vocal tension. She is accompanied by the alternating rhythms of the *buluh limbong*, consisting of a longer lower-sounding tube known as "father" and a shorter higher-pitched tube known as "mother" which are both struck on a long block of wood. The two tubes are pitched approximately a minor third apart. Although the keyboard and electric guitars play western chords, they emphasise the minor 3rd interval and the rhythms of the bamboo stampers, thereby keeping harmony to a minimum. The bamboo flute and electric guitar are also given melodic interludes. The song describes the joys and hardships of roaming the forest for days in search of jungle cane (*manao*) for the furniture stores.

Akar Umbi performed *Hutan Manao* live at the benefit concert for Bosnia at the Shah Alam Stadium on 16 September, 1994 and a series of other songs at the Second Sarawak Rainforest World Music Festival (28–29 August, 1999). Since the Shah Alam concert, which had an audience of 42,000 and was broadcast live on national television, Mak Minah has become a "cultural representative" for the marginalized *orang asli* community.

## Guardians of the Rainforest

Mak Minah's songs portray the love and reverence the indigenous people have for the forest, river, and mountains that surround them. Indirectly, Mak Minah's songs advocate the cultural autonomy of the *orang asli* at a time when two Temuan villages were to be relocated and Temuan sacred sites and ancestral heartland flooded to make way for a 400 feet high dam across the Selangor River. Mak Minah opposed the building of the dam strongly. The Temuan believe that they were placed on earth to be guardians of the rainforest. Legend says that "when the *orang asli* are no longer visible, the world will end." Experts have emphasised that the wetlands and the

# The Orang Asli: The Guardians of the Rain Forest

Researchers and other information-seekers agree that when it comes to identifying those who have the most intimate knowledge of an ecological niche, especially forest areas, the fingers point to the peoples who reside in those areas—those who depend on the resources found therein for their subsistence and well-being, and who derive their culture and identity from that geographical space. In most cases, these would be the indigenous peoples. . . .

In the case of Peninsular Malaysia, these peoples are the Orang Asli. . . . Numbering 149,000 today, about half of them live mainly in the forest and forest-fringe areas on both sides of the central mountain range. The peninsula is also the setting for several research efforts in various disciplines concerned with the management of protected areas. . . .

Without exception, however, the role of the Orang Asli in these protected areas have been, for the most part, mainly as temporary employees of individual researchers or of well-funded research projects. But, as far as I know, no Orang Asli is currently, or has been, in any management position or who is, or was, responsible for decision-making of any sort in the management of a protected area.

Why is this so? How did it come to this state of affairs?

The reason for this is two-fold: One, the divergence between western values and methods of forest conservation from that of indigenous systems of forest use and management. Two, the non-recognition of Orang Asli and other indigenous peoples as the owners and guardians of their traditional territories.

*Colin Nicholas, "Who Can Protect the Forest Better?"*
*Paper presented at the International Symposium on Eco-Human Interactions in Tropical Forests, Kyoto University, June 13–14, 2005.*

famous firefly colony near Kuala Selangor would be affected by the dam project. Despite protests, work on the dam began in February 2000. When logging and rock blasting began, the Temuan families living in Pertak and Gerachi had not been properly resettled.

*Sungai Makao* (River Makao) is a lyrical song with Minah Anggong on vocals, Rafique on acoustic guitar, and Antares on Balinese flute. Mak Minah sings about the Makao River, which flows through Pertak Village where she was born. The Temuan believe that the Makao River has its source in Gunung Raja, the sacred mountain, and regard it as the symbol of abundance and good health. Mak Minah incorporates into the lyrics a reproof against the destructive logging activities at the Temuan reserve.

In *Kuda Lari* (Running Horse), Minah Anggong warns those who intend to disturb the spirit guardians of the river that some mishap might occur. *Kuda Lari* is a Temuan nursery rhyme and a humorous account of how Cecil Ranking, the first magistrate and revenue collector of Kuala Kubu Baru, fell off his horse and had to chase it all the way to Pahang. According to legend, Ranking attempted to kill a crocodile *penunggu* or sacred guardian of the river in 1883. This may have triggered a dam disaster which killed Ranking and flooded the town of Kuala Kubu Baru. It is believed that rivers are guarded by dragons, snakes, and crocodiles, which will cause chaos if their homes are destroyed.

*Songs of the Dragon* has been produced the DIY way so that Akar Umbi has complete control over the production and distribution of the CD. Some of the tracks such as *Burung Meniyun* were recorded by Rafique in his home studio, using a four track cassette, MIDI sequencers, and a programmable drum machine. Other tracks featuring traditional bamboo ritual music such as *Raja Perahu* were recorded on a portable digital audio-tape (DAT) during rehearsals at Antares' house at KKB with a relaxed ambience. Additional tracks featuring the voice of Awa Anak Lahai (sister of Mak Minah), who has taken over the lead singing, were recorded at a private studio. Antares has been raising funds from friends and private funding agencies to pay for studio time, musicians, and other aspects of album production. Distribution is being done mainly through the website and through friends in the music world.

---

*Helping individuals achieve something in the field of culture and sports is the most effective way of raising the* orang asli*'s self-esteem.*

---

## Learning to Value Traditional Music

Antares says that the CD has helped "to keep Mak Minah's memory alive through her beautiful songs, and encourage the younger generation of *orang asli* to cherish and value their traditional songs". Through the album, "the Temuan in particular and *orang asli* in general have begun to feel a sense of pride in seeing one of their own become a singing celebrity ... The overwhelming response of the crowd at the Shah Alam Stadium to Mak Minah's singing has shown the Temuan that other people do value their traditions and believe there is much to learn from their culture."

By presenting the songs in a modern setting, younger Temuan have been inspired to learn these songs and play them at weddings and other festivities. Using modern instruments such as the guitar and keyboard and the world music idiom also helps the younger generation to connect and engage with modernity. Ten percent of the proceeds from the sale of the CD go towards a Mak Minah memorial fund for the children, widows, and old folks of Pertak Village. Antares says that part of the memorial fund will be used to help young *orang asli* with athletic or music potential. He is convinced that helping individuals achieve something in the field of culture and sports is the most effective way of raising the *orang asli's* self-esteem. This is in contrast to state Jabatan Hal Ehwal Orang Asli officers who try to "assimilate *orang* asli into modern Malay society by destroying their natural habitat and their spiritual links to the land."

Through their own version of world music, Akar Umbi has generated an awareness that the survival of Temuan culture is dependent on the forests, rivers and land around them. The Akar Umbi performances and CD have stimulated concern about the destruction of the Temuan's ancestral land and environment (due to the construction of the Selangor Dam) and action on their behalf. The Temuan songs assert that Temuan identity and the intimate relationship of the people with the natural resources of the forest are the basis of the continued existence of present and future generations.

# Canadian Indigenous Peoples Must Preserve Their Languages

## Muriel Draaisma

*Muriel Draaisma reports in the following viewpoint on the endangered status of many Canadian indigenous languages. Although 2008 was named the United Nations International Year of Languages, little has been done in Canada to mark the event. Indigenous peoples are attempting to protect their languages through Cultural Education Centres that organize educational materials and experiences to assist in language preservation. Elders representing the First Nations, Métis, and Inuit urged their members and the government to protect their languages. Draaisma is a writer for the Canadian Broadcasting Corporation news division.*

As you read, consider the following questions:

1. What kinds of language policies should governments develop, according to Koichiro Matsuura?
2. What Canadian indigenous languages are considered to have the greatest rate of survival? Why?
3. What happened in November 2007 regarding language preservation?

Muriel Draaisma, "Endangered Languages," *CBC News*, February 22, 2008. Reproduced by permission.

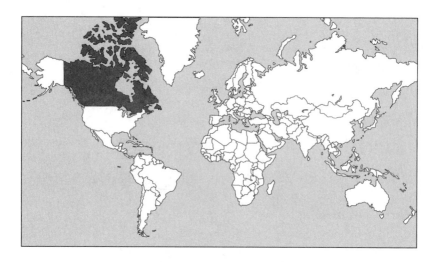

A language dies on average every two weeks somewhere around the world, according to the United Nations—and many aboriginal languages in Canada are among those considered in peril.

On Feb. 21, 2008, the UN [United Nations] Education, Scientific and Cultural Organization (UNESCO) officially launched the UN International Year of Languages to promote linguistic diversity and multilingualism while drawing attention to endangered languages.

"Languages matter!" is the slogan of the new international year. UNESCO says there are a multitude of languages spoken around the globe—an estimated 6,700—but more than half of them may become extinct over the long-term.

The Department of Canadian Heritage says it is not funding or organizing any official events or activities to mark the year.

Canada remains a linguistically diverse country. There are two official languages recognized on the federal level, English and French, and even more are recognized in some parts of the country. (The Northwest Territories leads the list, with 11: English, French, Gwich'in, Cree, Dogrib (also known as Tlicho), Chipewyan, Inuinnaqtun, Inuktitut, Inuvialuktun,

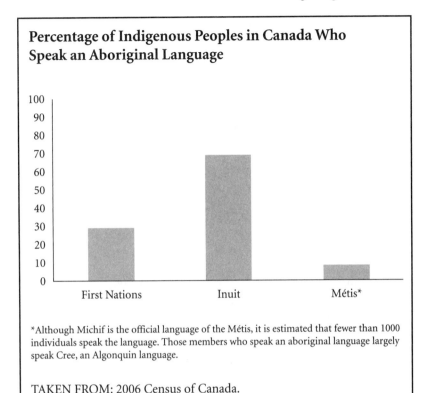

Percentage of Indigenous Peoples in Canada Who
Speak an Aboriginal Language

*Although Michif is the official language of the Métis, it is estimated that fewer than 1000
individuals speak the language. Those members who speak an aboriginal language largely
speak Cree, an Algonquin language.

TAKEN FROM: 2006 Census of Canada.

North Slavey and South Slavey). Apart from the official languages, more than 90 other languages among immigrant communities and there are 50-plus aboriginal languages spoken from coast to coast to coast.

Yet Statistics Canada says only three aboriginal languages in Canada—Cree, Ojibwa and Inuktitut—remain viable.

## Reasons to Preserve Indigenous Languages

Koichiro Matsuura, director-general of UNESCO, says there are good reasons to fight to preserve languages.

He said languages are key to cultural identity, linguistic diversity is closely linked to cultural diversity, and languages play an important role in the fight against poverty, hunger and disease. Indigenous languages in particular, he says, are crucial to preserving indigenous knowledge.

But he says thousands of languages around the world will likely disappear in the space of a few generations because they are not used in schools, in the media or on the Internet, or they have few very speakers left. Many are used only sporadically. UNESCO estimates that 96 percent of the world's languages are spoken by four percent of the world's population.

"We must act now as matter of urgency," he said in a statement released for International Mother Language Day on Feb. 21. The day has been celebrated since 2000.

---

*Languages are the key to cultural identity, linguistic diversity is closely linked to cultural diversity, and languages play an important role in the fight against poverty, hunger, and disease.*

---

Matsuura says governments should develop language policies that encourage linguistic communities to use their mother tongues as widely and often as possible.

He says governments should also encourage speakers of a dominant language to master other languages to promote cultural understanding.

UNESCO urged governments, educational institutions and professional associations to organize activities in 2008 to promote and protect all languages, especially endangered ones.

"Only if multilingualism is fully accepted can all languages find their place in our globalized world."

## Indigenous Peoples Must Protect Their Own Languages

Claudette Commanda, of the Ottawa-based First Nations Confederacy of Cultural Education Centres, told CBC [Canadian

Broadcasting Corporation] News she is not surprised that Canada is not officially celebrating the UN International Year of Languages.

Commanda, who is executive director of the national non-profit organization, said she wonders whether the UN General Assembly consulted community groups actively fighting to preserve languages before it declared the year.

"I think that protecting languages should not be in the hands of governments," she said. "After all, it was government policies that destroyed our languages. Governments need to support and to provide adequate resources for language preservation, but in the case of our languages, it's up to First Nations to develop programs needed to protect, promote and revitalize First Nations languages at a community level."

Commanda said the confederacy has a mandate to protect languages it defines as belonging to First Nations, meaning status and non-status Indians, while other groups focus on preserving other aboriginal languages, of the Inuit and Métis peoples.

Eighty-seven cultural education centres, which receive funding under a federal cultural education centres program administered by the confederacy, are developing tools to increase knowledge and use of traditional Indian languages. The confederacy, set up by Indian and Northern Affairs Canada, has an annual budget of $8 million.

The centres are producing dictionaries of First Nations languages, CD-ROMS, software, audiovisual tools, cultural awareness kits, and second-language acquisition programs. They are also organizing cultural activities, ceremonies and summer camps to promote First Nation languages. And they are working with band-operated schools to develop culturally relevant curricula.

"Our languages are dying rapidly. Our languages are in a critical state," Commanda said. "Our position is that all First Nations languages are endangered."

# All Indigenous Languages Are Endangered

Commanda says Cree and Ojibwa—along with Inuktitut, spoken by the Inuit—are considered to have the greatest rate of survival because they have large numbers of speakers. But even Cree and Ojibwa are endangered, she says, because they're not spoken in all of their respective communities.

"We need to bank the languages. Our elders are telling us that all are endangered."

She acknowledges that families, not just language tools and cultural education centres, play an important role in passing on languages. However, she says many First Nations families across the country are not in a position to ensure their children speak their native tongues because many are dealing with a host of problems, from poverty and unemployment to the legacy of residential schools.

"There's another reality to this. We need to provide them with support to help them pass on First Nations languages and culture," she said.

According to the confederacy, there are 52 First Nations language groups in 10 language families in Canada. The language groups include dialects.

---

*Many First Nations families across the country are not in a position to ensure that their children speak their native tongues because many are dealing with a host of problems, from poverty and unemployment to the legacy of residential schools.*

---

## Language Statistics

Statistics Canada says its 2006 census found that there are 60 aboriginal languages spoken by First Nations people, grouped in distinct language families, which include Algonquian, Athapaskan, Siouan, Salish, Tsimshian, Wakashan, Iroquoian,

Haida, Kutenai and Tlingit. Cree is spoken by the largest number of First Nations speakers.

It found that there are five primary distinct Inuit language dialects spoken throughout Canada, and while Michif is the traditional language spoken by Métis people, the most commonly spoken aboriginal language among the Métis is Cree.

Inuit were most likely to speak an aboriginal language, according to the 2006 census. Just over 32,200 Inuit, or 64 percent of the total, said Inuktitut was their mother tongue.

About 29 percent of the First Nations people who responded said they could speak an aboriginal language well enough to carry on a conversation, while only about four percent of Métis said they spoke an aboriginal language.

## Many Languages Are Nearing Extinction

According to Indian and Northern Affairs Canada, in a 2002 publication entitled *From Generation to Generation: Survival and Maintenance of Canada's Aboriginal Languages Within Families, Communities and Cities*, aboriginal languages already extinct include Huron, Petun, Neutral in the Iroquoian family, Beothuk, Pentlatch and Comox in the Salish family, and Tsetsaut and Nicola in the Athabaskan family.

More than a dozen aboriginal languages are near extinction, the 2002 report said.

In 2002, the federal government—then under the Liberals [a Canadian political party]—announced it would spend $172 million over 11 years to preserve aboriginal languages. The funding led to the creation of a task force on aboriginal languages and culture that produced 25 recommendations.

The task force said aboriginal languages range from "flourishing" to "critically endangered."

"Even languages with a large number of speakers may be flourishing in some regions and be in a critical state in others," it reads.

It concludes: "Some are spoken by only a few elders, others by tens of thousands. Large language groups like the Cree, Ojibwa and Inuktitut are viable, having at least 25,000 speakers, ranging from the young to the elderly. However, all languages, including those considered viable, are losing ground and are endangered."

---

*[The Aboriginal Languages Initiative] is designed to support projects that increase the number of language speakers, encourage language transmission from generation to generation, and expand the use of languages in family and community settings.*

---

## The Elders Speak

In November 2007, the federal government under Stephen Harper's Conservatives cut the $172 million earmarked by the Liberals for aboriginal language preservation, saying aboriginal organizations had not come up with plans on how to spend the federal money. At the time, the Assembly of First Nations said the claim was not true.

Currently, the Department of Canadian Heritage manages what it calls its Aboriginal Languages Initiative, which provides about $5 million in annual funding to aboriginal communities across Canada to support community-based language projects.

The department says the initiative is designed to support projects that increase the number of language speakers, encourage language transmission from generation to generation, and expand the use of the languages in family and community settings.

Commanda says there is no question that more money is needed to preserve endangered languages—and that they are key, as UNESCO says, to cultural survival.

Elders, when consulted by the task force, said the same thing. According to the task force report, they said: "Do not forget our languages. Speak and write our languages. Teach and learn our languages. Respect each other's dialects and do not ridicule how others speak. Focus on young people. Start in the home to strengthen the will of the people to bring back our languages. Work together to build a foundation for our peoples. Speak with a united voice."

# Periodical Bibliography

*The following articles have been selected to supplement the diverse views presented in this chapter.*

| | |
|---|---|
| *Aboriginal Affairs* | "About New South Wales Aboriginal Languages," New South Wales Government, September 9, 2008. www.nsw.gov.au. |
| Vanessa Baird | "I Will Return . . . and I Will Be Millions," *New Internationalist*, no. 410, April 2008. |
| John Beaucage | "Message from Grand Council Chief John Beaucage," *North Bay Nugget*, January 4, 2009. www.nugget.ca. |
| Daniela Estrada | "Chile: Keeping Indgenous Langauges Alive," Inter Press Service News Agency, September 13, 2008. |
| *Indigenous Peoples, Indigenous Voices* | "Indigenous Languages: A Fact Sheet," United Nations Permanent Forum on Indigenous Issues, April 21, 2008. |
| *SIL International* | "Why Languages Matter: Meeting Millennium Development Goals Through Local Languages," 2008. www.sil.org. |
| Sid Spindler | "Empowering Aboriginal Communities," *Arena Magazine*, vol. 93, February–March 2008. |
| Nick Squires | "Australia Taps Aboriginal Weather Knowledge," Telegraph.co.uk, July 27, 2007. www.telegraph.co.uk. |
| Novaline D. Wilson | "Tribal Consequence of Urban Indian Relocation: Case Examination of the Existing Indian Family Exception and Adoptive Placement under the Indian Child Welfare Act," Occasional Paper Series, *Michigan State University College of Law*, March 2007. |

# For Further Discussion

## Chapter 1

1. Do you think it is possible to define what the writers of this chapter mean when they use the term "indigenous peoples"? If not, why? If so, what would your definition be? List four or five key factors that would allow you to identify a group as indigenous.

2. Most of the viewpoints in this chapter discuss past wrongs perpetrated against indigenous peoples. Summarize the historic wrongs discussed by the writers, then consider what, if anything should be done now. Do you think that the non-indigenous descendants of Europeans should offer apologies or reparations to indigenous peoples harmed by colonization? Why or why not? Do you think land illegally taken from indigenous peoples should to be returned to them? What would be some of the problems that would arise from doing so? What do you think that justice demands in these situations?

## Chapter 2

1. According to several viewpoints in this chapter, some of the most pressing issues facing indigenous peoples today include poverty, ill health, and racism. Find a copy of the United Nations Declaration on the Rights of Indigenous Peoples and read it carefully. Do you think passage of this declaration by all nations of the world will address the concerns presented by the writers of this chapter?

2. Climate change is affecting indigenous peoples all over the world. Can you give examples of how indigenous

peoples will have to adjust their lives to adapt? Who do you think will be most affected by climate change and why?

## Chapter 3

1. What is the nature of the relationship between indigenous peoples and their traditional lands, according to the writers of the viewpoints in Chapter 3? What are some of the consequences for indigenous peoples who have either had their lands taken from them, or have been forced to move from their lands?

2. Should indigenous peoples have the right to natural resources found on their traditional lands, such as water, minerals, and wildlife? Support your answer with evidence from the viewpoints in this chapter.

## Chapter 4

1. What are some examples of the ways that indigenous peoples are working to preserve their cultures, according to the viewpoints in this chapter?

2. Should the traditional knowledge of indigenous peoples be protected as intellectual property? For example, should indigenous peoples be able to hold the copyright on their art or music and demand royalties from those who purchase or use this intellectual property? Likewise, should indigenous peoples receive payment from pharmaceutical companies who use indigenous traditional knowledge to produce new drugs and medicines?

# Organizations to Contact

*The editors have compiled the following list of organizations concerned with the issues debated in this book. The descriptions are derived from materials provided by the organizations. All have publications or information available for interested readers. The list was compiled on the date of publication of the present volume; the information provided here may change. Be aware that many organizations take several weeks or longer to respond to inquiries, so allow as much time as possible.*

**Center for World Indigenous Studies**
1001 Cooper Point Road SW, Suite 140
Olympia, WA   98502-1107
(360) 586-0656 • fax: (253) 276-0084
Web site: www.cwis.org

The Center for World Indigenous Studies in a nonprofit, international research and education organization. One of its important activities, according to the organization's Web site, is to "foster better understanding between peoples through the publication and distribution of literature written and voiced by leading contributors from Fourth World Nations." The organization's Web site includes the *CWIS Newsletter*, full-text reports of research, and access to the media center with documents and video clips.

**Cultural Survival**
215 Prospect Street, Cambridge, MA   02139
(617) 441-5400
Web site: www.culturalsurvival.org

The stated purpose of the nonprofit Cultural Survival organization is to "partner with Indigenous Peoples to protect their lands, languages, and cultures; educate their communities about their rights; and fight against their marginalization, discrimination, exploitation, and abuse." The organization works around the world in public education programs, field projects, and advocacy campaigns. Included on the Cultural Survival Web site are news of their project and educational information. The group also publishes a journal, *Cultural Survival Policy*.

## doCip: Indigenous People's Center for Documentation, Research, and Information

14 ave de Trembley, Geneva  CH-1209
  Switzerland
41-227403433 • fax: 41-227403454
e-mail: docip@docip.org
Web site: www.docip.org

doCip: Indigenous People's Center for Documentation, Research, and Information is a Swiss nonprofit organization supporting indigenous peoples as well as serving as a documentation and information center. Activities include providing translation and technical services to indigenous groups and working for indigenous rights. Its most important activity is to "constitute the collective memory on the recognition of indigenous people's rights at an international level, notably for the younger generation," according to the group's Web site. doCip publishes a quarterly update on indigenous issues and maintains links and information on the subject.

## First Nations Confederacy of Cultural Education Centres

666 Kirkwood Avenue, Suite 302, Ottawa  K1Z 5X9
  Canada
(613) 728-5999 • fax: (613) 728-2247
e-mail: info@fnccec.com
Web site: www.fnccec.com

The First Nations Confederacy of Cultural Education Centres (FNCCEC) is a nonprofit advocacy group working with eighty-seven First Nations cultural centres across Canada. Included on the Web site are descriptions of programs undertaken by the FNCCEC as well as links to individual First Nations cultural centers.

## Indigenous Law and Policy Center

Michigan State University College of Law
East Lansing, MI   48824-1300
(517) 432-6939
e-mail: indigenous@law.msu.edu
Web site: www.law.msu.edu

The Indigenous Law and Policy Center at Michigan State University provides support for students wishing to become lawyers in the field of Native American law. The Center maintains a blog, Turtle Talk, containing up-to-date information on indigenous issues, links to other publications, and insightful editorials. In addition, the organization posts publications and research conducted by scholars in the field.

## Indigenous Law Centre

The Law Building, Sydney, NSW   2007
  Australia
61-293852252 • fax: 61-293851266
e-mail: ilc@unsw.edu.au
Web site: www.ilc.unsw.edu.au

The Indigenous Law Centre, located at the University of New South Wales in Australia, provides support for students engaged in indigenous studies, particularly in relation to the law. The Centre is also the home of the *Australian Indigenous Law Review*. The Centre's Web site contains news articles, analyses, back issues of the *Australian Indigenous Law Review*, and *Indigenous Law Bulletin*, and links to many other valuable resources, including the Australian Indigenous Law Library, and an up-to-date database of articles concerning indigenous peoples and the law.

## Inuit Circumpolar Council

ICC Greenland, Nuuk   DK-3900
  Greenland
299-323632 • fax: 299-323001
e-mail: iccgreenland@inuit.org

Web site: www.inuit.org

The Inuit Circumpolar Council is an international organization representing Inuit peoples living across the far north of Alaska, Canada, Greenland, and Russia. Its goals and activities include promoting Inuit and worldwide indigenous rights, developing and preserving Inuit culture, and working to preserve the environment. The council's Web site includes reports from working groups and commissions, news articles, and information concerning Inuit culture and education.

**Inuit Tapiriit Kanatami**
75 Albert Street, Ottawa, Ontario  K1P 5E7
  Canada
(613) 238-8181 • fax: (613) 234-1991
e-mail: info@itk.ca
Web site: www.itk.ca

Inuit Tapiriit Kanatami (ITK) is a large national organization representing Canada's Inuit population. Its Web site holds a wealth of information regarding Inuit culture, land, heritage, and rights, as well as a history of the Inuit people and the creation of Nunavut. The group publishes *Inuktitut Magazine* in both Inuktitut and English; back issues of the magazine are available on the Web site.

**Kalahari Peoples Fund**
PO Box 7855, Austin, TX  78713-7855
(512) 453-8935 • fax: (512) 459-1159
e-mail: information@kalaharipeoples.org
Web site: www.kalaharipeoples.org

The Kalahari Peoples Fund is a nonprofit organization founded in 1973 that includes volunteer professional anthropologists, development workers, linguists, educators and others who work with the indigenous peoples of the Kalahari at their request. The organization states that it provides "responsible information and research on the Kalahari peoples for lawyers, students, volunteers and eco-travelers interested in southern Africa." The Web site contains full descriptions of projects and information about the San peoples.

**Living Tongues: Institute for Endangered Languages**
4676 Commercial Street SE #454, Salem, OR   97302
(503) 540-0090 • fax: (503) 540-0900
e-mail: ContactUs@LivingTongues.org
Web site: www.livingtongues.org

Living Tongues: Institute for Endangered Languages is a non-profit organization whose mission is to "promote the documentation, maintenance, preservation, and revitalization of endangered languages worldwide," according to materials published by the group. One of its main projects is "Bringing Voices to the Future: Assisting Indigenous Communities in Their Struggles for Cultural Linguistic Survival." On the organization's Web site, students can find descriptions of the group's projects, papers and publications, and a map of the "Top 5 Language Hotspots" where indigenous languages are most endangered.

**United Nations Permanent Forum on Indigenous Issues**
2 United Nations Plaza, Room DC2-1772
New York, NY   10017
(917) 367-5100 • fax: (917) 367-5102
e-mail: indigenouspermanentforum@un.org
Web site: www.un.org

The United Nations Permanent Forum on Indigenous Issues is the international organization charged with the oversight of indigenous issues for the United Nations. As such, it is the premier human rights, social justice, and sustainable development organization in the world. On its Web site, students can find a wealth of materials relating to indigenous peoples worldwide.

# Bibliography of Books

Rodolfo F. Acuña   *Occupied America: A History of Chicanos.* New York: Pearson Longman, 2007.

Keith G. Banting and Thomas J. Courchene   *Belonging: Diversity, Recognition, and Shared Citizenship in Canada.* Montreal: Institute for Research on Public Policy, 2007.

Kara Briggs and Ronald D. Smith   *Shoot the Indian: Media, Misperception and Native Truth.* Buffalo, NY: American Indian Policy and Media Initiative, 2007.

Barbara A. Brower and Barbara Rose Johnson   *Disappearing Peoples?: Indigenous Groups and Ethnic Minorities in South and Central Asia.* Walnut Creek, CA: Left Coast Press, 2007.

David G. Campbell   *A Land of Ghosts: The Braided Lives of People and the Forest in Far Western Amazonia.* New Brunswick, NJ: Rutgers University Press, 2007.

Claire Charters and Andrew Erueti   *Maori Property Rights and the Foreshore and Seabed: The Last Frontier.* Wellington, New Zealand: Victoria University Press, 2007.

Ward Churchill   *Kill the Indian, Save the Man: The Genocidal Impact of American Indian Residential Schools.* San Francisco, CA: City Lights, 2004.

| | |
|---|---|
| Ken S. Coates | *A Global History of Indigenous Peoples: Struggle and Survival.* New York: Palgrave Macmillan, 2004. |
| Ann Curthoys, Ann Genovese, and Alex Reilly | *Rights and Redemption: History, Law and Indigenous People.* Coogee, NSW, New Zealand: University of New South Wales Press, 2008. |
| N. Bruce Duthu | *American Indians and the Law.* New York: Viking, 2008. |
| Joan G. Fairweather | *A Common Hunger: Land Rights in Canada and South Africa.* Calgary: University of Calgary Press, 2006. |
| Matthew L.M. Fletcher | *American Indian Education.* New York: Routledge, 2008. |
| Josephine Flood | *The Original Australians: Story of the Aboriginal People.* Crows Nest, NSW, New Zealand: Allen and Unwin Academic, 2007. |
| K. David Harrison | *When Languages Die: The Extinction of the World's Languages and the Erosion of Human Knowledge.* New York: Oxford University Press, 2007. |
| Ben Kiernan | *Blood and Soil: A World History of Genocide and Extermination from Sparta to Darfur.* New Haven, CT: Yale University Press, 2007. |
| Julian Kunnie and Nomalungelo I. Goduka, eds. | *Indigenous Peoples' Wisdom and Power: Affirming Our Knowledge Through Narratives.* Burlington, VT: Ashgate, 2006. |

Kyra Landzelius    *Native on the Net: Indigenous and Diasporic People in the Virtual Age.* New York: Routledge, 2006.

Michael Ross Lee    *First Nations Sacred Sites in Canada's Courts.* Vancouver: University of British Columbia Press, 2006.

Frederico Lenzerini    *Reparations for Indigenous Peoples: International and Comparative Perspectives.* New York: Oxford University Press, 2008.

Peter Lourie    *Arctic Thaw: The People of the Whale in a Changing Climate.* Honesdale, PA: Boyds Mills Press, 2006.

Roger Maaka and Chris Andersen, eds.    *Indigenous Experience: Global Perspectives.* Toronto: Canadian Scholars Press, 2006.

Jerry Mander and Victoria Tauli-Corpuz    *Paradigm Wars: Indigenous Peoples' Resistance to Globalization.* San Francisco, CA: Sierra Club Books, 2006.

Beatriz Manz    *Paradise in Ashes: A Guatemalan Journey of Courage, Terror, and Hope.* Berkeley, CA: University of California Press, 2005.

Daniel McCool, Susan M. Olson, and Jennifer L. Robinson    *Native Vote: American Indians, the Voting Rights Act, and the Right to Vote.* New York: Cambridge University Press, 2007.

Henry Minde    *Indigenous Peoples: Self-determination, Knowledge and Indigeneity.* Delft, The Netherlands: Eburon Publishers, 2008.

Dominic
O'Sullivan

*Beyond Biculturalism: The Politics of an Indigenous Minority.* Wellington, New Zealand: Hula, 2007.

Kent Hubbard
Redford

*Protected Areas and Human Displacement: A Conservation Perspective.* Bronx, NY: Wildlife Conservation Society, 2007.

Lindsay Gordon
Robertson

*Conquest by Law: How the Discovery of America Dispossessed Indigenous Peoples of Their Lands.* New York: Oxford University Press, 2007.

John K. Roth, ed.

*Genocide and Human Rights: A Philosophical Guide.* London: Palgrave, 2006.

Damien Short

*Reconciliation and Colonial Power: Indigenous Rights in Australia.* Burlington, VT: Ashgate, 2008.

Jeffrey Sissons

*First Peoples: Indigenous Cultures and Their Futures.* London: Reaktion Books, 2005.

Laura Westra

*Environmental Justice and the Rights of Indigenous Peoples: International and Domestic Legal Perspectives.* Sterling, VA: Earthscan, 2008.

# Index

Geographic headings and page numbers in **boldface** refer to viewpoints about that country or region.